Half the World Away

Rebecca Banks

"Gorgeously warm and romantic"
Paige Toon

For Lennon
Dream big little one

CHAPTER 1

PERCHED ON A cold wooden bench in the police station waiting room alongside Dave Jones, the London Town Football Club manager, Abbie waited in silence for Henry Smithson to work his magic. She stayed silent because she could see that Dave's cheeks had gone so red, he was about forty-five seconds away from spontaneously combusting. She didn't want to make a peep for risk of him exploding in her direction.

Quite how Henry, the club's lawyer, was going to get one of the country's top premiership players smuggled out of the cell he was currently occupying after a seventeen-year-old girl reported him for sexual assault was beyond her. And how she was going to keep the press off the scent of this was another thing she hadn't quite got her head around.

Exactly what she needed on a Saturday night. Actually, scrub that. This wasn't even something to be sarcastic about. She never needed this, ever.

When had it become commonplace for a professional person earning a hell of a lot of money to behave like a complete bloody idiot? And it was her job to hide it and make it all go away so he could continue in his job as a pseudo god, earning squillions for kicking around a ball and, more often than not, missing the sodding net.

She'd paid her own way through university, worked her arse off ever since, and still struggled every month to pay for a flat and a life in Central London, while this guy didn't know any words longer than two syllables, regularly behaved like a complete Neanderthal and was sitting pretty in his Surrey Hills mansion. She didn't feel bitter, just completely at the end of her tether. She also sadly believed that there was a chance the girl was telling the truth. She had seen enough over her years in the sport to know what went on. But this girl would get paid off or made to look like she was asking for it, and everything would be swept under the carpet as usual. Her younger sister Lily was the same age, and she couldn't imagine something like this happening to her. It didn't bear thinking about. It made her feel sick to her stomach.

The door to her right clicked and Henry emerged, looking grim-faced. He was dressed in a grey pinstripe suit, the lighter grey vertical stitching seeming to lengthen his lofty frame even further. Abbie wondered how he looked so together at 4:00 a.m. It was as if he'd just popped out from his Chancery Lane offices. She knew her hair was dishevelled, her face make-up free and her clothes creased, but she was not one of those girls who shot up out of bed looking like they'd just stepped out of a shampoo advert.

Looking around to check nobody was in earshot, Henry spoke. 'They will let him out but not until the morning when he's sobered up. I have an emergency injunction meeting scheduled for first thing Monday, but don't worry, they can't name him before then because he hasn't been formally charged. Don't answer your phones for now and I'll draft you a formal response for when the calls start to come in.'

'What has the little bastard got to say for himself?' growled Dave through gritted teeth.

'He's not denying that he was with the girl, but he's saying she said she was in her twenties and it was all consensual. It's a bit of a tricky one, his word against hers. No damning evidence either way.'

'Alright, enough, I don't want to bloody hear any more. We had none of that back in my day, I tell you. I'm going to absolutely throttle him.'

Abbie looked at her chipped caramel-painted nails as she listened to Dave's northern lilt and wondered if she pinched herself really hard she would find herself waking up again. Sort of like a double nightmare, *Inception* style. Another minute and Leonardo DiCaprio would hurtle through the doors to save her and whisk her away to a paradise island. She grabbed the skin between her left thumb and forefinger. No, she wasn't sleeping. She looked up again as Henry spoke.

'We should all go home and get some sleep now, there's nothing we can do until the morning. I've warned them that if this gets out we'll sue everyone at this station, so hopefully we can avoid pictures. I'll organise a car to collect him first thing in the morning from the back exit and take him home.'

Dave looked over at Abbie and sighed, rubbing the bridge of his nose. 'Get yourself home, pet, you shouldn't be sitting in a bloody police station in the middle of the night. It's no place for ladies.'

Nodding, she arranged to speak to Henry in the morning and trudged out of the building into the freezing January air.

As she ordered a taxi, the wind whipped at her face, and she pulled her scarf and winter coat tighter but still felt body parts beginning to go numb. In fact, the only warmth she could feel was the tears that had started to prick at her eyes.

She wasn't sure if it was the cold breeze or her frustration at the situation, but she bit the tears back and breathed a sigh of relief as the cab pulled over in front of her. She sank into the seat and the warm air inside the car started to defrost her frozen form.

Twenty minutes later, she pushed open the front door. As she pulled off her coat and scarf, a giggle from the lounge told her that her flatmate Polly was home for once, but that she probably had company, so she quietly slipped into her bedroom and flopped down on top of the duvet, rubbing her eyes. She was asleep before she got around to taking off her clothes.

ABBIE SHIFTED POSITION and opened her eyes as the bright winter sunlight shone through the blinds. Her taste buds went into overdrive as the smell of frying bacon reached her nostrils, and taking note of the angry growl of her stomach, she quickly changed her now very crumpled trousers and shirt for jogging bottoms and a hoodie and made her way to the kitchen.

Polly was singing along to the radio wearing her signature black from head to toe with a patterned headscarf tying back her long, currently ruby red, locks. She turned as she heard Abbie enter.

'Good morning, you dirty stop out. Don't think I didn't notice you sneaking in at all hours this morning. Tell me, what was his name? It's about time you got back in the saddle.'

Leaning against the kitchen counter, Abbie sighed. 'Sadly, I was out at a work emergency. No men involved. Well, none worth talking about anyway. I was more surprised to see you home but figured you had company so thought I'd leave you to it.'

'My little Scouse beauty, you need to get out more. You know what they say about all work and no play.' Polly said this over the noise of sizzling bacon that she was pushing around the frying pan with a fork.

'Yeah, I know, I know. I need to come and see you play soon. How was last night's gig?'

'It. Was. Epic.' Polly mimed playing her electric guitar while headbanging. 'You have to come soon. We've got so many new songs that you haven't seen us play, and you used to come to so many nights.'

'I know. I'm a terrible friend and I need punishing.

Give me your worst.'

'Ah, I love you too much for that. You can have a bacon sandwich instead. If you're going to work like a boring old cow all the time, then you need to eat.'

Abbie grinned as she took the plate Polly offered, squeezed on some brown sauce and sat down at their little kitchen table.

She had moved in with Polly two years ago. She never knew how Polly paid her rent. Her 'job' was that of guitarist in struggling pop rock band The Flame Effect, and she spent most nights out performing or going to other gigs. It meant they passed like ships in the night most times, with Abbie at work during the day.

She took a huge bite of the sandwich, wiped the sauce that trickled down her chin and savoured the taste of the salty bacon, quickly satisfying her hunger.

'I'm out for drinks with Violet tonight if you want to come along, Pol. It's been ages since we've all caught up.'

'Out with Damian tonight, I'm afraid, but keen for next time,' Polly replied, through a mouthful of bacon.

'Which one's Damian?' Abbie asked, raising her eyebrows up and down a few times and leaning towards Polly on her elbows.

'The artist. He wants to paint me. How romantic is that?'

'Sounds like an excuse to get you to bare your beautiful body, but go ahead, you're only young once.'

'I hope that's what he wants!' she squealed.

The two girls collapsed into giggles and Abbie felt a

million miles away from the cold bench she had been sat on just hours before.

EIGHT HOURS LATER Abbie occupied a corner table in the White Horse, nursing a glass of pinot grigio the size of a fish bowl. She was deep in thought, dreading tomorrow at work, when she was disturbed by a loud commotion. She looked up to hear Violet shouting apologies as she ran in from the drizzle and cold towards the table. Despite having just made a mad dash across town, Violet still looked her impeccable self. Her perfectly coifed auburn hair fell in loose curls around her porcelain face. She always reminded Abbie of a perfect little pixie, and she had lived up to that by bewitching boys ever since they first met at university in Liverpool. The boys had loved her Dublin lilt and petite features, and Abbie had loved her full stop.

'I'm so sorry I'm late, darling. It's bloody impossible to get a taxi in this weather. I'll get us some drinks.' And she was off again like a firecracker, tearing towards the bar. The barman didn't know what he had coming, Abbie thought with a smile.

Violet seemed to return to the table before she had even left, and Abbie could see a young man scurrying behind her carrying a tray with two drinks on it, another wine for her and a Johnnie Walker, straight up and on the rocks for Violet. Unbelievable. They were in the local pub, not The Ritz, yet Violet had got them table service. She suppressed a laugh as Violet motioned to the boy where she wanted the drinks placed, throwing him a thankful grin as he retreated towards the bar, barely able to take his eyes off her, which Violet didn't seem to notice.

'So, tell me what's happening. You said you were having a shocker, I thought you were going to cancel on me.'

Abbie sighed. She seemed to be doing a lot of that lately.

'It's just work. One of the players has been up to no good and I've had to spend some of my weekend with the lawyer.'

'Leave! You haven't liked it for ages. You're just dealing with selfish prima donnas. You're better than that, darling, and I hate to see you so down. You look like crap.'

Abbie felt tears pricking at her eyes again, and she looked down before grabbing her glass and taking a large gulp.

'I can't just give up. I've been working so hard and it's a good job. People would kill for it. It's just stressful sometimes, that's all.'

'No, that's not all. Honestly, Abbie, I've wanted to give you a good talking to for a long time but I just think that you're going to burst into tears so I've been avoiding it. You can't go on like this. You've done nothing but work since, well, you know, and I'm really worried about you.'

Abbie couldn't speak. She knew if she did, she wouldn't be able to stop an emotional outburst and she couldn't deal with that on top of everything else that was going on.

Violet never could leave a silence, and Abbie saw concern shoot to her face as she waited for a response and saw she wasn't going to get it.

'Don't you agree, Abs, you've not been yourself? All you do is work. You never go out anymore. When was the last time you dragged me to one of your grungy underground music dives to listen to groups that look like they need a good scrub?'

She grinned, and lifted her brows.

'Don't worry, I'm okay really. I've just been busy.'

Violet's grin fell.

'Don't give me that shit. More than ten years I've known you, Abigail bloody Potter, I know you better than you know yourself. We've got to do something. This has been going on too long, and it's killing me watching you live this empty life. There's never any light in your eyes anymore.'

Violet let the ensuing silence continue while she stared at Abbie, a mixture of frustration and concern etched across her face.

Abbie sat there. She felt the bubble of the upset, the one that she tried hard to keep squashed, building in her stomach. Yes, Violet was right, but was it going to do any good to bring all her past crap back to the surface?

Violet continued to stare at her. Abbie looked up and Violet folded her arms across her chest.

'We're not going anywhere until you start talking so you may as well just get it over and done with. It's time.'

That did it. The tears started slowly, then began to cascade, and Abbie was grateful she'd picked a discreet corner table.

'I just can't make it go away, every day I think about what happened. If I work it makes me think about other stuff for a while and it's the best way to cope.'

'It's clearly not because you haven't dealt with it. It's been two years now since the divorce and six years since, well, you know, and you're getting worse, not better. I don't know how many times I have to tell you that you didn't do anything wrong. It was his fault. He's the fuckwit. God, Abbie, I love you more than life itself, I need to help you get out of this hole.'

Abbie swallowed and breathed deeply, trying to calm down before the people in the pub started staring at the slightly tipsy girl who was ruining the ambience of their relaxing Sunday evening.

'What we need is a plan,' Violet stated simply.

Sniffling away, Abbie stopped delving into her handbag where she was searching unsuccessfully for a tissue and looked up. She wiped her eyes with the back of her hands instead.

'I know you're right, Vi. I'm bloody miserable, but I just don't know how to get out of it. I'm completely lost. And part of me thinks I deserve to be miserable.'

Violet left her chair to join Abbie on the bench seat and put her arms around her, drawing her in for a hug. 'We're going to get you a fresh start, it's what you need. First of all, the job. You have to leave that awful place with those feckless idiots. And you have to start leaving the house for something other than work.'

Abbie nodded and took another gulp of wine while Violet continued explaining her plan of attack.

'And men. You have to get back out there and get on a date.'

'No way. I am drawing the line at that one, Violet. I don't need or want a man.'

Violet sighed dramatically, exasperated at her best friend. 'You do, you're just scared. It's like riding a bike though, once you get back out there it will all seem so easy again.'

'Easy! It definitely wasn't easy the last time, was it.'

'Quit this bullshit, Abbie, this stops now. Josh the tosspot is not going to ruin the rest of your life. I won't let him.'

'I'm hardly the most baggage-free of prospects though, am I? Sad and lonely old divorcée who hasn't had so much as a sniff at a man for too long to remember. It's hardly attractive.'

'Don't be so bloody ridiculous.' Violet slapped her on the arm. 'Who doesn't have baggage nowadays? You're nearly thirty. You've been married before. So what? Elizabeth Taylor was on her fourth husband by the time she was your age. Really, you're underachieving.'

Abbie felt butterflies of anticipation in her stomach. It felt very much like a mixture of absolute panic combined with a small slice of hope. She looked at her friend and, on a whim, agreed to the plan. Things couldn't get any worse, could they?

'Okay, so let's do it like this. I know you're right. I'm absolutely petrified of all of it, but I know I have to do something. Let's sort out the job and getting my social life back first, and phase two can be the man thing. I can't quite think about that at the moment. I need to do this in manageable chunks.'

Violet smiled, the triumphant grin of someone who had got her own way and was very pleased about it. Like an Irish pixie who'd found a pot of gold.

'This is going to be so much fun,' she said, clapping her hands with glee.

Abbie felt the niggles of doubt but she knew something had to change and, now Violet had the bit between her teeth, there was no going back now.

CHAPTER 2

O N MONDAY AFTERNOON, Abbie sat in Dave's office. John Sullivan, the player in trouble, occupied the chair to her right while the manager leaned against his desk, looking down at John with an expression of pure fury that threatened to make his mood on Saturday night look like a mere flicker of annoyance.

The room was deathly silent, with John looking more and more uncomfortable by the second. He was trying to portray that he was calm and collected but it looked like he couldn't bring himself to meet his boss's eyes.

Abbie kept her own eyes fixed on her notebook. She was ostensibly writing work-related things down but, in reality, was jotting down song lyrics from The Traps, one of her favourite bands, in a bid to distract herself from the awkward silence.

There was palpable relief when the door swung open and Henry strode in, his calm aura sending soothing waves across the office. John managed a tight smile at the lawyer.

Henry stood next to Dave and cleared his throat.

'Right, I don't want you to think that what has gone on is not very, very serious. Innocent until proven guilty and all that, but I've spoken to you and I've spoken to the girl, and we all know what went on in that room.'

'Like I said, mate, I didn't do nothing wrong,' John said in a defensive voice.

'Let me finish, please,' Henry asserted.

Dave jumped in, anger flashing across his face. 'Don't you bloody dare interrupt him again or I'll have you packed off to Accrington Stanley quicker than you can say free transfer.'

Abbie silently fist-pumped the air in admiration for her boss before turning her attention back to Henry.

'Now, what is spoken about in this meeting shall go no further than this room,' he said. 'We have had some, shall we say, discussions with the girl to check that she was sure this hasn't all been a big misunderstanding. We're taking care of her to make sure she's okay and we've got an agreement that there were maybe some crossed wires and a bit too much alcohol all round, and she's withdrawn her statements from the police. I've also got an injunction preventing the press from naming you. You're off the hook this time, but I suggest you have a long hard look at what went on and make sure that nothing like this happens again. The repercussions on the club could have been disastrous, and you have a duty to represent your place of work in the best possible way. You're a role model, whether you like it or not.'

John started to get up from his seat.

'Sit back down now,' Dave shouted, making Abbie jump with the ferocity of his order. 'Do you really think you get to behave like that and walk out of my office with no consequences? Do you really? I am fed up to the back teeth with the utter lack of respect from you. I don't know what you did and what you didn't but, whatever happened, you put yourself in this position with a total lack of thought or care because you think you can do whatever you want. You've got the morals of an alley cat and you never have to face up to your actions. Well, I'm fining you. Three months' wages. How do you like that?'

'Maybe he could donate it to a women's group for victims of abuse?'

Oh, shit. She had said that out loud. Shit, shit, shit.

'That's a bloody great idea, Abbie. That's exactly what we'll do with it. It's a hell of a lot of money, that'll make a big difference, even if this idiot treats it like it's going out of fashion with his new Bentleys and fancy watches and whatnot every five minutes.'

Turning to face John again, he growled, 'Now get out of my office. I can't stand the bloody sight of you right now.'

Knowing he was beaten and there was no use trying to fight back, John trudged out of the office, but not before throwing a look of anger in Abbie's direction as he left. She feigned nonchalance and focused on Dave, who was leaning against his desk shaking his head.

'What a bloody disaster. I'm so bloody angry. He's lucky he got out of here with his limbs still intact. I feel like skinning him alive.'

Henry put his soothing lawyer's voice to use trying to calm Dave before turning to Abbie. 'Let me finish up here and then let's you and I head into one of the meeting rooms and go through the press strategy in case you do get any calls. You shouldn't with the injunction in place, but we'll cover every possibility so you're armed and ready.'

Abbie offered her thanks and left the room, leaving Dave and Henry to wrap up their conversation on the whole sorry mess.

SCROLLING THROUGH HER inbox later that afternoon, Abbie couldn't really focus on the job at hand. The task of responding to emails seemed trivial when she thought of what the teenage girl might have gone through on Saturday night, and how she must be feeling now having been coerced with a lot of money and, probably, thinly veiled threats. Abbie didn't blame her for making the decision that she had; she'd have enough money now to set herself up with a house and would have a good level of financial security, but she'd always know that she didn't get justice and the snake had got away with it.

Her thoughts were interrupted when the mobile on her desk started to ring.

'Abbie Potter.'

'Hello there, Abbie, how's it going?'

'Hey, Michael, not bad thanks. Actually, that's a complete lie. I'm in a horrible state and it's all down to your better half.'

'Yes, I heard you had rather a rowdy Sunday night.'

'Ah, Michael. Violet and I rowdy? Never.'

Abbie liked Michael. He and Violet had been together for years. On paper it shouldn't work. Michael was relaxed, while Violet was a total whirlwind, but they just fit together right, and for all the henpecking and the fights that Violet picked, Michael never rose to the bait. He adored her, craziness and all.

'What can I do you for, Michael? Need some birthday present advice for our Vi?'

'Actually, not this time, no. Violet mentioned you were in the market for a new job, and quite coincidentally we've had an interesting role come in this week at MD Recruitment. I wondered if you'd like to chat.'

Abbie moved quicker than she had all day to run and close her office door before settling back down at her desk. 'That sounds interesting.'

'I think you'd be perfect for this. It's in football and it's a very rare opportunity. I'm not sure how much you know about the industry in America, but the Utah Saints are looking for a communications director and I think you'd be absolutely perfect. They want to take someone from an English premiership club to really bring them up to scratch. I couldn't imagine anyone better than you, and from what Violet is saying, you need a great new challenge and you need it quickly.'

'I don't know what to say. I'm really flattered, Michael. I don't really understand how that would work though. Why on earth would they hire someone in the

UK when they're based god knows where in America?'

'That's the thing, Abbie, it's not England based. They want someone to move to Utah to run the whole operation.'

'Aha, that makes more sense now. I have to say it's slightly annoying as the job sounds amazing, but I can't move to America.'

'Are you sure? It's a real once-in-a-lifetime opportunity and they're only looking for a one-year commitment to start with. You could interview here, and just see what happens.'

'Really, Michael, thanks, but this one's not for me. I've never had any big ambitions to work abroad, and it feels like it's too far from home. What would I do if something happened to Mum or Dad and I needed to rush to be there or look after Lily? I couldn't do that from the other side of the world. I've got to run as I'm heading to the training ground to meet a TV crew, but could we catch up later about any other ideas you've got?'

Michael sighed down the phone.

'Of course, but give this one some thought. I can get you an interview next week.'

As Abbie put the phone down, she looked at her computer screen and saw the time. She closed the computer down and layered up in preparation for the bracing January temperatures, then hurried out of her office.

SHE TRUDGED INTO the training ground building and said hi to Mavis, the catering lady who had worked there for twenty-seven years and watched many a youth player grow up to either make it to the first team or have their dreams shattered and their contracts torn up. There wasn't much Mavis hadn't seen, and the boys (for the most part) adored her.

'You be careful out there on the pitch this morning, Abbie dear, you'll catch your death. Here, come and get a nice hot cup of tea before you go out, it will do you the world of good.'

Abbie took the tea appreciatively, giving Mavis a hug. Things weren't all bad here, she thought. Unfortunately, her time had been taken up recently dealing with awful events that overshadowed the good people and players. She cursed John Sullivan for ruining things. Although he wasn't the first to cause her drama, an incident like the one he'd caused made her tar the rest of the not-so-bad bunch with the same brush because it took up so much of her attention.

She would try to remember that and be patient dealing with things this morning. She wouldn't let her anger spill into her work today.

Heading out onto the training pitch, attempting to put a spring in her step, the first face she saw was John, scowling as usual as he knocked a ball around the damp grass. Unfortunately, he was the TV crew's number one request to interview that day. It pained her to facilitate putting him in the living rooms of millions of children, holding him up as a hero and a role model. But it wasn't for much longer, if her plan of escape worked. She just needed to grin and bear it for now.

A commotion behind her indicated that the TV crew had arrived, and she walked over to talk to them about the shoot. When they were settled and ready, she headed towards John.

'John, can you come over here please? Sport TV are here to interview you about the derby.' Unsmiling, he walked alongside her as they headed towards the crew. 'Now remember, don't discuss the team selection even though it's already decided. Some quick stats for you are that this derby has been held seventeen times and we've won the last fifteen of them, so we're confident the winning streak will continue.'

John nodded and sneered at her again. This was a fun morning. He leaned in and Abbie moved her ear closer to him. Often the players would want to ask her something before being interviewed – checking a fact, or what they could and couldn't say – so she was ready for questions.

'You need to watch yourself, with your smart-arse comments. Girls like you need teaching a lesson.'

Abbie's blood ran cold. He threw her a menacing smile then quickly moved away and walked straight to the TV crew, all charm and laughter.

She was completely shocked. He had just threatened her, unless she was very much mistaken. The familiar tears pricked at her eyes but then the anger took over. That bastard was never going to change and she needed to get the hell away from characters like that. As much as there were nice boys in the squad, there were a few too many bad eggs, and for her sanity, she had to get out.

As she walked past the TV crew, she told them something had come up and she had to get back to the office. They were welcome to carry on interviewing John but she wanted no part of any of it anymore. Let him fuck it up when he didn't know the answer to a question. She didn't care any longer.

CHAPTER 3

'SO, YOU'VE ACTUALLY done it? Without a job to go to?' Violet was incredulous when Abbie called her that evening to tell her she had handed in her resignation to Dave.

'Yep, I couldn't bear it anymore. What John said to me today was the last straw. Dave was amazing, he totally understood. He said he would be sad to see me go, but he's happy for me to see out my notice, which gives me a month to find something.'

'Abs, I'm so happy for you. You've got the fire back in your belly.'

'It definitely feels like I've taken a step towards something,' she said, smiling as she talked to her friend. 'I'm chatting to Michael about what he's got available so hopefully things will get sorted pretty quickly. Things are looking up, Violet. It already feels like a weight's been lifted.'

'That's amazing.'

Something had shifted in Violet's voice, which unsettled Abbie. She thought Violet would be delighted for her, but her reaction had turned flat and Abbie told her as much.

'Um, I don't know how to say it. It's shitty timing,

and I was going to come over later, but…'

'Spit it out, Vi. What's going on?'

Her friend paused, hemmed and hawed, and then suddenly blurted it out.

'Josh and his wife are having a baby.'

Abbie remained silent at this unexpected news about her former husband.

'I'm so sorry, love. I didn't want you finding out from someone else or seeing it on bloody Facebook or something.'

Clenching the phone, Abbie realised she was holding her breath.

'Are you okay, Abs? I can come over there right away. In fact, I'm going to get in the car now, don't move.'

Quickly pulling herself together, she moved to reassure her friend. 'Don't be silly, Vi. I'm absolutely fine. We're starting over, remember? It's been two years now. It's time I moved on. I'll be fine.'

Violet hesitated. 'Well, if you're sure. Call me anytime, okay? I'm keeping my phone on loud all night.'

Abbie said her goodbyes and let out a deep breath. She was exhausted after a hell of a few days and now, hearing her ex-husband's news, she wanted to curl up in a ball and sleep for a week. The notion of letting purposefully repressed memories bubble to the surface didn't bear thinking about, so she turned her thoughts back to her conversation with Michael and how it wouldn't hurt to take an interview with the American company he'd mentioned. Letting all her attention turn to the possibilities she might have in front of her, she let herself relax down into the couch, pushing all the unwanted thoughts out of her head.

She switched on the TV to try to distract herself, but found it difficult to focus on the holiday home search programme that flickered onto the screen. As she worked to concentrate on the couple looking at the Spanish beachside apartment, she felt the lids of her eyes getting heavier and heavier until, finally, she dozed off.

SLOWLY MOVING HER cricked neck, it took Abbie a minute to realise that she was still on the sofa.

A wave of loneliness hit her as the quiet night allowed noisy thoughts back in and the phone call with Violet came flooding back into her mind. Josh was going to be a father to someone else's baby. She had always envisaged that future for them, but it would never be.

With the metaphorical door cracked open, physical pain engulfed her as the memories she tried so hard to block out came crashing back into her consciousness. How he would slowly entwine their fingers and gently stroke her palm with his thumb. The way when he was tired, he would nestle his head into her chest, murmur words of tenderness to her and make her feel so loved and needed. And how he used to draw her to him in the still of the night. Now he was doing those things, the things she thought were special between them, with wife number two.

She brushed away a tear that started to escape and tried to feel some fury towards Josh. The anger was there somewhere but, too often when she allowed herself to think about him, she felt only her own sense of deep failure and sadness.

She had met Josh when she was just twenty-two and in the first year of her job as an assistant music publicist. Having the time of her life, going to gigs almost every night of the week, the last thing on her mind was a relationship. Then one day she was sent to the coffee shop near her office to buy a round of drinks for her hung-over colleagues. As the barista pushed her order of four double espressos, two skinny lattes and two Americanos towards her, she realised she'd forgotten her purse.

'Oh, shit,' she said to the barista, feeling awkward as she knew a queue had built behind her because of the big order. 'I'm just from the record company around the corner, I'll be back in five minutes.'

As she went to turn around, a suited arm reached past her with a credit card.

'I've got this,' she heard a man say. 'Add a double espresso to that order.'

Abbie reddened as she looked up at him. 'Oh no, I couldn't. Let me go and get you the cash. My office is close by.'

The man smiled at her. 'Mine too. How about you just buy me a drink after work and we'll call it even. Meet me in The Crown at six?'

He was cute. And he had kind eyes. And he was helping cure eight people's hangovers. So it seemed he was thoughtful too. Why not?

'See you there,' she said, smiling as she juggled the cardboard drinks holders while leaving the coffee shop.

He swept her off her feet and he wanted to take care of her. A year later they walked down the aisle of a church in her hometown of Liverpool, one of his hedge fund colleagues as the best man and Lily and Violet as her bridesmaids.

There was no catalyst for their breakup that she could pinpoint. They hadn't been arguing. She had still loved him, and he seemed to feel the same.

One day he just told her he was leaving. That he was sorry but he couldn't be in a relationship at that moment. He'd never given her the decency of a conversation for 'closure' but she was pretty sure he felt they'd settled down too young and didn't want to be tied down anymore. He said she could stay in their riverfront apartment for a while and he would stay with a friend, but she needed to get away from the daily reminders of their five years together, four of them married. She searched for a place as different to Josh's city pad as she could find and was out within days, living with a Swedish painter and decorator and a Lebanese chef for a few weeks until she found something more permanent.

Twenty-seven years old and heading for divorce. She had been ashamed.

A year later she heard on the grapevine that he was

engaged to someone else, and his profile picture on Facebook now showed him happily walking under a shower of confetti next to a beautiful blonde in a wedding gown.

She knew it was time to move on and she knew she couldn't go back, but it hurt like hell to feel like you weren't good enough, yet the next girl to come along was. They'd now taken their relationship a step further than Abbie and Josh ever did, and the thought made her close her eyes and curl up in the foetal position. He had found someone new who was good enough to be the mother of his children.

She knew she had to find a way to make the pain stop.

A WEEK LATER, Abbie walked purposefully into a meeting room at The Ritz, facing Utah Saints board director Hank Henderson (the third, apparently) and two of his fellow board members. They didn't introduce themselves and stayed mostly quiet throughout. She was slightly daunted as the room setup resembled how she imagined a firing squad would look. She nervously smiled, with only one of the men facing her returning the gesture, and mentally prepared herself for a grilling.

Hank was friendly though, and she immediately felt at ease in his presence. The other two middle-aged men were impossible to read, so she tried to block out their presence and focus on the man sitting in the centre. The interview was flowing nicely and she forged an easy rapport with Hank as he explained the vision for the Utah Saints soccer team and American soccer as a whole industry. She couldn't help but be utterly enthused at his ideas. The plans to develop the team were solid and his excitement was infectious.

When he asked about her career starting out in music and why she made the switch to football, her response flowed freely.

'I loved the music industry, I really did. My father was a music producer before he retired and I definitely inherited his passion for music. I got into promoting bands, which was fantastic and I really enjoyed doing that for a couple of years.'

Hank nodded, seeming interested. 'So why make that jump from music to sport?'

'Something about sport intrigued me and it's as much entertainment as music or television and has just as much impact on people, if not more. There's nothing like sport that resonates with a community, a team of supporters or even an entire country. Remember when Bubba Watson won the Masters for the first time a few years ago? Well, I cried. I'm a casual golf watcher at best, but the magnitude of the occasion and Bubba's reaction caused an emotional tidal wave for the general viewer, and that's the power of sport.'

'That was some day,' one of the other board members agreed. It was the first time she had received a reaction of any type from one of the other men facing her, and Abbie took it as encouragement to continue.

'And the Olympics over here in London. It changed the attitude of a whole country. We were watching sports we had never heard of, cheering athletes who until that day had been strangers to us. And everyone in London was smiling. It really felt like a different country we were living in for those weeks – we were united as a nation and it has left behind a real legacy. Cycling got a real boost and you couldn't move for a while in London for new adoptees biking to work.'

She paused for thought and saw the three men smiling at her. Finally, she seemed to have cracked the other two. She blushed. 'I'm so sorry, I get a little carried away sometimes.'

'Don't apologise at all. Your passion is fantastic to see, and we need someone like you with us at Utah Saints,' Hank said. 'We need someone who lives and breathes sport and has the knowledge and skill to put us firmly in the spotlight, as soccer is still very much evolving in the US.'

She walked out of the room at the end of the interview with as much purpose as she had walked in. She knew it was likely nothing would come of it but it had felt good at least, and helped her remember why she followed the career path she had.

AT HOME LATER that day, Abbie's mental playback of the

interview, while she was finishing eating her dinner, was interrupted by the ring of her phone and she jumped to retrieve it from her bag, seeing Michael's name pop up on the screen. Swiping the phone to answer, she started speaking as soon as Michael had said hi.

'Thanks for setting today up, Michael. It was great practice and they were a really interesting bunch of guys to chat to. It really did help get me fired up a bit so I'm ready for other ideas now. And bless you for phoning to see how it went.'

Michael laughed loudly. 'I'm not phoning to see how it went. I didn't have time to think about it before Hank phoned me to offer you the job. They want you to start as soon as possible, and they're offering you an absolute shitload of money and an incredible move package. Before you say no, promise me you'll take a day or so to really think about it?'

The sound of silence filled the airwaves.

'Abbie, are you there?'

'Yes, yes, sorry. It's a bit unexpected, that's all.'

She listened, stunned, as he ran through the details of the package. Her mouth dropped open when he mentioned the salary. She barely heard the rest as she was still processing the figure. It was more than double what she earned now and it would be a promotion. Her mind started racing. She couldn't really do it, could she? How good would it look on her CV though? It was only for a set period of time, and her parents were still young.

She brought herself back to the call as Michael asked

if she had any questions. 'No questions, but I do need some time to think. This really wasn't in my life plan and it's come out of left field.'

'Look, I totally understand. Take a couple of days. Let me know any questions that crop up while you're thinking and I'll help. I certainly don't want to push you into doing something you don't want to do but, equally, I don't want you to miss what could be not only a great career opportunity, but an amazing life experience.'

Ending the call, she walked back into the kitchen and started doing the washing up, the dull task acting as the perfect antidote to her whirring mind. Could she do it? Did she want to? She had to admit it was an exciting idea, but she didn't think she could make the move from her home. It would be a huge change. She was contemplating moving to a place that not only had she never visited, but she'd barely heard of. She'd only ever been to America once, to New York, and everyone said that wasn't like the rest of the country. She had to be mad.

Finishing drying and putting away in the kitchen, she remembered that an old football colleague of hers had attended a couple of American Major League Soccer games the year before on an extended road trip. She'd send him a message and get a bit of intel.

While her laptop fired up, she clicked onto Facebook and started scrolling through the recent photos of dogs and holidays and cat videos reposted from YouTube. The seemingly harmless 'people you may know' section came into view, and there he was. Josh Hawthorn. Like a car crash that you know you shouldn't look at but you just can't help yourself, Abbie clicked on the name. Oh god, his profile image. It had changed from the picture-perfect smiling wedding day confetti shot to one of a baby scan.

Clicking on the photo, she saw ninety-seven likes and fifty-three comments. The last comment was from Josh himself. 'Thanks everyone!!! We couldn't be happier. Baby Hawthorn is due in July, making our two into a perfect three. Love Josh and Hannah xxx'

Abbie slammed the laptop shut. She refused to cry. He'd had enough of her tears, and two years down the line she had to pull up her boots and figure things out.

Life had to change, and she had to change.

Picking up her phone, she navigated to the text icon and composed a message.

I'll take the job. Consider me a fully signed-up member of the Utah Saints. Let's talk tomorrow about the details, but I trust that you've got the best you can for me. Thanks. I think you're about to change my life!

CHAPTER 4

THE TASK OF sorting out her belongings and deciding which to throw out, donate or pack was upon her before she knew it. She was doing a little bit each night after work, and tonight she was confronting the boxes under the bed, hastily packed when she left the apartment she shared with Josh. She could barely remember what they contained, and if she hadn't needed them in the last two years, she couldn't think what might be useful in them now.

One box contained books. She carefully went through, putting aside the ones she hadn't read to take to America, and separating the ones she had read into a bag that would go to the charity shop. That was quite a good find. A pile of books would no doubt be handy for evenings in her new home. Maybe she'd start exercising when she got out there. She could find some classes, maybe join a running club. Her excitement was growing on a daily basis as she thought of how she could shape this experience just how she wanted to. Salt Lake City really was going to be her oyster.

She had been sent her ticket and she left on Sunday. Four more days at work and a final Saturday in London and she would be leaving on a jet plane. The days were flying by faster than she had anticipated. She had to get everything done.

The next box was filled with old music magazines. She had kept them as they all had articles or reviews of her clients from her time as a publicist at the record label. She opened one at random and smiled at the memory of the photo shoot with a band at a mad hatter's tea party. The lead singer was sporting a tall hat worn crooked while the bass player had his pinkie sticking out while holding a teacup that looked ridiculously small in his large hand. There was a live rabbit perched on the table with them and the drummer was dressed as a Cheshire cat. They'd all fallen about laughing when the rabbit decided it needed a bathroom break just as the drummer had perched him on his lap.

She'd leave that box with her parents in Liverpool. The magazines were worth keeping; a record of a great time in her young career and a lot of fun times. Her parents were coming down with Lily on Saturday to stay overnight and wave her goodbye at the airport the next day.

Reaching back under the bed, she retrieved the final box. All at once, she remembered what was in there.

This was the history of her and Josh, all neatly packaged up in a box. There was a stack of photos, which she quickly flicked through. Under that was their wedding album. He had kindly and sweetly told her she could keep it, and not knowing how to respond, she had packed it and moved it out with the rest of her things. Turning the pages, she noticed how young they looked. The expression on their faces was so innocent and happy, she never would have guessed looking at those photos that they wouldn't survive even four years.

Next up was a large envelope containing their wedding certificate and, of course, the resulting divorce papers. Ironic that the paperwork could coexist quite nicely for years gathering dust when their owners couldn't manage it. A dark blue velvet box held her simple gold wedding band which Josh had secretly engraved with the date of the wedding and the inscription 'And I Love Her', a surprise he had revealed at the altar in reference to the first dance they had picked for their reception.

She was about to put the lid back on when she noticed a final small envelope at the bottom. She knew what was inside, and her heart started beating faster. She was facing up to things. Exorcising demons. She needed to see it again. She lifted the flap of the envelope and pulled out the photograph. The small typed letters in the top corner were still clear on the scan. Baby Hawthorn. The first one. He or she would have been five now.

She put the scan back in the envelope and tucked it inside one of the books that she was taking to America. She put aside the marriage and divorce paperwork, making a mental note to find somewhere safe to keep it with the rest of her life admin. She repacked the rest of her old life into the box, replaced the lid, then walked outside and threw it all in the wheelie bin, dusting her hands off afterwards as though she had been handling something unsavoury.

ABBIE'S FINAL DAY in London was reserved for her goodbye dinner. Her mum, dad and sister Lily came all the way from Liverpool to see her off.

On Saturday evening, she left them with Polly to go out and buy wine while they deliberated over takeaway menus. She walked back into a flat full of people and a shout of 'surprise'. Polly had taken it upon herself to organise a going away party. She didn't feel a departure like this should go without fanfare. Abbie soaked up the atmosphere, grateful to Polly for doing something so lovely for her.

Polly's bandmates were over in the corner, obviously in charge of the playlist. Lily was in the kitchen with Damian the artist, who was teaching her the intricacies of mixology and how to make the perfect mojito. A couple of her old university friends were over talking to her parents and some of her colleagues from the music days were attempting to find common ground with her newer work pals from the football club, which included Dave and Mavis.

She swallowed back a lump in her throat as the reality hit that she was giving all this up. She'd been sleepwalking through life for two years yet she had all these wonderful people around her, who she'd been neglecting as she threw herself into work. She owed it to them as much as herself to make the most of Utah and to come back at some point more like her old self. And she needed to start being a bit more like the old Abbie right now.

She decided to join her sister. She wouldn't see her for months and twenty-nine was probably a good age to learn how to make the perfect cocktail. It seemed like a useful life skill.

Fifteen minutes later she was giggling away with Michael and Lily as they tasted an awful pink concoction, which they were planning to trick Polly into trying. Just as Abbie placed the finishing touch of a green cocktail umbrella on top with a flourish, a voice from behind made her jump.

'Don't give up your day job will you, that looks like an abomination.'

Her head flew around at the sound of the Irish lilt and she grinned as she saw Violet.

'Come on then, don't just stand there, I've spent thirty minutes on the Northern line to get here, someone needs to put wine in the hole in the middle of my face and quick. Sorry I couldn't come earlier with Michael, I had to pick something up and so I told him to come ahead without me.'

'Don't worry,' Abbie smiled. 'I'm so glad you're here now. Lily, can you grab Violet a drink please?'

Lily grabbed a wine glass and poured it almost to the brim, handing it over to her sister's best friend.

Then Violet motioned to Abbie and the pair walked through to the bedroom, Violet closing the door behind them. Taking in the nearly bare room and the two suitcases standing next to the wall, she said, 'So, this is it then, you're really off?'

'I really am.'

Violet's lower lip started to wobble. 'What am I going to do without you, Abs?'

With that she put down her glass, threw her arms around Abbie and started to cry.

Abbie wiped away her own tears as they moved apart to look at each other again.

'I'm going to miss you so much, Vi. But you know I get to come home four times a year, you can visit me, we can Skype and I'm sure I'll be back before you know it.'

Abbie nodded, smiling at her friend to reassure her that she was right.

'I know this is great for your career and you seem really set on it, so you should give it a bloody good go. Now, let's go get me a whisky. This wine tastes like shite.'

Laughing, they returned to the party where, by this point, the lead guitarist from Polly's band had started chatting up Lily, who seemed to be enjoying it. Definitely time for Abbie to intervene like an embarrassing older sister has the divine right to do.

'HAVE YOU GOT everything?'

'Yes, Mum.'

'Have you got your passport?'

'Yes, Dad.'

'You will phone when you get there, won't you?'

'I promise I'll phone.'

'You'll come back if you hate it, won't you?'

'Yes, Vi, I promise I'll come back if it's awful.'

'You'll tell me if you meet any film stars?'

'Yes, Lily, although, like I've told you, I'm not anywhere near Hollywood. And you'll stay away from wannabe rock stars in my absence?'

'Well, I can't promise that. Dad says the music business is just in us. We can't help it. I'm probably meant to be a muse.'

'Amusing more like,' piped up her dad.

Everyone laughed and it helped to break the slight tension in the air that their little motley crew had felt the whole way to the airport.

'Let's do it now.' Lily looked as if she was going to burst with excitement as she looked at her mum and dad in turn with a pleading look on her face. A face that was clearly used to getting its own way.

Her mother rolled her eyes. 'Go on then.'

Lily took out a small wrapped box and handed it to Abbie.

'Go on, open it,' her little sister urged.

'What's this?'

Her dad cleared his throat before he spoke. 'We wanted you to have something that whenever you look at it, you'll think of home. Just a little something to say good luck.'

Smiling, Abbie untied the carefully fixed bow and removed the pink wrapping paper. Sitting on a burgundy velvet bed inside the black jewellery box was the daintiest of silver charm bracelets.

'It's beautiful,' she exclaimed, studying the charms that were already hanging from the links.

Lily leaned in, pointing at the charms one by one. 'You see, there's the Beatles so you'll remember Liverpool, the Camden Town tube sign to remember your flat with Polly, a football for your job, a skirt cos you used to dress trendy and a treble clef cos you like music.'

'It's perfect, I love it so much. Thank you.'

She gathered everyone into a group hug and then her mother helped her clasp on the bracelet.

Violet scooted forward. 'I got this for you to add onto it.'

She handed a little package over and Abbie emptied into her hand a tiny shamrock charm.

'So you'll never be able to forget me.'

'As if I ever could.'

Abbie could sense that much more time together would see them all get maudlin, and as much as she wanted to squeeze every moment of time in with her loved ones, she didn't want everyone to start crying, so she told them she had better head through security. After many tight hugs and kisses, and despite their best efforts, a few tears, she went through the security gate.

She felt like a child who had just had their training wheels taken off their bike. A bit wobbly, but after a few paces she gathered her confidence and felt like she was flying.

The airport was a blast. She bought some new sunglasses, a multicoloured silk scarf, some too-high heels and a bright blue maxi dress. What was it about airports that made it seem like you had monopoly money in your purse and you weren't spending real cash?

Glancing up at the screens, she noticed her flight was boarding. This was it.

She strode purposefully towards the gate. Armed with her passport, boarding pass and an address scribbled down on a piece of paper to take a taxi to at the other end, she was ready for her next chapter.

CHAPTER 5

STANDING ON TIPTOE to stretch her legs and reaching her arms to the sky as she got out of the taxi, an utterly exhausted Abbie stood on the pavement outside her new temporary home. It was difficult to see much, with the street shrouded in the darkness of the late hour, but Abbie didn't have the energy to look at her surroundings anyway; it had been a hell of a journey. After leaving her old flat in London nearly twenty hours ago, she'd flown across the Atlantic all the way to Las Vegas, and then waited for nearly three hours in the airport for her connecting flight.

She'd amused herself for ten minutes on the slot machines (net loss four dollars but, hey, she was in Vegas), watched a whole lot of stag and hen parties walk back and forth (or bachelor and bachelorette was the correct terminology here judging by the t-shirt slogans: MEGAN'S BACHELORETTE DOES VEGAS! WATCH OUT BACHELOR ABOUT!) and finally settled down with a Utah travel guide she found in the bookshop, scanning the glossy pages until her flight to Salt Lake City boarded. Reading the statistics about where she was heading, she wondered if it would feel like there was so much more space around her, going from a city with six million people crowding around each other in the ultimate rat race to a place with just 190,000 inhabitants. Was it going to be the proverbial breath of fresh air? Or would she be bored, missing the hustle and bustle of England's capital? Would she pine for the jam-packed tube and the teeming streets?

Now she looked up and located the apartment number of the place that the Utah Saints had arranged for her to stay in for three months, until she found a long-term solution. The low, single-storey modern building was covered in light cream horizontal vinyl strips of siding with a grey slate gable roof. A dark grey solid wood front door was the entryway to her new home and she couldn't wait to get through it.

The taxi driver carried her two cases up the four steps to the front door and Abbie used the last bit of energy in her body to offer her appreciation and hand him a tip.

'No problem, ma'am. Have a nice day now.' The driver left her with a friendly wave.

Wow. So, it really was like that. What a difference from the grunting London cabbies she was used to.

The email from Hank Henderson's secretary had told her that the key would be under the doormat, so she fished around in the dark until her hand closed around the cold piece of metal.

Fiddling it around in the lock, she finally heard a click and the door swung open. She lifted her cases inside, leaving them near the door, and feeling along the wall, she located a switch that suddenly bathed the dark entrance hall with soft light. Through the door to the left was a large kitchen and living space. The kitchen was modern, all silver appliances and dove grey units. The lounge area was carpeted in a soft-looking dark grey pile, with a lighter grey corner sofa and an ash wood dining table with four chairs. A matching bookcase sat against one wall while a huge television was mounted opposite the sofa. It looked like something from a catalogue, and she couldn't believe her luck.

On the opposite side of the hallway was the bathroom. Another modern-looking room, this one was all white, with a huge shower cubicle and two sinks. She couldn't quite comprehend why one sink wouldn't be enough, but this was America – everything was bigger and better, she'd been told.

The room next to the lounge was a decent size with a queen bed, decorated like the lounge in neutral tones, with the same dark grey carpet. Built in closets filled the length of one wall with a dresser on the opposite side of the room. It was bigger than her room in London, and she knew she would love staying here.

As much as she wanted to explore her new place, root about in the kitchen drawers and cupboards and start writing a list of things she'd need to buy, tiredness engulfed her. She couldn't even think about opening a suitcase so she stripped off her shoes, jeans, jacket and jumper and crawled under the grey covers in her t-shirt. She faintly recognised that she still had her make-up on, but before the thought could fully form, she let the marshmallow-soft mattress and sheets envelop her and fell into a deep slumber.

WAKING UP TO the sun streaming through the window, Abbie mentally cursed herself for being too tired to close the curtains. She shut her eyes again but quickly realised she was now wide awake and had zero chance of going back to sleep. She glanced at her watch and saw that it was 5:23 a.m. Got to love jet lag. Although she supposed it was better having the whole day to get to grips with the area before she had to report for work the next day.

First things first though. She needed a shower after the trip she had made yesterday. It was the farthest she'd ever travelled and she felt a long, long way from home.

Heading into the entrance to get her suitcases, she noticed a fourth door that she hadn't got around to opening last night. In the thick fog of tiredness that had descended upon her, she'd barely noticed it was there.

Opening the door, her jaw dropped. It was bright and airy and decorated in the same style as the other bedroom, but this room had taken steroids. In the middle was an enormous bed. She didn't really know what king size was, but this must be even bigger. President size? Along an entire wall ran wardrobes with mirrored sliding doors. She didn't have enough clothes to fill even five per cent of it. Another huge TV was wall-mounted opposite the bed above a long chest of drawers, and to the side of that, a dresser with a mirror and stool. But the pièce de résistance was at the other end of the room where a huge window opened out to the view of a beautiful park filled with trees. In front of the window was a chaise longue in the same dove grey as the lounge sofa.

'Holy shit.'

After a moment of stillness she screamed, ran and launched herself into the middle of the bed. This whole thing had to be a dream. There was no way she could be living here. She'd find out it was all a horrible mistake later on and they'd move her to a studio flat above a kebab shop or something.

Sitting up and looking around the beautiful room, she saw some paperwork on the dresser. Scrambling over, she picked up the note, which was handwritten in perfect cursive.

Hello Abbie!!

Welcome to Salt Lake City! We're all looking forward so much to meeting you! In the meantime, here's some information for you to help you on your FIRST DAY in Utah!!

- The key to your company car is in the drawer of this dresser. The car is parked right in front of the apartment in space 4B – that's your allocated spot.

- Also in the dresser is your new cell phone and charger. I've programmed in a few numbers for you, including mine, so don't hesitate to call if you need <u>anything</u>! Your number is 555-586-

8294. I checked for you and your family can dial it from the UK by putting 001 in front of that number. ☺

- Your email address is already set up on your cell phone and you'll get your laptop at the office. Your email address is abbie.potter@utahsaints.com.

- The apartment has Wi-Fi. The network is 'Liberty4B' and the password is 'UT4H4EVA'. (I set that up!)

- Your closest grocery store is two blocks away. Just head north on S 500 E (north is if the park is on your right ☺) and you'll reach it. I've marked it on the map I've left with this letter. There's a Walgreen's drugstore next to it in case you need to buy any medicines. I did put a little survival kit in the kitchen with some basics such as painkillers, Band-Aids, vitamins, sleeping pills, etc.

- There's a gas station right across the street from the grocery store if you need to fill up. Your car is <u>DIESEL</u> so be careful to fill with the right gas!

- If you have any problems with the apartment please call me and I'll make sure to resolve it with the management agency. We want you to be so happy here so let me know <u>any</u> issue at all!

- If you come to my office when you arrive I'll give

you an orientation, go through your paperwork and make sure you're settled in. I thought we could have lunch together too to get to know each other so I've booked a table at a restaurant close by for 12.30 p.m. I can't wait!!

Have a <u>GREAT</u> day!

Yours
Kitty McIntire
Senior Personal Assistant to Mr Hank Henderson III &
President of Utah Saints Internal Social Committee

Dear God. Abbie enjoyed friendly, but this sounded like a Disney princess had swallowed a factory-load of pink cupcakes and flown into town on a multicoloured unicorn.

Mean Abbie, she chastised herself. This was a different country and a different culture. It wouldn't do her any harm to enjoy some friendly faces and helpfulness. She was always moaning that Londoners weren't as friendly as where she came from up north. These guys were obviously incredibly welcoming – she simply needed to get used to it. And she needed to make some friends in this town if she was going to live here. Spending every evening and weekend alone wouldn't be any fun.

Thinking of having fun, she jumped into action. There was a whole city at her fingertips that she knew nothing about and only a day before she had to go to work.

After emptying the entire contents of her suitcases onto the bed in 'The Royal Suite' as she had dubbed it, and finally washing off the drudgeries of long-haul travel, she decided to explore the lush green grounds next to her apartment. She only had to cross the street and she was inside, passing a sign identifying it as 'Liberty Park'.

It was barely six forty-five when she got to the park but she could see quite a few people on the running tracks and cycle paths and, beyond that, lots of dog walkers on the grassy fields. She didn't stop to look at the map but instead decided to meander wherever her feet took her. Walking through the park, which was lined with huge trees, she felt a real sense of being grounded. It was a beautiful wintery morning, with shafts of light from the rising sun helping to warm the air a little.

She walked past the entrance of an aviary, hearing the early morning call of hundreds of birds, and carried on walking until she saw a swimming pool. There was so much to do in this park alone. She'd seen runners, cyclists, swimmers and dog walkers and she'd barely been out half an hour. Further exploration revealed some tennis players getting a game in, she imagined before they went to work, and several mothers with children in pushchairs out for a walk.

She carried on exploring for a while and was about to work out how to make her way back to the apartment when she saw the glint of sunshine on water through some trees and wandered over to take a look. She emerged into a clearing on a grassy knoll that led down to a duck pond, and gasped at the view. Rising majestically above the trees was a range of breathtaking snow-capped mountains. It must be the Wasatch Mountains that she had read about in her guidebook, but she never imagined she'd be able to see such an incredible sight from the city.

She'd never seen anything quite like it. Standing by the water she felt like she'd made one of the biggest discoveries in humankind, yet this was something that the people who lived here must see every day. She felt like a very lucky girl at that moment. She wasn't sure why the gods were shining down on her but, so far, she loved everything about her new home.

As she walked backwards towards the path, not wanting to tear her gaze away from the vision ahead, it suddenly felt like she'd been hit by a freight train. Losing her balance and falling hard on her left side, she shrieked in shock as her arm made contact with the hard ground.

'Oh my god, are you okay?'

Looking up, way up, she came face to face with the freight train. Or rather, a tall, broadly built man who had knocked her over with the force of one.

'Well no, thanks to you, but I think I'll live.'

She brushed her hands off and started to struggle to her feet. The man reached down to help her up but she waved him away. 'I'm fine, just watch where you're going next time.'

The man raised his eyebrows.

'Hey, lady, I'm really sorry. I didn't see you. You did walk backwards onto the running track.'

'Well, you should have watched where you were going. I didn't know it was a stupid running track.'

She gingerly felt her upper arm, where a bruise was forming already and the top layer of skin was grazed.

'That looks painful. Want me to take a look?'

'I think you've done enough, thanks.'

With that, she started marching off in the direction of where she thought her apartment was. She paused as it didn't look familiar. She turned around and the freight train was still standing there.

'Where are you from? Australia?'

'England. Why are you still here?'

'Well, you kind of looked lost, and you sound like you don't come from around here, so I thought you might need some directions.'

'I'm not lost. I live here too.'

'Okay then. Well, I'll be seeing you, England.'

'I hope not. I don't know where the hospital is yet and who knows what would happen if you bumped into me again.'

The freight train laughed. 'I heard the British sense of humour was good. Now I've had it proven. When did you move here?'

'Yesterday. But I'm not lost.'

'Sure, okay. So, you're leaving then?'

'Yep. I'm just admiring the park for a minute then I'm going.'

'Cool. So, you definitely don't need me to point you in the right direction?'

She looked up at the freight train. 'I'm heading to S Five Hundred E Street. Which is this way, right?' she said, pointing.

'You're absolutely right. Just turn one hundred and eighty degrees from where you're pointing and walk that way. You'll be there in a heartbeat.'

'Exactly. I was just testing if you really were a local. See you.'

She could hear the freight train's laughter half the way back to her new home.

ONCE SHE WAS back and had washed the dirt off from her fall, she looked at the list she had made of places to visit from her guidebook. What would she do first? There was the temple, which she supposed she really should visit. The museum. Obviously, Salt Lake. She also needed to do some food shopping and should probably figure out where the football (sorry, soccer) club was in relation to the apartment.

She mulled it over for a while and then made her decision, circling it on her notebook. Sod all of it. She was off to The Gateway Mall. Utah wardrobe, here we come.

CHAPTER 6

PULLING INTO THE car park at the club the next morning, Abbie turned off the engine and rested her head and her hands on the steering wheel, her heart pounding and her breathing heavy. The fact that she would have to sit on the wrong side of the car and drive on the wrong side of the road had completely passed her by until she hopped into the car yesterday, excited about the shopping trip to buy new clothes.

She had remembered quite quickly that the only other time she'd driven like that was in France, where she was so jittery that after a few minutes Josh had made her pull over and had taken over for the rest of the journey, telling her that it was obviously something she didn't feel comfortable doing.

At that memory, she had resolved to conquer this bizarre upside-down inside-out world of driving and get herself to the mall. The task was made slightly easier by the fact that the executive-style Ford was automatic, so she didn't have to grapple with the gearstick on the wrong side, like in France with the little Renault they had hired.

Gingerly pulling out from in front of her apartment, she had thrown all her concentration onto making sure she stayed on the right side of the road. After a few laps around the block, where she only veered over the line a couple of times, she pulled over to set the GPS to the mall.

Happy that she only had three miles to drive, she pulled back out onto the road. No sooner had she accelerated than she was faced with a rather large truck coming at her head on. She screamed at the realisation she'd inadvertently and unconsciously been driving on the left and swerved quickly back to the right, her whole body shaking in shock.

After concentrating intensely for the rest of the short trip, which felt like it took an eternity, she gladly parked up and decided to block out the memory of the drive with some serious retail therapy.

This morning's journey to the club had been slightly less traumatic. On the upside, she had managed to avoid any head-on meetings with other motorists and, despite making slow progress, her over-the-line veering had reduced. All she needed was practice.

She focused on slowing her breathing and preparing herself to walk into her new place of work. Counting down from ten to one, she was at number four when she jumped out of her seat at a sharp rap on her window.

Standing on the other side of the window was a woman about her age, very slim with angular features, long blonde hair and a huge, white-toothed, perfect beam.

As she tapped again, Abbie wound down the window and smiled.

'You are Abbie! I recognised you immediately from

the photos I looked at on the internet. I'm Kitty. How is everything? Did you get everything you needed? Do you need help with anything from the car?'

Abbie laughed. 'Hi, Kitty. Everything is perfect, thanks. I was just taking a moment after my trip over. I haven't done much driving on this side of the road so it's taking a little getting used to.'

'Oh of course, I didn't even think. I'm sure you'll soon adjust. Let's get you into the office and get you some coffee and then we'll get you set up.'

Abbie climbed out of the car and gladly followed Kitty in through the glass double doors marked 'PER-SONNEL ONLY'. Her new colleague scurried down the long corridor, pointing out things at breakneck speed.

'There's the security office, that's human resources, through there is the staff cafeteria, although I hardly ever eat there as there's a lot of good places around. That's the assistant manager's office, those doors take you to the marketing suite where you'll be based, and I'm right along here next to Mr Henderson's office. Come in, and welcome.'

Abbie knew she would have to retrace her steps and look at the door signs herself as she'd had no chance to take anything in.

'Please sit down. Mi casa es su casa, as they say – you're always welcome in here. Let me get you a coffee. How do you take it?'

'Do you have tea?'

Kitty looked at her strangely. 'Not normally this early

in the morning but yes, we have some. Hold on just a second and I'll get you some. Do you like it sweetened?'

'No sugar for me, thanks.'

With that Kitty dashed out of the office and Abbie had a good look around. Hank Henderson III's PA clearly had OCD. There wasn't a piece of paper in sight – in fact there was nothing on her desk except for her computer screen, keyboard and a wrist support pad – and above the desk on the wall was a row of books all lined up in height order. Four tall filing units lined one wall, and on the facing wall, four equal-sized framed photographs hung. Three were of the Utah Saints in action during matches and a fourth showed a group of people in ski gear looking like they were having a whale of a time. She stood up to take a closer look. There were about fifteen people in the photo, all men with the exception of Kitty who stood out in her bubble gum pink salopettes, grinning front and centre in the frame.

Abbie started as the door flew open and Kitty came back in clutching a mug of steaming coffee and a lidded cup with a straw.

'I was just looking at your photos while I waited.'

'You've seen the skiing one? I don't know if I mentioned but I'm president of the social committee here. I plan fun things for us to do together outside of work and that was a ski day we went on in Park City. You'll have to come next time.'

'I've only been skiing once, and I wasn't that good so I haven't done it since. It scares me a bit,' Abbie said sheepishly.

'Oh. I don't think I know anybody who doesn't ski. Anyway, here's your tea.' Kitty brandished the cup with the straw and Abbie took it, confused. It was freezing cold to the touch and she could feel ice cubes clashing together in the cup. After the brief ski discussion, she didn't want to feel any sillier so she took a sip from the straw. Try as she might, she couldn't disguise the look on her face as she swallowed the bitter, freezing liquid that tasted nothing like tea.

'Oh goodness, are you okay? What's the matter?' Kitty exclaimed, eyes wide.

'Nothing, I'm so sorry. I didn't mean to be rude. Usually in England our tea is hot and it comes with milk. I was a bit surprised, that's all.' She quickly tried to straighten her features but she could feel her cheeks warming and she knew she must look red.

'You wanted hot tea! You should have said! When we say tea here, we mean iced tea, either sweetened or unsweetened. Have you never had it before?'

'It's safe to say that I haven't, no. I'm sure it's really nice though. As soon as you get used to it.'

'Well, you don't ski, you've never had iced tea. This is a real education for you over here, isn't it, Abbie!' Kitty seemed to think the whole exchange was hilarious and launched into peals of squeaking laughter. 'It's like your American version of Hogwarts.'

Abbie couldn't help but look at her like she had gone mad. What on earth was she talking about?

Kitty carried on laughing. 'You know, your name is Potter, like Harry Potter! And he went to Hogwarts and learnt all sorts of things. And now you're here learning about tea.'

Abbie forced out a laugh and decided she needed to get this conversation back on track.

'Kitty, thanks so much for organising everything for me with the apartment and the car. I couldn't have wished for a more perfect welcome. You really took the stress out of arriving here.'

'You're more than welcome, I'm so pleased it all worked out! Now, you'll meet human resources to talk through a lot of your stuff, but any problems with the apartment, let me know.'

'It's an incredible apartment. I'll have to start looking fairly soon, so I was wondering what the monthly rent would be on a place like that. I can even downgrade as I don't really need two bedrooms.'

When Kitty mentioned the figure, Abbie gasped as she did the rough sums in her head. The rental on her beautiful park-side unit was less than she paid for a room in a flat share in London.

'If you want to stay on at the end, the owner said you could probably extend if it makes it easier and it's within your budget.'

Before they could continue the conversation, there was a tap on the door and it swung open.

Abbie's jaw dropped when she looked up at the newcomer and came face to face with the freight train from the park the day before. He saw her straight away and looked surprised.

'What's up, England? Now this is a small world. Have you tracked me down to sue my ass?'

Abbie started to splutter out a plea, but then she noticed the twinkling in his caramel-coloured eyes and the grin on his face and she too broke into a smile.

'I work here, I'll have you know. I think it's you who's tracked me down. Wanting to make sure you didn't do too much damage so I don't sue, I'm sure.'

'You've met already?'

Having almost forgotten she was there, Abbie turned at the sound of Kitty's voice and then looked back towards the freight train as he spoke.

'Apparently walking backwards is a thing in England and so we had a bit of an accident yesterday in the park when I ran into her. She was a trooper though, got right up off the ground and told me right off.'

'What were you doing in Liberty Park, Kyle? You don't even live near there.'

'It's a nice place to run.'

As Kitty continued to engage him in conversation, Abbie took another look. So, Kyle was his name. He was so stereotypically all-American that he could have been in the movies. Good-looking, muscly, around six feet tall, with tanned skin that looked like he spent a lot of time outdoors and dark tousled hair, she guessed he was around mid-thirties. He was a walking, talking cliché. And she was a cliché for appraising him like a breakfast platter. She metaphorically slapped herself on the wrist and brought herself back into the room.

'Don't you think, England?'

'Sorry, what did you say?' Abbie cursed herself for switching off.

'I was saying to Kitty that it was pretty cruel of her to put you over East of Downtown. There's not much going on there. You're going to get really bored.'

Kitty threw him a dirty look.

'It's beautiful,' Abbie said. 'If I can wake up every day to the view of those mountains, I think I'll be just fine. And Kitty's been really helpful.'

'Thank you, Abbie. That's her name you know, Kyle: Abbie. So you can stop being rude and calling her England.'

Abbie eyed them both curiously. They were squabbling like brother and sister. She brushed it aside when she remembered where she was. She was sure people at American football clubs had just as much banter as at home. Britain hadn't cornered the market on humour.

'Oh simmer down, Kitty-Kat. England knows it's a term of endearment. We're old friends by now. In fact, because she's new to town I'm going to make it my duty to make sure she experiences all the fun stuff we have to offer.'

'No need, Kyle. I've got it under control. I've told her about the social committee and I've invited her to come skiing with us next time.'

Kyle chuckled. 'She can't even walk properly; I don't

like her chances skiing.'

As Kitty gave him daggers, Abbie couldn't help but burst out laughing. He had no clue how true his words were.

'Kyle, you can leave now, Abbie and I have things to discuss. What did you want anyway?'

'Hank's schedule for Friday. I need him to meet the new youth players.'

'I'll check Mr Henderson's schedule and let you know if he has a window,' she said primly.

'Alrighty, you do that. England, I'll catch you later.' With a salute he left the room, and it suddenly felt empty without him occupying the space.

Abbie sensed a tense atmosphere and rushed to fill the silence.

'So, small world isn't it? I can't believe that the only person I've spoken to since I got here works here too. What does he do?'

'Kyle Miller is an ex-soccer player and he runs our college scouting programme and youth team. You probably won't need to have much to do with him.'

'He seems nice, reminds me of some of the guys back home.'

'Well, appearances can be deceptive, Abbie, and I would be really careful if I were you. You need a friend here and I can be that person. I can see he's got his eye on you but let me just tell you that you're far from the first. I've seen this so many times before from him. He's what we call a major player and he'll hurt you. I promise you're better staying as far away as possible.'

Abbie was surprised at the openness of the girl she had met not thirty minutes previously, but thankful for the heads-up. Not that she was interested in a man right now anyway but, if she were, she absolutely didn't need another heartbreaker. Why were the good-looking, charming ones always the worst?

'Look, let me show you to your desk. I know you have a bunch of emails waiting for you, and I can get this paperwork to you later. Then we'll have lunch and get to know each other better.'

Kitty's voice had lost its severity, so Abbie threw her a grateful smile and followed her down to her new office.

CHAPTER 7

CLICKING 'SAVE' ON her document, Abbie crossed another action off her to-do list and looked up at the clock on the wall of the office. Technically she could have gone home an hour ago and started her Friday night, but she'd wanted to finish a few things and only had the quiet apartment to go back to. She was planning to do some exploring at the weekend but, after a week of information overload and trying her best to remember everyone's names, she was looking forward tonight to simply going home, putting on some jogging bottoms and ordering a pizza.

It had been a good week. Everyone had been welcoming and she was loving getting stuck into her new job and learning all about her new team. The culture did feel different to where she'd come from, and she was grateful for it.

She was missing Violet like mad but they had messaged every day, which helped ease any moments of homesickness. Violet had taken to sending her an email each morning with a summary of key British news, celebrity gossip and a weather report. She didn't have the heart to tell Vi that she could get all of that from Twitter as she never wanted the emails to stop.

She had also spoken to her parents, and hearing in their voices that they were totally fine made her feel better about her decision. It was as if she were still just a few motorways away. Lily was also apparently doing well, although her parents hadn't seen her much as she was in a whirlwind of starting her A level revision and also wanting to see her friends at every conceivable moment.

Feeling that she still had close connections to those who were important to her had made it easier to throw herself into the new job. She'd had a great meeting with Hank Henderson earlier in the week and his enthusiasm at having her there was only matched by her enthusiasm at getting stuck in. The season started in two weeks and her focus for the rest of the year was to increase publicity around the team. Hank wanted the Utah Saints to be operating at the top so it could mix amongst the big teams like LA Galaxy in the years to come. He told her that within the next year he wanted to sign a big-name Premiership player to show that they meant business.

After the meeting she had hidden herself away with a blank piece of paper and started brainstorming ideas on how to bring in new fans, and found the germ of an idea that quite excited her. She was working on fleshing it out in between getting to grips with everything else that she had to get a handle on. She had less than a fortnight to familiarise herself with the players, the game and the basics of her job, so at the moment, her head resembled spaghetti junction. She had been dreaming of player formations, fixture dates and the names of journalists in

Salt Lake City that she had yet to meet, so she knew she needed to take some time this weekend to clear her head or there was a danger it would explode before the first game. Then all that work would have been for nothing.

One thing that had surprised her was how well she was getting on with Kitty. Her first impressions had been that Kitty was a bit strange. She had been prickly, perfunctory and slightly overzealous, but Abbie couldn't criticise her for her friendliness since. She perhaps wouldn't be Abbie's usual cup of tea but, since that first odd meeting, Kitty had calmed down a bit and been awfully helpful. She had taken Abbie for lunch every day, showing her some of her favourite food spots in the area surrounding the football club. They had enjoyed spicy Mexican fajitas, one of the most mouth-wateringly delicious burgers Abbie had ever tasted, a huge grilled sandwich and soup combo and today, as a Friday treat, they had gone for Chinese. She'd have to curb these lunches or she would soon have to buy a whole new wardrobe as the current one wouldn't fit her. She didn't quite understand how Kitty stayed so slim if that was her usual diet. She must have a hell of a good metabolism.

Kitty had asked lots of questions, interested in finding out all about Abbie's life back home in England. She had asked about her past jobs, her family and her friends. Abbie had willingly answered, thinking how nice it was to have someone to talk to. Kitty was no Violet or Polly, and Abbie wasn't as comfortable as she was with them, but it was nice to have already made a friend and know that she wasn't going to be lonely across the pond.

At work Kitty was also proving a real gem. She had introduced Abbie to everyone, made sure she knew where everything was and been helpful whenever she had needed to ask a random question. Kitty had even managed to save the day yesterday when Abbie's laptop froze up and she couldn't get it restarted. Apparently, she doubled as the team's computer A&E, managing to solve most issues before it got serious enough to need to call their external IT company.

Realising she had just wasted time thinking back on her week, delaying her leaving the office, Abbie looked down at her notebook, mulling over what else she wanted to finish before going back to her apartment, when the door to the marketing office swung open. She looked up in surprise, as she thought she was the only one left in the building, and saw Kyle walking towards her, smiling.

She hadn't seen much of him this week since their meeting in Kitty's office, only a couple of times from a distance.

'Haven't you got a home to be going to, England? Why are you here so late on a Friday night?' Kyle perched on the corner of her desk, filling the space all around her as he seemed to do whenever he came into a room.

'I've got a lovely home, thank you. I'm finishing a few things up here then I'm heading back there for a thrilling night of box sets and pizza.'

'What?' Kyle threw his arms up with a look of horror on his face. 'Your first Friday night in the city and you're staying in? This can't happen. Come on, turn off the computer and we'll head out. There's this amazing Italian that does the best meatballs in the world. We can eat there then go onto this awesome bar—'

'I wasn't angling for a pity invite. I'm honestly fine. I'm still a bit jet-lagged and I have a ton of things I need to do,' Abbie interrupted, tripping over her words as she felt flustered.

'Garbage. What do you need to do on a Friday night that can't wait until Monday? I said I'd show you around the city and I meant it. There's nothing pitiful about it. You're new to town, hell, you're new to the country, and it's not that much of a hardship to spend time with a bright, beautiful woman, you know.'

Kyle's eyes twinkled as he delivered this last line and Abbie remembered Kitty's warning that he was a man who liked to, for want of a better phrase, sow his wild oats. She had been wavering on saying yes. She hadn't explored and felt a bit silly at the thought of going into restaurants and bars on her own, but getting into a situation with a guy like Kyle was not the way to go about building a lasting career at the club or finding friends for the long-term. And it went without saying that heartbreak was as far down the list of 'things to do' as it could possibly be.

'Really, I'm so tired I couldn't.' She looked down at her lap as she spoke, nervous to meet his eye.

'Shoot, sorry, England, I wasn't throwing you a line there. I genuinely want to show you around, no funny business. How about it?'

He seemed such a nice guy, but she knew that type.

'I promise you I'm not giving excuses. I wouldn't even be able to stay awake for the meatballs. Let me get on this time zone a bit more, then maybe I'll feel more like getting my social life on track. Is that okay?'

She felt a pang of regret at turning him down but she knew it was better this way. She could think of some better excuses in case he asked again. Not that she assumed he would. From the sound of it, he'd have someone else to take out for the world's best meatballs before her jet lag had managed to leave her be.

'Okay, I'll let you off this time, but I promised I'd show you all that Utah has to offer and I don't break promises, so this is just a rain check.'

Abbie grinned at him, her face uncontrollably giving him a reaction that her head was telling her not to give, and he smiled back at her.

'Alrighty, England. Get yourself packed up and out of here before I call security on your ass. Kitty must have told you that Friday overtime is prohibited in the state of Utah? She did tell you that, right?'

Abbie's eyes widened as she began to babble that she didn't know. She stopped in her tracks when she noticed that familiar twinkle in his eye.

'Oh, bugger off, I knew that wasn't true.'

'I had you for a minute there. Admit it.'

'I believed you for less than a second. And that's only because I'm jet-lagged. I never would have fallen for it otherwise.' She looked at Kyle and rolled her eyes, with a little smile on her face. Despite knowing she needed to keep him at arm's length, she couldn't help but warm to him and find herself comfortable in his presence. 'I'm heading off in a minute, I promise.'

'You better. I don't want to find you here on Monday morning still in the same clothes. We shower here in the US. I know you guys still have your outside toilets and share a tub once a week but over here we're clean.'

'That's enough of your cheek. Go on, get out or I'll never finish up and then I *will* still be here on Monday morning.'

Kyle hopped off her desk, took off his baseball cap, bowed and made for the door. 'Until later, England.'

'It's ABBIE,' she half-shouted, half-giggled, as he disappeared.

It suddenly felt empty in the office, as it always seemed to when he'd been around and then left. Deciding the best thing was to start with a fresh brain on Monday morning, she closed down her computer and headed out into the brisk Utah evening.

CHAPTER 8

ABBIE GOT READY on Saturday morning, took her guide book and left the apartment, deciding to wander the streets in her area in the hunt for a spot to have lunch.

She braced herself against the chill that hit her as she walked out the door, and headed north. The weather since she arrived had been crisp. It was cold, but the sky was a beautiful blue each day, meaning that each morning when she opened her curtains she was greeted by the same spectacular view of the park and snow-capped mountains. It felt so alien. Usually, the only thing she caught sight of on a clear day in London was the BT Tower, but in Salt Lake City, it felt like she was close to nature. It was calming, despite her being a stranger to these types of surroundings.

Keeping her eyes peeled as her stomach started to rumble, she scanned the street for an eatery. She had yet to come across another walker, but she'd quickly realised that people here seemed to drive everywhere. Whereas she would walk to Liberty Park, most other people would drive, park up in the lot there, then get out and be 'active'. The walking felt good, though, so she didn't want to fall into a habit straight away of hopping in the car to drive short journeys.

Out of nowhere, she spied a sign for an all-day diner. The building looked identical to the row of colonial style homes along the rest of the street but had been fashioned into a café. She pushed open the door and was met with a buzzing room containing about ten tables. She was ushered to a table in the window, prettily decorated with lace mats and a milk bottle filled with fresh yellow and white crocuses. The friendly waitress pushed a menu into her hands and Abbie scanned it with joy. Pancakes, maple syrup and bacon it was then. Maybe with a side of strawberries. God, she loved America.

WITH A FULL belly and a grin on her face, Abbie had no choice but to head home and fetch her car for the next item on her agenda. She had joked with her parents about the search engines throwing up nothing but information on Mormons, but it was a huge part of Salt Lake City's history so she decided to visit the famous headquarters of the Church of Jesus Christ of Latter-day Saints, which she had located in downtown.

She was surprised to find herself back in the same area where she had gone crazy with her credit card the weekend before. Crossing the street from the car park, she looked at the map in her guidebook and saw she was on the perimeter of the church – she was heading for Temple Square. To her, it looked like a whole mass of concrete office buildings, but then she saw a path splitting the buildings and headed towards it.

Suddenly it was as if she were in the midst of the Chelsea Flower Show. Everywhere she looked were beds of beautiful multicoloured blossoms, and towering trees filling the space with greenery. It was so lush and so peaceful. She meandered around and then looked to her left. Eclipsing the skyline was the most stunning church she thought she had ever seen. Towering above the rest of the city was an intricately built gothic-style temple with six stunning spires. It was breathtaking, absolutely huge, and according to her guidebook, over 125 years old.

Abbie didn't particularly think of herself as religious, but in the past she had enjoyed visiting the works of art that were some of the world's most famous and historic places of worship. From the Sacré-Cœur in Paris to the cathedral in Barcelona (which she still thought was stunning despite it being perpetually covered in scaffolding), and the one in Liverpool, which had embraced modernism and also now acted as a mini gallery, exhibiting a neon light installation by Tracey Emin, she loved them all.

She couldn't wait to get inside this beauty in front of her, and walked purposefully towards it. As she reached the tall black wrought iron gates, flanked by Victorian style lanterns, she spotted a security guard in her path. Approaching him, she asked if there was a payment required to enter and if there were formal tours and was surprised when he told her it was prohibited for her to go into the temple itself – it was considered sacred and only open to members of the church. However, she could tour the square, taking in the gardens and the visitor centre. She thanked him and headed back the way she came. Maybe she'd come back another day, but for now she had seen what she could and it was pretty impressive.

Leaving the square, she felt the need for some noise. It had been an eerily quiet area and, having been on her own all day, she craved some company as the evening started to draw in.

She walked several blocks away from the temple and started to see restaurants and hotels. She spotted a sports bar but couldn't bear the thought of filling her weekend off with talk of balls, goals and nets so carried on walking, looking out for something up her street.

She saw a sign up ahead, sticking out overhead above the path. The logo featured a piano and a guitar, with the name The Live Joint. There was still a padlock on the door and a sign telling her it would open at 8:00 p.m. Something about the place drew her to it, so she decided to kill some time in the Mexican restaurant next door.

Peering at the menu, she mulled over the fact that, despite nearing her thirtieth birthday, she still had no bloody clue about the difference between a soft taco, an enchilada and a burrito. She'd lost count of the times she had been to a Mexican restaurant and listened to the people around her convincingly ordering, yet it seemed that no matter what she ordered the bland plate arrived looking and tasting the same as every other time she'd ordered.

She decided this time to put her fate in the hands of the gods (or the chef to be more precise) and told the waiter to bring her whatever he would recommend.

A few minutes later, he proudly placed a plate in front of her.

'Let me present you our speciality – a BBQ chicken fajita with guacamole. Please, go ahead, I hope you like.'

Abbie eagerly speared her fork into the mixture and the next moment was caught up in what could only be described as a foodgasm. The taste of the tenderly cooked chicken marinated in a sweet BBQ sauce, mixed with flavourful onion, juicy tomato and the freshest avocado, worked to create an explosion of pleasure in her mouth.

It was the best thing she had ever eaten and she couldn't help letting out a groan of bliss.

She took it all back. Mexican food was absolutely not bland and she never wanted to eat anything else ever again.

With her taste buds well and truly satisfied and the waiter in possession of a rather hefty tip, Abbie made her way back to The Live Joint and was happy to find the padlock now released, the door open, and an inviting light beckoning her inside.

Walking in, she heard the strains of 'Free Bird' by Lynyrd Skynyrd playing and smiled to herself. It was as if they knew she was coming in and had captured the feeling she'd been wrapped up in since touching down in the city.

She looked around the room. It wasn't a big place but she could see a small raised platform in the back corner, complete with a drum kit, amps and microphone stands. Mix-and-match, scuffed-up wooden tables and chairs were dotted around the room, and to her left was a weathered bar with drip mats scattered along it bearing the logos of every conceivable whisky brand and a row of bar stools with torn black leather seats set in front. She loved how authentic it all felt.

Facing away from her, refilling bottle dispensers at the back of the bar, was a woman of about her age. As Abbie pulled a stool out, the woman turned and beamed.

'Sorry, I didn't see you there. We don't usually get many people in here this early.'

'No problem. I know you've only just opened. I was trying to find somewhere I could get a drink and maybe listen to some music.'

'Well, this is the place to be for that. We're famous for it. Where are you from? You're not from round here.'

Abbie explained her English roots and that she had now been a Salt Lake City resident for all of a week.

'That's just brilliant. Welcome to Utah. I'm Rose. Born and bred here. Barely left the city. Super jealous of you coming from England, home of so much amazing music. Why on earth have you come here?'

Both of them laughed then Abbie started to fill Rose in on her job and why she was there. 'Sorry, you must be busy and I must be boring you.'

'Are you insane? This place isn't going to get busy for

another hour and it's not often an interesting new gal arrives in town who sounds like an English princess but apparently works in the down and dirty world of sport. I don't know anyone else who can introduce me to fit soccer players, so you better believe we're staying friends.'

Something about Rose reminded Abbie of Polly, and it felt familiar. It felt nice.

They kept chatting and discovered a mutual love of a number of bands, from both sides of the pond.

'One of the reasons I like working here is we have some great indie bands playing most nights of the week,' Rose said. 'So, I basically get entertained and get paid for it. There's no downside. Except every so often when a couple of drunks need splitting up and throwing out, but I try to treat that like it's exercise and take the positives.'

Abbie was warming more and more to Rose and thanked the serendipity of stumbling across this bar. People had started to fill the room and Abbie made a move to leave the bar, but Rose stopped her. 'Stay here, we can watch the band together. It'll be good company for us both!'

Secretly thrilled, Abbie ordered another glass of wine and settled back onto the stool. Between serving, Rose told her that the band tonight was a young country rock outfit from Tennessee called Memphis Black, who were touring venues around the country. They were tipped for big things, and if predictions were right, she and Abbie would be able to brag one day about seeing them in a ramshackle bar with only a hundred or so other people, when by that point they would be selling out arenas.

By the time the band came on stage, Abbie was filled with the warm, woozy feeling that only three glasses of wine and a new friendship can bring.

The band was brilliant. With both a female and male vocalist, their delicious voices blended together like coffee and cream, while the drummer and guitarists filled the room with heart-pounding beats and chords.

Abbie felt exhilarated by the end of their set, clapping wildly as they modestly left the stage and made their way over to the bar for a well-earned drink on the house. She was exhausted by the combination of having been out all day and still trying to see off the remnants of her jet lag, but didn't feel quite ready to leave this bubble of fun.

Rose engaged the band in conversation, her natural ability to make people feel at ease once more coming to the fore.

'I'd like you to meet my friend, Abbie. She's just moved here from England and is working for the MLS soccer club here. She used to work in music in the UK and she's kind of a big deal.'

Abbie started as she realised Rose was introducing her to the band. They were friendly and seemingly interested in this weird foreigner moving to Utah to work in a sport that even Americans hadn't got used to yet. The drummer, Kevin, was quite excited though as he had spent some time as a child on an air force base in England and developed a love of Arsenal, so he quizzed her on the current state of the Premiership.

Rose distributed another round of drinks as the conversation continued to flow, all of them discussing their love of music and Kevin asking regular questions about the beautiful game.

Abbie left the bar when it closed at 1:00 a.m. having swapped contact details with both Rose and the band, and made promises to contact Rose to organise a night out and to invite Memphis Black to one of the forthcoming Utah Saints games.

She took a taxi home with a plan to collect her ditched car the next day, then fell into bed in The Royal Suite without taking her make-up off and was asleep before turning out the light.

CHAPTER 9

M ARCH ARRIVED BEFORE Abbie could believe it, and with it came the first game of the season. The Utah Saints would be playing the fearsome-sounding San Jose Earthquakes. The season opener was at home, and for Abbie, that meant one thing: she was launching her big idea.

She had spent her first weeks at her new job feverishly making phone calls, sending emails and pulling together plans for the fifteen minutes that she hoped would please her new bosses.

It hadn't left much time for getting to know her new city, but she was desperate to do a good job so she had thrown all her time and energy into quickly making a good impression. She had worked late nights and weekends, had eaten an inordinate amount of take out, and hadn't been back to The Live Joint, but had promised Rose they would meet up once this important day had passed.

Taking everything she had researched about American sport and what fans seemed to like, she had created The Half-Time Show, and now there was less than an hour until it began. She didn't have time to worry now, though, as she was in the press room talking to journalists, introducing herself in person after speaking to them on the phone and making sure they all had what they needed.

All the ingredients for her big idea were sitting in the marketing office and she had already double- and triple-checked everything was set for half-time so that she could focus on watching the opening forty-five minutes of her first Utah Saints match. She had lost count of the games she'd watched back in the UK, but she felt a frisson of excitement as the whistle blew for kick-off and she stood on the sidelines.

The game began in a fast-paced manner with the home side confidently driving the ball forward towards the San Jose Earthquakes goal. It looked like it was only a matter of time before the Utah Saints opened the scoresheet and, sure enough, in the twenty-third minute, Bobby Fox scored with an incredible volley from outside the penalty box. Bobby was a young hotshot, straight out of college and scouted by Kyle. Abbie felt her pulse race as she watched her new team celebrate and saw Bobby's eyes nearly pop out of his head with excitement as if he could hardly believe he had scored on his debut.

It neared half-time and the moment she had been working towards. She knew she wasn't reinventing the wheel, but she was introducing something new to this stadium that she hoped would bring the crowd alive. The whistle blew and she watched as The Half-Time Show unfolded.

A troupe of twenty cheerleaders in navy costumes bearing the team crest, together with a new club mascot,

Eric the Elk, ran out onto the sidelines. As soon as the last player had left the field they catapulted onto the pitch to begin a dynamic routine. There were girls and boys cartwheeling, backflipping and flying through the air while other members of the troupe were running around the perimeter, triggering the crowd to start a Mexican wave.

While all this was going on, her slick production crew assembled a simple platform in the centre of the pitch and rigged a microphone connected to a sound system. When the cheerleaders ran off, a local singer she had found on Instagram called Nicola George took to the stage with her guitar and performed two songs for the now enraptured crowd. As Nicola's gravelly country voice played out of the PA, Abbie watched the crowd closely and saw they were all listening to the young woman attentively, lots with their phones out filming and taking photos. This young performer was a complete unknown yet it still seemed to be working. The crowd were enjoying themselves, choosing to stay and buy hot dogs and beers from the roaming vendors rather than leaving the stands. She had wanted Memphis Black to play, but they were already booked, so she had earmarked them for something later down the line.

With the final five minutes approaching, Nicola wrapped up her set and walked back through the tunnel while Erik The Elk stood in the goal mouth. The cheerleaders had picked out three children from the crowd who all took turns in a penalty shoot-out against the large elk. His bulging costume made it difficult to nimbly defend against the ensuing shots, but must have eased the pain when the ball hit him smack in the stomach when seven-year-old Jessica hit the bullseye. In the background the stage was expertly and discreetly removed, leaving the pitch ready for the second half of the match.

It was all over before Abbie knew it and she went back to the press room to get settled in for the final part of the game, buzzing with adrenaline that everything had gone smoothly and seemed to have gone down well. A scroll through social media told her that fans were talking about and posting pictures and videos of The Half-Time Show, and her happiness improved even further as the final whistle blew with a 3-0 victory to the Utah Saints.

AS SHE WAS wrapping up work at her desk a little while later, the door opened and Hank, Kitty and Kyle rushed through it, all looking as happy as she felt.

'Abbie. You're a genius.'

She didn't know what to say as Hank beamed down at her, and was at more of a loss for words when he grabbed her by the arms, pulled her out of her seat and hugged her. The look on her face must have been a picture as Kyle burst out laughing, a deep, belly laugh that in turn made Abbie giggle as Hank plonked her back in her chair.

The three of them all perched around her on desk and

Hank spoke.

'Seriously, the partners loved The Half-Time Show, the fans loved it, and some of the season ticket holders have already bought extra tickets for the next game so they can bring their families along. It's exactly what we needed. The soccer we're playing is good and now we've brought in some extra entertainment that makes it fun for the whole family. I'd say we did the right thing hiring you, Abbie Potter.'

'Hank, you're so right,' grinned Kitty. 'Abbie has changed things around here and I love having her working with us. Anytime you need help on this, Abbie, you just let me know. Even if I have to do it in my own time I will because I think it's just brilliant. Today was brilliant. You're brilliant.'

She couldn't remember the last time she'd had such a rewarding day at work, and having Kitty and Hank praise her like that felt good. At that moment she wondered why she hadn't left her old job sooner. She felt like a different person and that she had her life back on some sort of track. She couldn't even remember why she had been so upset about Josh. That life seemed like a million years ago.

Hank was talking and Abbie tuned back in.

'I want you to organise The Half-Time Show for every home match this season and make sure the marketing guys are putting the info out to help sales. They need to pre-promote the music acts and get them promoting their appearance, so we can bring their fans in.

Get an application form on the website for kids to apply for the penalty shoot-out. And make sure that elk costume has a protective cup you know where or one of those kids is going to castrate the poor guy inside it.'

Kyle let out another belly laugh. It was obvious Hank didn't let loose like this often, but they were all riding high on the success of the day.

'Oh, and Abbie, for our last game, I want you to go big,' Hank added. 'That's the day we need to bring in a famous band. They can do a song at half-time and then we'll bring them back out at the final whistle for a few more songs. We'll have a sell-out crowd if we do that, and that will make my board happy. You have full authority to book whoever you want – I trust you.'

'I'm on it, boss,' Abbie grinned as Hank walked out of the room, closely followed by Kitty. She couldn't believe it had gone so well and wanted to call Violet to tell her all about it. That would have to wait until tomorrow, though, as Violet would long since have gone to bed. She mentally noted that she hadn't heard from Violet for a few days, which was strange as her emails had been daily since she had arrived, but her thoughts were quickly interrupted.

'Hey, superstar, are you wrapping up to go home soon?'

'You're a bit of a superstar yourself, aren't you? Spotting Bobby Fox at his college. He made quite the impression today.'

For the second time in as many minutes, Kyle looked

surprised.

'How did you know he's one of my guys?'

'I do my research, Captain America,' Abbie teased. 'I have to write about these players, I need to know where they came from. And I was also happy to find out during my research that you really are out there finding the next big things and not just attacking random women in parks.'

'Are you ever going to let that go?' Kyle covered his face with his hands in mock distress.

'Possibly not. I'm still waiting for you to make it up to me.'

She shocked herself with that comment as she knew she had opened the door, and Kyle didn't wait a second to walk through it.

'Then let me. You promised a rain check on me showing you around. Let me take you somewhere tomorrow. I know you won't have left Salt Lake City, and you've been working so hard on this game that I'm willing to bet you've barely ventured out of your apartment.'

'You would be correct,' she laughed. 'But it's honestly been fine. I came here to throw myself into this new job and that's what I've been doing as I really wanted it to go well today. But now I can breathe a bit and I do want to see the sights around my new home. I'd already told myself after today I would start to do some exploring.'

'So, let me help you. If you go on your own, you'll follow a guidebook you bought at the airport and go to all the dumb tourist spots and miss out on the good stuff.

Only a proper local knows all the hidden gems. I bet the first thing you did when you got here was go see that church. Am I right?'

'Have you been stalking me as well as tripping me over?' she exclaimed.

'I knew it. I just knew that's the only thing you'd have done.'

Laughing, she playfully pushed his arm and was surprised at how comfortable she felt with this newcomer in her life.

'What do you say? Will you let me show you around tomorrow? Make the most of your day off before another week at the grindstone?'

She was so conflicted. She knew he wasn't asking her on a date – he was being friendly to the new girl. On the other hand, she had been warned by Kitty what he was like and she was taking a risk going out for the day with him, even if it wasn't a date. But the way he made her feel comfortable was so at odds with the vision of him being a total arsehole. He seemed like the most genuine guy she had met in a long time, maybe ever. She supposed that's what made him so successful with the girls.

She realised he was staring at her as she sat having an internal conversation with herself, waiting for her to answer.

She felt her resolve sinking. Not only had she been lonely in the evenings and at weekends, but she wanted to go. She suddenly couldn't remember all the reasons not to.

'Alright, alright. You've worn me down. I will, for one day only, let you be my tour guide. Where are you going to take me?'

He fist-pumped the air and did a comedy jump, clicking his feet together, making her laugh.

'I'm taking you to Park City. It's the next city on the other side of the mountains, about forty minutes from here. Bring a warm jacket and a hat and gloves because it's cold near the snow. I'll pick you up at ten. You'll need your strength, so make sure to have breakfast.'

With that, he doffed his baseball cap and left her sitting at her desk, wondering how the hell that escalated so quickly, why on earth she would need her strength, and which of her new wardrobe items she was going to wear for an absolute non-date.

CHAPTER 10

ABBIE FELT STUPIDLY nervous as she waited the next morning for Kyle to pick her up. It was pretty much freezing so she wore her new light blue Levi's, cosy fur-lined brown boots and a chunky knit blue sweater the same hue as her eyes. She saw a pristine jet-black Honda pickup truck pull up outside and recognised Kyle getting out. She threw on her jacket, picked up her woolly hat, gloves and handbag and headed out the door to meet him.

As she made her way carefully down the steps, not wanting to trip and look like an idiot, she looked up and saw him clearly for the first time.

Fuck.

He looked fit.

'Good morning, England,' he grinned as he handed her a Starbucks. 'I thought you could use a hot chocolate to warm up. It's pretty chilly this morning.'

She thanked him as she greeted him and hesitantly kissed him on the cheek before gratefully taking the cup and using it as a hand warmer.

'Hop in, the car's warm and the heated seat is on for you.'

She opened the door and then used the step to hoist

herself up into the truck. Why does everything have to be so much larger than life in the US? she wondered, hoping Kyle hadn't noticed how inelegantly she hauled herself into her seat.

Strapping herself in, she asked what the plan was.

'It's a surprise. You'll see when we get there. It's not far but it's a super cool place.'

She laughed. 'Well, I did say I'd allow you to be my tour guide today, so it's over to you.'

As they settled into the drive, she relaxed into the warm passenger seat. She was surprised to see that just a little outside of Salt Lake City the road cut through the middle of the snowy mountain range. It was a new kind of landscape for her. Driving in England, everything was pretty flat, and having lived her whole life in cities, she had definitely never driven through the middle of a mountain range.

She looked over at Kyle and broke the easy silence.

'Kitty told me you guys all go skiing in Park City. Do you like skiing?'

'Yeah, Kitty organises trips every now and then for staff but I don't always go. They tend to stick to the pretty simple runs and head for the après-ski as soon as possible, whereas I'm more a black run kind of guy.'

He smiled as he delivered the line and Abbie raised her eyebrows, questioning the statement.

'I learned to ski when I was four. These slopes have always been my second home. We're lucky to have Deer Valley here at Park City – it's the largest ski resort in the

States, and the slopes are some of the best in the world. I qualified as a ski and snowboard instructor after I finished playing soccer, but then I got the job at the club. I do the occasional teaching gig here and there, but most of the time I come out here it's just me and the board. The best thing is getting out on the snow, feeling the adrenaline, out in the open air. It's pretty special.'

Abbie loved hearing his enthusiasm.

'When did you give up playing professionally? Surely you could play now if you still love it?'

'Sometimes life doesn't go the way you plan, unfortunately,' he said. 'I got a soccer scholarship to college in Indiana, which is one of the best places for that in the country, and everything went pretty well for a few years. I came back here to play for the Utah Saints but then I injured my knee and I just couldn't recover well enough to keep performing at the top.'

'I'm so sorry, that's crappy.'

'You know, it all turned out okay in the end. I had a blast for a few years playing all around the country. I always got on well with Hank so when this role came up, we got talking, and I was up for the challenge. Now I have a job I love. It's great working with the kids on the youth team and really trying to help them, and the benefit is I'm not banned from skiing and snowboarding like I was when I was playing.'

Abbie poked him in the arm and teased, 'Oh, so are you telling me you got injured on purpose?'

Kyle laughed as he expertly reversed the massive truck

into a spot that seemed too small on the side of a street, then they got out of the truck.

'So, this is Park City,' he said, throwing his arms all around. 'Home of the famous Sundance Film Festival, but for me, the home of epic skiing and snowboarding just forty minutes from home. My happy place,' he sighed.

Abbie looked around in awe at the little town as they started to walk down the main road. She'd never seen anything like it. The quaint street was peppered with brightly coloured buildings higgledy-piggledy in height. Green, yellow, blue and red. A movie cinema that looked like it could have been a hundred years old. Tiny bookstores, and little boutiques selling patterned throws, artworks and mementoes linked to the area's American Indian heritage.

And, of course, shops selling and hiring ski gear. A lot of shops.

Because, rising above the street on both sides, unbelievably close to where she was standing, were the snow-covered hills and peaks of the mountains that Kyle skied and boarded on as often as he could.

It was bizarre and breathtakingly beautiful.

'When it's the film festival, it's absolutely crazy. Can you imagine, this tiny town, bombarded by tens of thousands of people. You can't move.'

She couldn't imagine. It was so quiet and small. The thought of it being taken over by a sea of people seemed wrong.

Suddenly Kyle steered her to the right and through a doorway. She heard the tinkle of a bell over the door and looked around to see they were in a ski shop.

She heard Kyle greet the guy behind the desk like an old friend then he turned back to her.

'Ready for your lesson?'

'Are you serious?' she squealed.

'Never been more serious. Sit down on that bench,' he motioned. 'What size shoe are you?'

As she answered, Abbie was thankful she'd gone on her mall spree so she knew the correct US size to give him.

A few moments later, he headed towards her with a pair of stiff black boots in his hand that looked like the kind you hobbled around in if you had a broken foot. 'Deadly,' he grinned as he kneeled on the floor and started unzipping her own right boot and putting her foot in the new contraption.

'The only time I've ever skied was a school trip when I was a teenager, and I really didn't like it that much.' She sighed at the memory but didn't stop him from putting on the boot. Salt Lake City had made her feel more alive than she had in a long time, and even though she was nervous at the thought of going out on the snow, she didn't mind embarking on this spontaneous lesson.

'Did you like red wine when you were a teenager?'

'No, I was more of a Bacardi Breezer kind of girl.'

'And do you like red wine now?'

'Yes.'

She could see where he was going with the analogy.

'This is going to feel tight, but that's how it's meant to be,' he said as he started clamping the buckles closed. Her leg felt as if it was being forced into an awfully wrong position with each additional buckle closing and her face obviously showed her discomfort.

He laughed as he pulled off her left boot and repeated the buckling procedure on that side, essentially encasing her left leg in what felt like cement.

'Up you get then,' he said as he rose. 'The powder is perfect and I don't want you missing the best of it.'

Putting her hands firmly on the bench and pushing herself to standing, she went to take a step forward and wobbled on the unfamiliar soles of the boots. She couldn't help but let out a little exclamation of shock and Kyle, quick as a flash, steadied her by holding her by the arms firmly and setting her on the shop floor once again.

She felt electricity run through her whole body as she looked straight up into Kyle's twinkling eyes, and quickly looked down again.

'You okay there? I'm thinking maybe this isn't such a good idea. You really aren't good at staying on your feet, are you?' he laughed.

Crossing her arms with faux indignation, she tried to look serious. 'It's you. You keep putting me in these dangerous situations. If I was a more cynical person, I'd think you'd been hired by a mortal enemy to bump me off.'

'I have no intention of bumping you off. I'm going to

make sure you're as safe as can be.' With that he disappeared again and returned laden with a huge heap of items in his arms.

'Here we go; ski pants, gloves, some good socks to go under those boots, goggles and a helmet.' Kyle piled the items on the bench beside her. 'Oh, and here,' he said, reaching into his pocket and passing her some sunscreen. 'You're definitely the type to get burned aren't you.'

She stuck her tongue out at him, and he laughed.

'Get out of here.' He guided her towards the door, shouting goodbye to the sales clerk as they left and thanking him for the loan of the gear.

SITTING AT THE top of a snow-covered slope, Abbie wondered what on earth she was doing as Kyle set the snowboard on the ground and reached out to pull her to her feet.

'Now, step on the board, but not where you see the clips. I just want you to get used to what it feels like to stand on it. Put your weight slightly forward onto your toes, bend your knees and lean a bit forward into the boots.'

'This feels so weird. It doesn't feel natural at all.'

'You've been standing there for three seconds. Where's your patience?'

She concentrated and followed his instructions, getting used to the board and how to stand on it. Putting her weight onto her toes, then switching to her heels. Back and forth, again and again, until it started to feel like she knew how to balance.

'I think you're there. Let's get you in those binds.'

She felt her stomach lurch with anxiety. Why was it that things seemed so much scarier as an adult? She was pretty sure she hadn't been so nervous on that school ski trip.

'Kyle. I'm a bit worried about that slope. I don't know what I'm doing.'

'Lucky we're not going down there then. We're practicing in the other direction on the flat. Do you think I'd send you down a slope when you can barely walk straight? You're not even going anywhere for a while. First, we're going to practice falling. It's the perfect snow for it – soft, so it won't hurt much.'

Abbie raised her eyebrows.

'I'm serious. Before you learn to ride, you need to know how to fall correctly. I really don't want you to end up in the ER with a broken wrist. Now, fall forward on your knees, then onto your forearms.'

Resigning herself to bruised knees, all in the name of learning, Abbie did as she was told.

SITTING BACK DOWN on the snow a few hours later, Kyle unclipped his board and set it next to him. Abbie kept hers clipped to her boots. She couldn't be bothered to keep lifting it on and off.

'See, you're not so bad after all. And I'm pretty sure I see a smile hiding there somewhere.'

'This is actually a lot of fun, Kyle. Thank you. I'd never have done this myself and it's so beautiful up here.'

'You see all these little kids flying around on boards? If a bunch of five-year-olds can handle it, I'm pretty sure a badass woman from Britain has nothing to be scared of.'

She laughed as she looked further afield and, lo and behold, saw kids that couldn't have been long out of nappies flying down the beginner slopes on skis and boards.

'What do you say we have one run down this little slope before we wrap it up today. You're more than capable, you know.'

Filled with confidence from her lesson, she agreed. 'You're buying dinner after this, though. On account of you trying to frighten the life out of me today. That's if you have time, I expect you have plans.'

'Not at all. I told you, today I'm in charge and I've already got a plan, don't you worry.'

Abbie was pleased at the thought of the day stretching out even further, although she reminded herself she had to keep Kyle in the friend zone.

Suddenly desperate to get off the slopes and hunker down in a warm restaurant with a glass of wine in her hands, she pushed herself to her feet as Kyle had showed her, pointed her lead foot forward and pushed off.

'Abbie, wait,' she heard Kyle shout out, but she was

off.

Although it was a pretty gentle slope, it felt like she was going faster than she could cope with and she felt a sense of panic rising as she desperately tried to keep her balance. She was staying on her feet but the panic was making her wobble and she couldn't remember how to stop.

Suddenly, looming in the near distance she saw two pools of water next to each other, with a group of children standing around them looking at their reflections, or trying to spot fish.

She was heading right for them.

She was going to massacre a bunch of kids on a beginner's ski slope.

'Watch out!' she cried as she neared the children, who looked up and started darting out of the way left and right.

She tried to steer the board and somehow managed to skim between the pools, on a piece of snow only just wider than the board itself.

Realising she had managed to avoid mass murder, she tried to engage her brain to remember how to stop the bloody thing. Then she felt herself grabbed from behind and plonked on her bottom on the snow.

Kyle. Her rescuer.

She looked up at him, knowing her cheeks were stained red with half adrenaline, half embarrassment and her eyes were probably still showing shock and fear, and then she burst out laughing.

'What are you trying to do, England? Get my license revoked for bad teaching?' he laughed. 'Right, get up. You're trouble. I'm taking the board back and we're going to eat.'

'Aha. My tactics worked. I had it handled all along. I just wanted the wine.'

She scolded herself internally. This guy was impossible not to flirt with. She couldn't remember the last time she felt so at ease with a man. But he was off limits and she needed to take it down a notch.

'I know the most fantastic steak restaurant not far from here,' Kyle said. 'Amazing wine, ironed tablecloths, people eat with their knives and forks. Really quite fancy for these parts,' he winked, grinning.

Suddenly feeling things were escalating a bit too much into a formal date, Abbie replied, 'You know what? I'd really like a dirty pizza. Can we do that?'

He didn't seem upset as he agreed, and she took that to mean she'd been worrying unnecessarily and she should stop flattering herself that a guy as hot as Kyle would even look at her that way. He was just intrigued because she was foreign and new.

THIRTY MINUTES LATER they were sitting at an outside picnic table, snow boots and boards long discarded, eating huge slices of pepperoni pizza off of cardboard plates and drinking beer straight out of the bottles.

'Most girls would have wanted the tablecloths and the knives and forks, you know,' he said in that teasing voice of his.

'Yeah well, most girls hadn't nearly wiped out half a school and needed some comfort food,' she quipped and he responded to her with his rich laugh.

He collected their empties and went to dispose of them while Abbie stood up.

'Are you ready to go home?' he asked.

'Yeah, that's a good idea. It's getting late and it's back to the grindstone in the morning.'

As they headed towards the car, she thought how much more confident American men seemed compared to men from home. Kyle didn't seem to have a doubt about him. The way he walked, the way he held himself, the way he talked. He was completely comfortable in himself. She could take some lessons from that.

WHEN THEY ARRIVED back at her apartment, she turned to him as she unbuckled her seatbelt.

'Thanks for today. I really did enjoy it and I'm grateful you took time on your day off to show me around.'

'You're more than welcome, and believe me, I've got more on the list. Don't think you're getting away with it.'

'See you tomorrow,' she grinned as she jumped down out of the beast of the pickup.

Heading towards her front door she couldn't help but

be filled with reflections of him and their day. She knew she shouldn't be entertaining the idea, but she wasn't so unaware as to be able to completely ignore the frisson of electricity between them. But then she had to remember Kitty's warnings; he was flirtatious with a lot of people and she was fresh meat in town.

She tried to shake off the wave of conflicting thoughts as she headed into her apartment. She knew what she needed more than hours of overthinking; a hot bath.

CHAPTER 11

TWO NIGHTS LATER Abbie sat at one of the scuffed-up tables in The Live Joint across from Rose, two Bud Lights on the table in front of them. Rose had told her even though it sounded lame to hang out at your workplace when you didn't need to be there, she had enjoyed going there before she was hired and she still liked to go there and listen to the music – live or their playlists – when she felt like going out drinking.

Abbie completely understood why. This bar was welcoming. One of those places that felt like home the minute you walked in. And not a cheesy pop song to be heard within those walls.

She was enjoying listening to Rose tell her story with the background noise of the jukebox playing seventies rock.

'I was always the one who couldn't wait to get out of school to go and hang out at the venues that had bands playing. I'd pretend I was a bit older to see if I could catch the eye of a cute bassist here or there but, looking back, I must have looked fourteen. I never had a chance with any of those boys.' She laughed, taking a swig from the blue-labelled bottle of beer. 'I was smoking weed when it was still reserved for weirdos and loners, before it was

Californian and cool to do it.'

She'd told Abbie earlier that she was brought up by her mother, who worked shifts as a nurse. Her dad had walked out one day when she was three and never came back.

'Eventually my mom told me if I didn't get my act together, I was going to fail high school, and if that happened, I was on my own. The thought terrified me so I stopped the smoking and tried to get interested in something. I started writing music reviews for the school paper and that was pretty cool. That, and being petrified of my mom, got me to graduation. Then I worked in a music store for a few years until that closed down because everyone's downloading now. Two years ago, I got a job here at the bar and the rest is history.'

'It sounds like you're doing pretty well to me. Not many people actually like their job, but you're great with people and you get to see all this music every night for free.' Abbie smiled at her new friend.

'Yeah, I can't say I have any complaints really,' Rose said. 'What's your story? How did a nice girl like you end up wanting to walk in a place like this?'

Abbie laughed. 'I used to work in music PR before I was in football. My dad was a music producer so he gave me a love of bands. But then working in the industry, I started to get jaded and wasn't enjoying having to go to gigs all the time, so I decided it was better to keep the music as a hobby and try something different. That's how I ended up in football. I was at a football club in London for four years before I came here. And that's it in a nutshell,' she finished.

'I think that's badass,' Rose said as she got up and headed back to the bar. She returned a couple of minutes later with two more beers and put one in front of Abbie. 'I've not really left Salt Lake City. A couple of trips here or there with friends to see music mainly. It's pretty brave of you to move to the other side of the world.'

Abbie contemplated for a moment. 'Yeah, I guess so. But I needed a change of scenery. Something completely new.'

'Man trouble?' Rose's face gave off a look of understanding.

'Kind of yes and no. I was done with my job and I was looking for something new and this opportunity came up. Then I found out my ex-husband was having a baby with his new wife. It hit a few old nerves, so I decided I needed to get my arse in gear and my head together, and properly move onward and upward. And here I am,' she said, shrugging her shoulders and grinning.

It didn't feel like a sad conversation anymore. Just factual. This was progress. She took a swig from her bottle and mentally punched the air.

Rose then told her that she'd found her bassist after all. She was twenty-five, having a drink after a gig at The Live Joint with some friends, and suddenly felt a drink spill all over her, soaking through her t-shirt and jeans.

'I turned around to yell and found myself looking straight at the most beautiful girl I'd ever seen. You're surprised, right? I couldn't have been more surprised myself – I'd never felt anything for a girl before.' She laughed, looking at Abbie's face.

Abbie hadn't been expecting that after the confession earlier that she was fully in training to be a groupie as a teenager. 'Tell me more,' she urged, resting her elbow on the table and her chin in her hand.

'This girl. She was so apologetic, but I forgot I was soaked with beer when I started talking to her. She just had this soul, this aura, I was hooked straight away. She looked like Zoe Kravitz. Beautifully full lips, long black hair in tight braids and these crazy green eyes that I got lost in. I could see she had some tattoos on her arm so I asked her about them, just desperately trying to find a way to keep her talking.' She blushed. 'Turned out she played bass in a band who were touring and they had a gig at The Saltair, which is a cool venue over by the lake. We'll go there sometime. That was three years ago and we're still going strong. Probably because we don't see each other every day. Stella's still in the band touring around, and when she's not touring, she comes here and lives with me. It works for us,' she finished, shrugging. 'What about you? You must have had guys all over you since you got here, digging that British accent?' She giggled.

Abbie decided to get it off her chest. She still hadn't been able to get hold of Violet by text or phone to talk it through with her.

Peeling at the label of the beer bottle, she began explaining everything. 'Since my divorce I've been a bit useless, to be honest. Didn't want to go out much. Definitely didn't want to meet another man. I never really found out why Josh ended things so I think I was in this no man's land. You know how us females are – we like answers, but I never got them.'

'You're preaching to the converted, sister.' Rose sighed. 'I still don't get how a guy can think they can date you, sleep in your bed, be your best friend for six months or two years or five then just fuck off without so much as a goodbye. Every single one of my friends has a story.'

'I think we're just wired differently.' Abbie considered it. 'We like to talk, they like to… run a million miles away at the slightest whiff of a problem. Sometimes problems we don't even know exist.'

They both laughed.

'Sorry, that's a sweeping generalisation, but I'm the same, Rose. So many friends of mine have stories like that. Gahhhh. Anyway, coming here, things have shifted. I'm feeling good, I'm having fun, I'm loving work. And I think I've sort of met a guy.'

Rose lifted her hand for a high five. Abbie met the gesture, but told her to slow down.

'I know I'm hesitating a bit because of Josh. But it's not really holding me back that much anymore because I feel a million miles from all that here. The real problem is that I've already been told by a friend of mine at work that he's a real player and a heartbreaker, and I think it's idiotic to walk with my eyes wide open into a situation where I know I'm going to get hurt. Why would I want to do that to myself?' Looking down, she realised she had peeled off the entire label of the bottle in front of her. She knew there was some meaning behind that.

Rose sat quietly for a minute, thinking it over.

'Well, look. There're two things here. First of all, okay, I get it, you don't want to get shit on all over again. But you don't know for sure he's like that and, who knows, you could be the one to change him. All that British charm and poise.'

Abbie gave her a faux side-eye. 'The weird thing is that he seems like such a genuine, stand-up guy. He took me for a snowboarding lesson at the weekend up to Park City and we had the best time. And he was a perfect gentleman, he didn't try anything on.'

'Exactly. Give him a chance. And here's the second thing. You could always just have your wicked way and treat it like some fun and don't get all emotional about it. That way you can't get hurt if you're the one calling the shots.'

'As good as that sounds, we work together. Oh yeah, that's the next issue. They always say you shouldn't mix business with pleasure.'

'Is he hot?'

'Stupidly.'

'So, what if the pleasure is totally worth it?'

They collapsed with laughter and Abbie said she'd get the next round.

RETURNING WITH A bottle of Argentinian red wine a few minutes later, Abbie plonked down the bottle and two sturdy glasses. The Live Joint didn't do delicate glassware.

'I thought it looked like we were making a night of it and getting a bottle means fewer trips to the bar.'

'But more trips to the bathroom.' Rose winked as she got up and headed towards the back of the bar.

When Rose returned, Abbie was reading through a copy of the local newspaper.

'These music reviews are crap. It has to be a joke. Listen to this, Rose. *I was invited to watch The Temperamentals at Saltair. It was a pretty cold night so that was the first problem. Then I didn't think the band were great. I didn't know any of the songs and it wasn't my kind of style. It was a bit too much rock and I prefer pop.* Is this for real?' She stabbed her finger violently at the page.

'Oh yeah, that column is renowned. They've got some kid writing it for free. It's comedy gold a lot of the time. One time he said he left a Kings of Leon concert early because his ears were ringing from the volume.'

'So, if you really want to read up about what bands are gigging around here and coming here on tour, and then proper reviews, where do you go? Surely some people are actually interested and are as horrified at me at this shit?'

Rose pondered the thought. 'I guess there isn't anything. Which is weird as there's a good music scene here, but not many people know that. There's a bunch of live venues, all fairly small but still there, and you have to know where to go to listen to the stuff you like. There're rock places, Indie, blues, garage, a bit of country. And it's all Salt Lake City style; you have to listen to get it, we have our own thing going on here. Then we have big artists coming through when they're on national tours, obviously.' Abbie loved how animated Rose was talking about it. 'Some of the outdoor places are so fun in the summer. We can see a lot of bands this year if you want. I always pretty much know who's passing through because of this place.'

Abbie was struck with an idea and, without even hesitating to think a bit more, blurted it out.

'Why don't we start a music review blog for the area? We could preview bands heading here, and do reviews. If you used to write for the school paper you know what you're doing, and I did this kind of thing back in my music PR days.' Saying it out loud, she surprised herself with how excited she was at the prospect.

'You know, I think you could be onto something.' Rose's eyes lit up.

'It would be a hobby rather than a job, so if we didn't fancy doing something one night, we'd just give it a miss. But it could be really cool. It would probably mean we could wangle free entry to everything as well.'

Running away from the table, Rose picked up a stack of cardboard beer mats from the bar, then took her chair opposite Abbie and rooted around in her bag until she drew out a brown eyeliner.

'I haven't been this excited about something in a long time, Abbie. Let's get going. Most important thing first.

What do we call ourselves?' She was literally bouncing in her seat and Abbie felt herself getting more and more enthusiastic by the second.

'Ooh, something linked to the city and a music term? Like… The SLC Beat?' Swigging from her wine glass, Abbie felt the cogs turning. The Salt Lake Review?' Rose nodded as Abbie spoke, scribbling the options down on the beer mat with her eye pencil.

'The Salt Scene?' Rose suggested.

'That's the one. The Salt Scene.' Abbie reached out to high five Rose and then they clinked glasses and both took a glug.

Rose ran back to the bar, this time going behind it, and returned not a minute later with two shot glasses of tequila, two lemon wedges and a salt shaker.

'It feels like we need to celebrate. And what better way to toast The Salt Scene than with a salty beverage.' Rose reached across the table, grabbed Abbie's hand and shook the salt onto the back of it before handing her a wedge of lemon.

'Here's to The Salt Scene, and to having too much fun this year,' Rose said, clinking glasses with Abbie again before they both downed the strong liquid, the alcohol burning the back of Abbie's throat as it hit.

They both winced at the taste, with Abbie sticking her tongue out. Then they both sucked the lemons, laughing as they slammed the shot glasses back on the table.

'I have to work tomorrow, Rose, this was not in the plan,' Abbie said, shivering as she felt the tequila taking effect.

'We're on a roll now, we can't stop. Come back to my place and we'll get onto my computer. We'll register the domain and start to build the site. I know how to do it; it can be up and running by tomorrow. Let's plan a bit together then I can carry on during the day while you're at work.' Rose's excitement was palpable.

Abbie, too, was excited as they left the bar. She realised she didn't know what part of town Rose lived in and started to open the taxi app on her phone, but Rose stopped her.

'We don't need that,' she said as she put a key in a discreet black door next to the bar. 'As part of my deal when I started work here, they rented me the apartment upstairs.'

Rose's place was exactly what Abbie would have expected. Eclectic and cosy. Walking straight into the open plan kitchen and living space, Abbie was met with the sweet lingering scent of a vanilla candle. A huge multi-coloured woven wool rug took up most of the floor space with an inviting-looking soft dark purple corner sofa.

Grabbing her laptop from the kitchen counter, Rose urged Abbie to sit down as she fired it up.

'It's super easy to register a domain. Watch this.'

In minutes they were the proud owners of www.thesaltscene.us and Rose was showing Abbie how you could create your own website using templates that looked ultra-modern and super professional.

They decided on red for the main theme colour. Red was impossible to ignore and really strong. They mixed it with white and black and picked an old typewriter text for their font. It was looking good.

Immersed in what they were doing, they decided on the pages they wanted. They needed a listings page to detail upcoming gigs, with links to buy tickets. Then they clearly needed their reviews page. They also created a page about themselves, writing tongue-in-cheek biographies and adding their favourite photos from their Facebook pages.

'Maybe we should add a review, to get us started?' Abbie suggested.

Rose agreed. 'And it has to be Memphis Black, because none of this would have happened if you hadn't come into the bar the night they played.'

The feature wrote itself. They took it in turns to tweak and play with the copy as they launched into the story of how the blog was born after an unlikely American-Brit duo met in a live music bar in Salt Lake City one night and saw future stars play in front of fewer than a hundred people. They tipped them for big things.

Rose said she'd call around venues the next day and find out who was playing where for the next month so they could do their listings. And Abbie planned to write a review about Nicola George, the young songwriter who had played at the football game just a few days before.

Then, looking at her watch, Abbie jumped up. 'Shit, Rose, it's four a.m. I have to be at work at nine.' She took out her phone and ordered a taxi before grabbing her coat and bag. 'This has been the best night. I'll call you tomorrow.' Rose hugged her as she let her out.

And, just like that, The Salt Scene was born.

CHAPTER 12

ABBIE FROWNED AS she looked at her phone. She hadn't received an email from Violet in weeks now and her texts were being replied to with short, perfunctory messages, with her friend seemingly not wanting to get into a conversation.

Over the last month she had been busy organising The Half-Time Show for the fortnightly home soccer matches, then spending several evenings a week with Rose working on their website, going to gigs or updating the listings. That, combined with the seven-hour time difference to London, meant that Abbie hadn't realised the weeks were passing by so quickly with Violet being distant.

Abbie knew that Violet missed her. She missed her like crazy too. Maybe her friend was finding it easier to stay away. But, deep in her heart, Abbie knew that wasn't Violet and something was going on. She wanted to update her on everything that was going on in her new city; she craved her familiar voice and wanted news from home.

She made a mental note to call her in her lunch break.

Looking up at the sound of the door opening, she smiled as Kitty entered her office, where Abbie had been waiting for her.

'Abbie, you're here early.' She smiled as she swept in and started discarding bags and taking off her coat.

'Yes. I knew you always got here early and wanted to talk to you before work. How was your weekend?'

Even though they had formed a steady sort of friendship by this point, with Kitty regularly helping on The Half-Time Show and nothing being too much trouble, Abbie still couldn't relax entirely in her presence. It hadn't been the fast, easy bond that she'd made with Rose, or even with Kyle.

She hadn't seen him around for a couple of weeks as he'd been off around the country on a scouting mission, and she found herself missing him as she looked for him each day. She daren't ask Kitty when he was due back, though.

Kitty seemed delighted that Abbie had asked. 'Great, thank you so much for asking. I was invited to check out a ghost-hunting experience. I'm earmarking it for a social committee activity for Halloween. Doesn't that sound so fun?'

'So fun.' Abbie nodded, even though you wouldn't get her going hunting for ghosts if you paid her. She would find a way to get out of that. 'I wondered if I could talk to you about my apartment,' she asked, offering Kitty a blueberry muffin that she'd picked up on the way to work, which she politely declined.

'Of course. Is there a problem? I can get on it straight away.' Kitty already had her mobile phone in her hand poised to dial, a concerned look on her face.

'No, the opposite actually. I really love living there and I can afford the rent. I wanted to know how to go about staying on longer term. I could commit to it for the duration of my current contract.' Abbie had come to the decision she didn't want to go anywhere and she wanted to sort it as, unbelievably, her initial three months were coming to an end in just two weeks' time.

'I just knew you would be happy there.' Kitty grinned. 'Let me make some calls and see what I can do to keep you in your dream house.' She waved the phone at Abbie. 'Scram. Let me do my thing.'

Abbie stood up and uttered her thanks, brushing the crumbs from her own muffin from her sweater into her hand and into Kitty's bin on the way out of the office.

A couple of hours later the ping of an incoming email titled 'Apartment News' indicated that Kitty had an update. Excitedly opening the envelope icon, Abbie scanned the text and then felt her heart sink with disappointment.

Abbie

I'm so sorry. I've tried everything. I even shouted at the realtor but there's nothing I can do. The apartment has already been rented to a new tenant and the contract is watertight.

I'll help you with anything you need to find a new place. I'm devastated this didn't work out! I know how much you love the place!

Lunch? We can talk about it some more? Start

searching for somewhere even better for you?

Kitty (at your service)

x

Ugh. She was already so busy that the thought of finding a new place to live – all the admin that went with that, and then moving – was exhausting. She had thought, probably naively, that she could simply stay on where she was.

She quickly sent a thank you email back to Kitty, turning down the offer of lunch as she now needed to spend her time researching apartments for rent. Checking her diary, she hoped that there would miraculously be more than two weeks for her to do all this but, no, the dates were clear.

She parked the housing crisis for the rest of the morning as she got on with some work. Then, as the clock signalled 1:00 p.m., she took the sandwich she'd made that morning out of her bag and opened up a browser to search realtor websites for properties that were available immediately.

She focused her search on where she was living now as she loved waking up each morning to the view of the Wasatch Mountains and being close enough to walk to the park. She'd been doing that most weekends to try to keep vaguely active as she drove everywhere the rest of the time.

There seemed to be a few options. Nothing as spectacular and stylish as she had now, and all of the ones she could find were unfurnished. That would add an extra job, and a lot more expense, to the list if she needed to furnish an entire apartment.

She did what she always did in these kinds of circumstances and started to write a list of all the things she needed to achieve in the next fourteen days to have a fully functioning new place to live. It was all doable if she focused on the task for approximately twenty-five hours each day. She sighed.

Looking at the top of her computer screen, she was surprised to see nearly an hour had passed. She fired off a few emails to realtors enquiring about available properties; she didn't have time to lose. The hunt would have to continue this evening.

She suddenly remembered she'd meant to call Violet, so quickly dialled her as her lunch break neared its end. It would be nearly eight at home now, and her friend would normally be at home with Michael on a Monday night.

After ten rings, the phone went to voicemail. 'This is Violet, you know what to do.'

After the tone, Abbie put on her most upbeat voice. 'Have you been eaten by London street foxes? Kept prisoner by Michael as he ravishes you? Where the hell are you? Call me. I have so much to tell you.'

Hanging up, a funny feeling in her stomach, she returned to her long list of jobs.

EXHAUSTED AT THE end of a long day, Abbie finally decided she had to sign off or the hunt for a house wouldn't happen. She decisively closed all her programmes except for the web browser and focused on looking for realtors that she hadn't already searched through, since she'd received two replies already saying the apartments she was looking at were now unavailable.

She supposed worst case, Rose would let her sleep on the sofa for a few days, but she really preferred to find a new place as she didn't much fancy waking up each morning with a stiff neck.

She widened her search around the city as nothing new was showing up in the East of Downtown area that she had been focused on.

She sighed. This was going to be a long night, and she was going to need a shit ton of coffee. Picking up her empty mug – the LTFC 4 LIFE one the boys had given her when she left London City, which was a fond reminder of home – she went to leave her office and go to the kitchen. As she started to open the door, it flew back and she felt the weight of another freight train hit her as she crashed into someone who was walking into the room as she was trying to leave it.

This time though, Kyle grabbed her before she had a chance to fall to the ground. 'We must stop meeting like this,' he laughed, and let her go after making sure she was steady.

She returned the smile. 'You're determined to put me in the hospital, aren't you?'

'I figure the only way I can impress you at this point is to get you injured then swoop in to rescue you.' He wiggled his eyebrows up and down and then left them raised in a question.

'The only way you can impress me right now is by coming to the kitchen with me and making me a coffee, because I need it to give me the energy to get through the evening.'

He took the mug out of her hand and started towards the kitchen. 'Your wish is my command, England. I also owe you for leaving you in this place with Kitty for weeks while I've been roving around the country.'

Abbie flicked his arm. 'Stop being mean. She's been really helpful. She's supported me loads with The Half-Time Show and she's tried to sort out my apartment woes.'

'What's happened?' He looked concerned as he paused while heaping instant coffee into two mugs.

'Oh, don't worry. I need five minutes not thinking about it. Tell me about your trip. Distract me,' she encouraged him as she hoisted herself up to sit on the counter. She wouldn't normally, but it was after hours, and she was pretty sure they were the only two on the premises.

The culture was different at this club, and people didn't tend to work late. It was very different from every other job she'd had, where people were pretty much expected to do unpaid overtime every day or their dedication was questioned. It was taking some getting used to, but she was enjoying the ability to leave guilt-free when she had plans.

'It went pretty well actually.' Kyle stirred the coffee and handed Abbie a steaming mug. 'I visited ten colleges, a different one almost every day, and saw a bunch of matches. I also found a few kids I'm going to offer a place in the youth team, and there are two that I would move mountains to get here,' he said, his happiness obvious.

'That's amazing news,' she said, offering up her coffee mug to clink with his.

'Did you miss me?' he teased.

'To be honest, I didn't even notice you weren't here.' She winked, sticking out her tongue. Dear god, he was easy to flirt with. She didn't even know she still had it in her. She was rusty as hell.

'Rude. I'll be taking that coffee back then.' He made a mock grab for her coffee and she found herself looking straight into his eyes. The atmosphere felt charged and she looked down, taking a sip of the coffee.

He broke the silence. 'Tell me about the apartment then. What's wrong? I thought you loved it?'

'I do love it. I only had it for three months, though, and that's up in two weeks. Kitty tried to extend the lease but someone else is already moving in. So, I have two weeks to find a new place, sort a contract, find furniture by the look of it as everywhere is unfurnished, do all the utility stuff, blah blah blah, and that's on top of being crazy busy here. I'm panicking a bit as I don't really have enough time to sort everything, and the places I'm finding online are all gone when I talk to the realtors.' She felt her shoulders drop as she finished her rant.

'Wow. Okay. Well, England, what you need is a local, and lucky for you I'm one of those, and I'm ready and willing to help.'

'I couldn't ask you to do that. Kitty already offered to help, but this is on me. I was stupid and didn't ask to extend the lease soon enough, so it's my fault I'm now running out of time.'

Kyle frowned. 'Don't be an idiot and decline help because you think you're being a burden. You're not. I love a challenge and I have local contacts. I have at least three buddies who are realtors, I have a pickup truck to carry furniture around so you don't have to wait weeks for deliveries, and I know much better neighbourhoods to look for a place than Kitty, who put you over in retire-mentsville. Okay?' he asked, even though it wasn't really a question.

She hesitated, even though she knew she was going to accept. It felt like an impossible task otherwise, and she really did need the help, as much as she didn't like to put people out.

'Okay, you're on. But you have to tell me if I'm being a pain in the arse.'

'No question about that. I'll tell you.'

'And if you can't help with something you have to tell me and not be a moving-in martyr.'

'You don't know me that well if you think I'm going to be anything other than upfront with you.'

'And I can pay for your time, gas or anything because I really don't want to be a massive inconvenience.'

'Abbie?'

'Yes?'

'You're being a pain in the ass.' He looked at her, mouth stern, one eyebrow raised.

'Sorry.' She grimaced. 'One more thing?'

'Shoot.'

'Can you please not tell Kitty you're helping me?'

He crossed his arms and waited for her to continue.

'It's just, I turned down her offer of help, and I don't know how she would take it if she knew you'd stepped in.'

'My lips are sealed,' he said, miming zipping his mouth closed. 'So, are we going to get this thing going?'

She nodded and he took both mugs and started to refill them. As they headed back to her desk, he took his phone out of his pocket and started tapping.

'Oh god, I'm inconveniencing you already, aren't I? You're having to cancel a hot date?' she asked, realising that she was digging for information.

He paused, glancing at her. 'Important question. Do you like pineapple on your pizza?'

'What?'

'We have a long night ahead. I'm ordering pizza. This is your last chance. With pineapple or without pineapple?'

'With pineapple.' She smiled, relieved he wasn't cancelling personal plans because of her.

'Wrong answer. You're unbelievable, you Brits. Pineapple on pizza.' He tutted and she swatted him on the arm.

The next few hours passed quickly as she continued searching for properties online, while Kyle hit the phones to his estate agent friends. The priority was finding the place, he said. Everything else could be sorted at short notice. They ate pizza as they pored over the options that Abbie was finding and the ones that then started coming through to Kyle, with him advising her on the best locations and the pros and cons of each property.

She saw one apartment that looked beautiful. It was modern, like the unit she was in at the moment, but he vetoed the location as he said it had had a spate of crime recently and he wasn't having her live there. She thought he was being dramatic and told him so, but he just shrugged and told her it was a no-go.

Just after eight, his phone rang. There was a two-bedroom house available in the Liberty Wells area. It wasn't on the market yet and had just been completely renovated with a new kitchen and bathroom. She heard Kyle ask his friend to text him the address and said they would be over at five thirty the following day.

'What do you think?' she asked him nervously.

'I think we'll go take a look, but it sounds like it could be a real option. Noah wouldn't have offered it if it wasn't good, it's the same price you're paying now and it's in a good location. He knows the couple who are leasing it out and basically said if you want it, it's yours.'

She felt her shoulders drop about a foot. She had been

incredibly tense about the whole situation.

'Thanks, Kyle. I don't know what to say. You don't have to come with me to see it, though, I've taken enough of your time. If you give me the address, I'll let you know how it was.'

'Are you kidding? As if I'd let you go alone. You'd probably trip up the stairs and be eaten by wild dogs and be found in a week when the next house hunters visit. That, or agree to pay twice the going rate. I told you, you need a local.'

She looked at him, her eyes searching his expression to see if this really was okay. For the first time, she saw a flicker of uncertainty cross his face.

'Sorry, Abbie, I just realised I came into this like a steamroller and you might not want me prying and getting over-involved.' She saw him falter and her heart did an involuntary jump.

'That's not it at all,' she said. 'I just don't want to put you out, and you're doing so much for me. I would love if you could visit the house with me tomorrow. Make sure I'm not signing up for a rat-infested deathtrap.'

He visibly relaxed. 'You're on. I'll bring the tape measure so we can figure out the biggest sofa we can get you for the family room. Now, we have homes to go to, and we have to be back here in twelve hours. Finish your disgusting pizza.'

She deliberately picked up the slice loaded with the most pineapple and made a point of making satisfied noises as she chewed.

CHAPTER 13

STANDING ON THE pavement looking up at the house the next day, Abbie was excited. She tried to temper it, knowing that this wasn't a done deal. But it was gorgeous.

The cute cream Craftsman style house was on a tree-lined street, set back from the path with a freshly mown lawn in the front and a few steps leading up to a small porch. The left half of the two-storey house was shaped like a turret and had lilac wisteria creeping up it, and she could see a wooden balcony coming off the upper floor. She was already in love and she hadn't yet walked through the front door.

She waited for Kyle to head back over to her with his realtor friend, Noah. He didn't look like she expected an estate agent to look. In fact, he resembled an American football player. He was absolutely enormous.

'Abbie, meet Noah. He was one of my sports buddies at college. Noah, meet England.'

'Hey, Abbie, it's really nice to meet you.' As he shook her hand, she was fairly sure she felt bones crack and thought he was going to wrench it off her wrist as he pulled away.

'Thanks so much for giving us the heads-up on this

place,' she said, genuinely grateful. She was eager to get inside and was happy when Noah headed to the front door, which was black with a gold handle and knocker.

'The landlord has just finished renovating so they're looking to rent it as fast as possible. It's got new carpets throughout, and they put in a new kitchen and upstairs bathroom,' Noah explained as he walked them straight through the hallway and into the large, circular lounge on the left, which was in the turret section of the house.

The kitchen was at the back of the house and had a hardwood floor, big single-pane sash windows and was fitted with cream country style cabinets, a matching island, a range cooker and a cream SMEG fridge. It was the kitchen of her dreams.

A utility room with an industrial size washer and dryer and a small guest bathroom off the kitchen completed the ground floor.

At the end of the utility room was another external door leading to a small rear garden, which was half lawn and half decking. She dreamed of barbecues and cosy nights sitting outside until the sun set. With May on its way, the temperature was already close to what it was most summer days in the UK. She could live with that.

'I'll take it. Where do I sign?' she said, as Noah and Kyle laughed.

'Let's at least look upstairs first,' said Kyle. 'Maybe that's where the rats are hiding.'

Practically skipping up the stairs, she first went into the master bedroom, which was directly above the lounge.

She could imagine piling up a ton of cushions on the fitted bench seat that ran the length of the bay sash windows along the curved wall of the room, and a bed facing the windows that let in the natural light.

A second, smaller bedroom was across the hall with the newly fitted family bathroom sandwiched between.

She'd thought she loved her Liberty Park apartment. She realised now it was just lust. This was real love.

'Noah. I'm scared. I want this place. I have to have it. Who do I have to bribe?' She smiled wide, the gesture masking the very real fear she felt at the thought of this place slipping through her fingers.

Noah returned the smile. 'Abbie, if you want it, it's yours. The owners are friends of mine, and they've met Kyle a couple of times. I've told them what you're doing and how quickly you can move in, and Kyle already told me he can get you a reference from work, so they're good to sign if you are.'

She looked at Kyle. 'This is too good to be true. I'm taking it.'

'Let's get it done then, England. Noah, can you draw up the lease?'

'Of course, man. And look, stay as long as you need to measure up. I know you need to move in within a couple of weeks. Just drop the keys back at the office tomorrow.'

As Noah left, Abbie went to go down the stairs.

'Wait.' Kyle gestured to her. 'You haven't seen the best bit.'

A glass door off the upstairs hallway led to the balcony

she had seen from the pavement but had forgotten all about in her excitement at everything else. Stepping out onto the balcony, she looked up and saw the Wasatch Mountains in all their glory.

'I still have this view,' she whispered, hardly believing.

'I know how much you love it, and you're only a few blocks from the park so you can still go running into people whenever you want.'

She squealed and, without thinking, threw her arms around Kyle's neck. 'I thought you said Kitty had put me in the wrong part of town?'

He chuckled as he put his arms around her to hug her back, before releasing her. 'I was just winding her up. It's too easy. You were kind of too far south, though. Where you are now, you're also only a few blocks from Central so you can walk to the bars and restaurants. It's a good place to be.'

She couldn't believe he'd managed to swing this for her. Within a day and a half, he'd turned it all around. That was a hell of an effort.

'Enough daydreaming then, England. We've got a lot of work to do. Get out your notebook and a pen, we're going measuring,' He pulled out a tape measure from his pocket and ushered her back inside.

Over the next hour they went room by room, making a list of furniture she needed and the space she had.

Ending up in the lounge, she finished writing the final measurements down then lay down on the carpet. Unable to suppress her happiness, she squealed while making angel movements with her arms on the newly laid soft grey carpet. The lilac maxi dress she was wearing, a new spring purchase in her bid to keep bolstering her wardrobe with colour, complemented the flooring. She thought it must be a sign this was the place if she matched the fixtures and fittings.

She turned her head to look at Kyle. He was sitting with his back leaning against the bay wall, legs stretched out in front of him.

'Happy?' he asked, returning the tape measure to his jeans pocket.

'More than you could imagine.' She sighed with contentment.

The atmosphere charged as they looked at each other and Abbie met his gaze for slightly longer than she had the last time. Suddenly feeling spontaneous, she sat up. 'Do you feel like grabbing something to eat before it's too late?'

'I never say no to food,' he answered, taking the keys out of his pockets. 'Let's go.'

He led the way in his pickup and she followed in convoy in her company sedan. They parked in a quiet street about ten minutes from Abbie's new house of dreams.

She followed him into a cosy Italian trattoria, where he greeted the waiter by name. There were only about fifteen tables in the small room, which had exposed brick walls and a beamed ceiling. Running along the top of each wall was a black wrought-iron shelf crammed with red wine. The tables were covered in red and white checked tablecloths, each with a candle in a Chianti bottle in a straw basket, years of dripped wax set solid down the dark green glass.

A handful of tables were already taken. An elderly couple in one corner, bickering over a basket of bread. A couple with two teenagers and a younger boy in the centre, the teenagers glued to mobile phones and the boy colouring in a drawing while the couple chatted. And a group of three women in the corner, chatting ten to the dozen over steaming bowls of pasta and glasses of Prosecco.

The waiter, Rafaele, led them to a table next to the window and handed them both menus.

'Allora, welcome to San Giovanni. Tonight, we have the special of lobster ravioli or a Fiorentina steak, cooked in rosemary and served with roasted potatoes and roasted vine tomatoes. Can I start you with some wine?'

Kyle and Abbie both asked for a glass of red wine and Rafaele briskly walked off with their order.

'This place is so nice, Kyle.'

'Wait until you try the food,' he said excitedly. 'This is the place I told you with the meatballs from heaven.'

'I swear I'll be double the size I was when I arrived by the time my contract is up. All I seem to do is eat,' she said as she absentmindedly picked a chunk of bread out of the basket and started nibbling at it.

Kyle swiped the bread basket from under her. 'There's nothing wrong with a good appetite, but please do share.'

He winked.

An hour later, their bellies full of pasta, red wine, and, indeed the best meatballs in the world, Abbie realised she'd had more fun since she left work today than the last time she could remember. They'd laughed a lot over dinner, and he'd teased her relentlessly over her near miss on the snowboard at Park City. They'd talked about where they both went to school. And he had checked that she'd been okay while he was away and that Kitty hadn't been giving her a hard time.

'She's been really nice to me. What is it with you two?' she asked. 'You're like brother and sister or something, constantly sniping at each other and winding each other up.'

'I've known Kitty a long time. We went to high school together. There's nothing in it really. I guess you could say it was kind of a brother–sister thing. She's just easy to wind up, as you put it.' He shrugged, taking another sip from his wine glass.

It was the least enthusiastic he'd sounded about anything since she met him. She knew Kitty was a bit of an acquired taste, so she figured maybe she just wasn't his cup of tea, but if they'd known each other for over fifteen years, it kind of made sense. She changed the subject. She felt bad talking about Kitty when she'd been so helpful.

'Where do you think I should go to look for furniture? Since you're smashing recommendations out of the park right now.'

'Don't you worry about that. Are you free Thursday

after work?'

She nodded yes.

'Perfect,' he said excitedly. 'I know this hidden gem where I'm sure you'll find some of what you need for the house'

'Sounds great. Thank you, seriously.'

As she went to stand up after they'd paid the bill, he stopped her. 'The game this week is Friday. I was wondering if that meant you had a free weekend?'

He said it so earnestly and, for the second time, she saw a chink in the confident armour.

'I'm free,' she said, gently.

'Would you be up for a road trip on Saturday? I want to show you more amazing places, and it's the perfect time of year to see this one spot. There's a little catch, but I need you to agree first.' He smiled at her.

She quickly agreed to go. 'Even though you keep trying to kill me with all your crazy activities, something fun on Saturday would be great to take my mind off the house stuff, especially now you've lifted a massive weight off my shoulders finding that incredible place. But what's the catch?'

'I'll tell you on Friday. You'll need to wear sneakers and hiking clothes, and bring sunscreen and a baseball cap. But I'm not sending you flying down any slopes this time, don't worry.' He stood up and Abbie did the same.

'Okay, mysterious one. In the meantime, let's go test out sofas on Thursday,' she said as they walked out of the door and towards their cars, which were parked next to each other.

She pulled her keys from her bag and thanked him again, moving towards Kyle to give him a hug. She had done it without even thinking and, feeling embarrassed, withdrew before saying goodbye and quickly opened the car door.

Kyle didn't take his eyes off her as she put on her seat belt, and he stood next to his truck while she drove out of the parking lot, waving when he noticed her looking in her rear-view mirror.

Walking through the door of her apartment she looked around, thinking what a good start to life in Salt Lake City it had offered her, but that she couldn't be happier to be moving into her beautiful new place. It had been a good move to let Kyle help her. She knew she was pushing things by spending so much time with him, but she was enjoying his company and she felt more alive than she had in years with their easy conversation. And she hadn't crossed any lines.

THE FOLLOWING NIGHT, after doing a mass order on the IKEA website for kitchenware, bathroom odds and sods, pillows, towels, linen and a hell of a lot of coat hangers, Abbie closed her laptop and crossed a few more items off the 'moving to a new house' to-do list. Once she was moved in and a bit sorted, she'd work out anything extra she needed. But she'd made a major dent in organising the essentials and, with any luck, she'd find some furniture the next day at Kyle's secret shop.

As promised, Noah had sent through the lease for the house earlier that day and, apparently, Kyle had sorted all the paperwork she needed from the club. So, a mere forty-eight hours after having pretty much a complete break-down, she was signed and sealed on the Craftsman house with the mountain view. What a difference a day could make.

She turned the oven on, got a pizza out of the fridge and started throwing together a side salad while the grill warmed up.

As she was adding sliced yellow bell peppers into the bowl, the doorbell rang, and she hurried to let Rose in. She was coming over so they could do some more work on the blog.

Her friend entered, clutching a bottle of Four Roses bourbon in her hand.

'That's pretty heavy for a Wednesday.' Abbie laughed, taking it from her and putting it on the counter by the side salad.

'Well, Abbie. This seems like an appropriate time to tell you the old adage: no good story ever started with someone eating a salad.'

Looking at the bowl of leaves, tomato, cucumber and pepper, Abbie conceded, 'You're right.' She got two tumblers from the cupboard and passed them to Rose to do the honours.

'Besides, we're celebrating,' Rose said, her tone not

altering as she poured the amber liquid into the glasses. 'I've had a call from Dexter McFarlane.' She handed one of the glasses to Abbie, who looked at her questioningly. She had no idea who Dexter McFarlane was.

'He's an entrepreneur in town. He owns three bars that play live music, and we've been listing who's playing at his venues. He's apparently heard interest in our blog and he wants to offer us a deal. We'd get ten per cent commission on any tickets that he sells that link through from our site to his.' She lifted up her glass to clink Abbie's.

'What? We could make money out of this thing?' Abbie was surprised, and Rose had to prompt her to bring her glass to meet her own before taking a sip.

'Yes. And think, if this guy is offering already, we can go to all the other venues we're listing when we've got some good visitor numbers and try to get deals out of them too. It seems like we're getting some traction already. And apparently that idiot at the paper is pretty mad that he's losing invitations to gigs because people are reading our site instead and treating it seriously.'

Abbie felt a thrill as she pulled the pizza out of the oven and started slicing, then handed a piece to Rose as she let the news sink in. 'We really might be onto something here, right?' she mused, taking a bite out of her own slice of pepperoni.

'Abso-freaking-lutely. And it's happening so fast. Who knew we had our best ideas when we were drunk, hey?' She made her point by taking another swig from her glass.

The rest of the evening passed by with them planning

what they'd do over the next month for the blog, updating the listings, replying to invitations to gigs, and posting their latest review of an indie band they saw the week before.

Wrapping up, they refilled their glasses for a nightcap and moved to the sofa.

'What's cooking for the rest of your week?' Rose asked.

'Going furniture shopping with Kyle. No big deal.' Abbie mimed filing her nails.

Rose raised her eyebrows. 'That escalated fast.'

Laughing, Abbie explained what had happened the past few days with the new house and how Kyle had swooped in to save the homeless, helpless maiden in distress.

'Would you guys just get it on already. All this non-touching foreplay is getting boring. You're going to try out beds with this dude and you've never even kissed him. Are we in a Jane Austen novel?'

Abbie covered her face with her hands, shaking her head. 'I still don't know if this is a good idea. I fancy him, no point me trying to deny it. But on paper, it's got disaster written all over it. He's also taking me out for the day on Saturday. Some surprise place he won't tell me about until we arrive.'

'You're totally going to kiss,' Rose teased as she downed the last of her bourbon. 'Text me as soon as it happens. Like, literally the moment it ends I want you to pick up the phone. I want to know if this epic build up has been worth it.'

CHAPTER 14

'**F**UUUUUCK' ABBIE SWORE as she stubbed her toe on the corner of the chest of drawers in her bedroom.

Three a.m. was not her preferred alarm clock time. In fact, she was pretty sure the last time she woke up at that ungodly hour was the dreadful night she had to go to the police station when John Sullivan was arrested. That felt like a lifetime ago. Even though it had only been three months, the longer she was in Salt Lake City, the further away from home she felt. She was happy she'd settled quickly and embraced the challenge, but she did feel every so often that she was forgetting her old life. She remembered again that Violet had been evading her messages and pushed the thought away. She didn't have time to worry about it right now; Kyle was picking her up in half an hour.

That was the catch, it turned out. A 3:30 a.m. departure. What kind of a monster was this man? She was still worried it was all an elaborate practical joke.

He had broken the news of the early alarm call as they went their separate ways after a very successful shop on Thursday. He'd taken her to a huge warehouse outside of the city that had hundreds of pieces of end of the line and old season high-quality furniture. She found everything she needed at a fraction of the cost she would have normally spent, and they were going to deliver it all on the day she moved in.

If Kyle ever wanted to retire from football, he could make a fortune selling his moving house skills.

They hadn't had time to hang out afterwards as they both had a lot of work to do ahead of the big Friday night televised football game, so his parting shot was to tell her that she wasn't getting the lie-in and lazy Saturday morning that she'd expected.

It was chilly, as it was still the middle of the bloody night, so now she threw on a pair of light blue jeans, white Nike running shoes and a white cotton racer-back vest. She threw a soft grey hoodie over the top and tied her hair into a low ponytail, and then packed her bag with the baseball cap and sunscreen Kyle had told her to bring. She also threw in some denim shorts for when the bite was out of the air, some make-up and a few other things she thought she might need in the bottom of her handbag. Who knew what she needed, as he'd been so vague?

She should be nervous that she didn't know where the hell she was going and was being taken away in the middle of the night by someone she'd only known a few months, but she was excited. Every bit of time she'd spent with Kyle so far had been fun, easy and comfortable, and it felt natural to be heading out socially again with him.

Her phone pinged with a text, which told her he was outside. She double-checked she had what she needed, even though she didn't really know what that might be, and headed out the door.

She looked for the black Honda pickup, but couldn't see it. Then she saw the headlights of an unfamiliar car turn on and she frowned in confusion. The lights flashed at her and she could see Kyle waving to get her attention.

He got out to come and join her and gesticulated at the car.

'She's a beauty, right?' It was a proud statement delivered with a big beam, not a question.

The car was long and sleek and looked like it had driven straight off the set of the Grease movie. Bathed in light from the street light above, she could see that the bottom panels were a light cream, almost white, while the top panels and roof were a bright turquoise. Running the length of the wheelbase and horizontally down the centre of the sides of the car were gleaming silver metal panes. A huge silver grill housed double headlights either end of the huge bonnet. The detail was incredible and it was pristine.

'What is it?' Abbie gasped.

'That, my sweet England, is a 1958 Chevy Bel Air, and she is the love of my life.'

Abbie glanced sideways at him, suppressing the desire to laugh. Men and their motors.

'Will it fall to pieces?' she asked. 'That's a pretty old car.'

Kyle clutched his hands to his chest in mock horror. 'You're going to hurt her feelings. She's a perfectly maintained classic. She's never let me down.'

'It's beautiful, Kyle. I've never seen anything like it.' Abbie dropped the teasing because what she was looking at was a thing to be admired. Even though she knew nothing about cars, she could appreciate that it was special.

'I know. She's beautiful. But you'll have to admire her properly later because if we don't get a move on, we're going to miss the main event. Hop in, England.' He opened the door for her as he said it and she slid in, onto the turquoise and cream stitched leather bench seat. It was as beautiful inside as out.

Although, she still wasn't sure something this old would get them very far. Maybe the departure time had to be so early because it would take them an extremely long time to get there in this. She amused herself with this thought as she clicked the seatbelt in and, at the same time, Kyle carefully closed her door.

Sliding in the other side seconds later, his frame filled the space which felt much more intimate than when they were in his truck. He passed her a hot Starbucks cup, which she could see had the word 'England' scrawled on the side with a marker pen.

'Thought you could do with something to keep you awake after the early call,' he said as he put the key in the ignition.

The beast roared as he turned the key. Abbie could feel the steady vibrations beneath them as the car came to life and the engine turned over. The sensation ran through her body and her heart pounded from the sound. This was already an experience worth waking up for and he hadn't released the handbrake yet.

'You're going to wake the neighbours.' She put her index finger to her mouth and shushed him, but he laughed at her and began driving away from the apartment.

Sipping at her coffee, she looked at him as he drove them in a comfortable silence. He really was ridiculously good-looking, and she felt a jolt in her stomach. 'Are you going to tell me where we're going now?'

'Nope. You just sit back and enjoy the ride. No clues.'

As they left the city, there was complete peace, bar the soft growling purr of the car. The streets were empty at this time and the morning was still dark. Abbie found herself sinking lower into the padded seat and she shifted so she was facing towards Kyle. The glint of the street lamps lit up his face. He was all jaw and cheekbones underneath the well-worn dark grey baseball cap pulled low over his eyes.

She had thought it before, but this was a man completely at ease with himself, and he made her feel like she could be totally herself. She felt relaxed and carefree when he was around, and he never failed to make her laugh. She couldn't believe she'd only met him a few months before. He was the kind of person who had that rare ability to make you feel you had known them forever.

Resting her arm along the back of the bench seat and leaning her head on it, she thought about the niggling doubts she still had about him. Leopards never changed their spots, and she knew he had a reputation, but that knowledge didn't stop her feelings for him deepening, especially during the last couple of weeks when he really had come through for her. And the way she felt herself opening up whenever he was around was almost beyond her control. She knew it made her vulnerable, but she couldn't fight it.

As the car continued to warm up, her eyelids started getting heavy. She tried to battle it but a wave of exhaustion passed over her, and before she knew it, she was asleep.

'WAKE UP, SLEEPYHEAD. You're going to miss the best bit.' Abbie groaned as Kyle gently shook her awake. The smell of fresh coffee and pastries hit her nostrils and she stretched and winced, feeling the crick in her neck from sleeping awkwardly. The engine was off and she realised they were now parked.

'Shit, did I sleep the whole way?' She sat upright, looking at Kyle and feeling mortified that she'd flaked out and left him driving without company all the way to their destination. Given that it wasn't completely dark anymore, that must have been quite a distance.

He laughed, handing her a paper bag with a cream cheese bagel inside. 'I don't think a herd of charging animals could have woken you up. Although your snoring kind of sounds like a wild boar. You didn't even wake up when I restarted the engine after grabbing this breakfast.'

'I don't snore.' She felt the heat rise in her cheeks.

'That's for me to know, isn't it?' He winked. 'Anyway, I didn't bring you here to look at me. I brought you to look at this.'

He pointed out of the windscreen and Abbie followed the direction of his finger.

She was speechless.

The first shimmer of sunrise could be seen on a mountainous horizon. The glittering rays from the emerging yellow orb were captured perfectly in the centre of an enormous natural red rock window in the middle of a rocky desert, dotted with dark green shrubs. As she took in the alien landscape, she saw windows and arches made out of orange and red rock everywhere she looked, from small curves to enormous constructions reaching high in the sky and everything in between, rising out of the rocky ground. The sky above was turning blue and was peppered with soft pink clouds, the changing light creating a real show.

'What is this? Did we go by rocket ship to another planet?' she whispered, not believing what she was seeing with her own eyes.

'Pretty much,' Kyle murmured, contentedly. 'This is Arches National Park. We're a few hours' drive from Salt Lake, and the nearest town to here is a place called Moab. Do you like it?' His voice faltered a little, as if it meant a lot to him that she did.

'It's the most beautiful place I've ever seen,' she said, unable to take her eyes off the incredible spectacle in front of her.

They sat in silence watching the sun continue to rise above the rocks, the vista bathing in the growing light as the reds and oranges gained in intensity and depth. The detail of the sandstone arches became more visible with the emerging day. Making any noise would have broken the peaceful magic.

It felt like they sat there for hours, drinking in the sunrise. Abbie knew this was a special moment in her life. She felt an appreciation for the simple things, like a rising sun that had the power to take your breath away. And she felt small as she looked out at the rock arches all around as far as the eye could see. The world was a big place, and she was sharing what had to be the most beautiful spot on earth with someone who was rapidly becoming extraordinarily important to her.

They both seemed to shake out of their shared trance-like state when a flock of jet-black birds swooped past the arch framing the sunrise, breaking up the stillness of the view.

'Ravens,' Kyle stated simply.

Abbie glanced at him and he returned the look before speaking again.

'Sorry for all the mystery. I didn't want you to google this place before you got to see it for real. It's too awesome.'

'I'm glad you didn't,' she replied, briefly resting her

hand on his own down on the bench seat. A ripple of excitement rushed through her as she felt the soft skin on the back of his hand with the tips of her fingers for the first time. 'It's the most spectacular thing I've ever seen. Photos couldn't have done it justice.'

'My dad and I used to come here a lot when I was growing up, and it never gets old. There are more than two thousand arches here. Indigenous people had lived here for thousands of years but it was only about a hundred and forty years ago that European settlers started to spread the word that it could be a good tourist spot. And less than a hundred years since it caught the attention of the National Park Service. How could something so big stay hidden from the world for so long?'

Abbie swallowed. She knew exactly how you could keep something big hidden for years. Even from the people closest to you.

She pushed the thought away. She wouldn't let that ruin things.

Not today.

'Ready to see some more?'

She nodded eagerly.

'Okay, now we're going by foot though. And it's going to get hot.'

They both changed into shorts, Kyle respectfully standing a distance from the car while she switched her clothes. He ordered her to slather on factor fifty and then emerged from rifling around in the boot with two canteens of water.

She wished he would have warned her they were going to be hiking in a desert. She might have got her arse to a gym a few times to work up to it.

'Okay England, let's go.'

She followed him as they crossed the clearing where he had parked and took a dusty, rocky path that could just be made out. She felt like she was walking on the moon with the arid red land spread all around her with little shoots of dark green foliage popping up from the cracks in the surface here and there.

The temperatures were rising quickly as they continued hiking the trail, and she was astounded that, no matter which direction she looked in, the park stretched out beyond where the eye could see.

A little while later she was out of breath and dripping in the searing heat.

When he told her, eventually, they had arrived, before she could look up she bent, rested her hands on her knees and tried to catch her breath.

Kyle, who didn't even seem to have broken a sweat, burst out laughing. 'You idiot. We only walked a mile.'

She sat on the ground and looked up at him with mock indignation.

'Yeah, well, you didn't tell me you were taking me on yet another one of your missions to try to kill me. The snowboarding didn't work so you thought you'd try to make me spontaneously combust by putting me on a boot camp in the bloody desert.'

'You think this is boot camp? You haven't seen anything. Get up, you need to see this.' He reached down and she stretched her hand up to meet his so he could pull her to her feet. He seemed to pick her up off the ground awfully frequently.

As he led her around a rock, the view suddenly opened up to another spectacular arch. At the top of the formation was a large window looking up to the blue skies, with a smaller circle beneath it.

'This is the Double O Arch. Pretty awesome, right?'

Abbie nodded. She still couldn't really find the words to express how she felt in this place. It was otherworldly. It was like they had been catapulted onto another planet. This couldn't exist on earth.

She tried to explain it to Kyle. 'If you've been coming here all your life, I don't know if you can understand how this is for me. I feel like we're on Mars.'

He laughed. 'That's exactly what I was hoping. Believe me, I know how special Arches is.'

'I don't even understand how it's possible for the world to make these things,' she said, shrugging her shoulders.

'Well, if you really want an explanation, take a seat, Miss Potter.' Butterflies swam in her stomach as he called her the unfamiliar new nickname in a low voice, and he sat down beside her on a large flat rock. Before going on, he pulled two chicken sandwiches wrapped in tinfoil out of his bag and handed Abbie one. She was struck by his thoughtfulness as she started to eat.

Looking at her, he took a drink of water then started

talking. 'If you're paying attention, I'll begin.'

She rolled her eyes. 'Get on with it.'

'Okay. Once upon a time, more than three hundred million years ago, before even the dinosaurs were a twinkle in their mothers' eyes, there was a huge salt bed right where we're standing, from when this whole area was part of a sea. The salt bed formed when the sea evaporated. And I'm talking salt beds upon salt beds upon salt beds. You think the chick from the Princess and the Pea had a high bed? That's nothing. Some of these parts had deposits over a thousand feet high. Are you with me?'

She laughed. 'Continue, Mr Geography Teacher, please.'

'Your wish is my command. But it's Mr Miller to you.'

'Come on. If you don't hurry up, we'll be here when the sun sets and we'll never find the car.'

'So keen to learn. I'm proud of you, England. Okay, so, over millions of years debris continued to collect from floods and winds and oceans and all types of bipolar, Targaryen Mad King level crazy weather conditions. This happened for many eras, and it all turned into rock. The salt bed got weighed down by this super-heavy rock, some weird geological shit happened and the salt beds threw themselves up and formed into a bunch of dome-like shapes. Still with me?'

'You're hardly explaining it to me like Stephen Hawking would, but I'm with you. How many millions of years are left in this story?'

'Millions.'

'Get on with it then,' she teased.

'So, all the crazy rock shapes started to get eroded. Then there was the small matter of a tiny little ice age that broke down that rock even more. The domes and shapes started collapsing into walls. Then there was even more wind and water. Like damn, you'd never have known how to dress for the weather here. Is it icy? Is it dry? Is it wet? Anyway, the wind and the water eroded the walls and all these magnificent arches formed that you, my lady, have the privilege to see today.'

'Wow.' She hadn't enjoyed geography at school, but she hadn't wanted this story to end. 'You're just full of surprises, aren't you? Footballing legend, snowboarding superstar and now historical nerd.'

'Hey, you watch out there with who you're calling a nerd. You haven't even heard the best.'

'Tell me.'

'There were dinosaurs here. Shit loads of them.'

She swatted him on the arm. 'You took me for a ride there, didn't you? This whole story is just a load of crap you made up to try to impress me.'

'I swear.' He held his hands up then reached down to take her hand in his and pull her up. 'Follow me.'

They continued walking through the stark desert. She tried to push away her breathlessness and looked around at everything, drinking it in. The red sandstone rock formations, etched with millions of years of life, contrasted with the bright blue sky that the day had brought.

Every now and then a fluffy white cloud broke up the endless azure.

'AHA.' She jumped as Kyle's voice boomed. 'I knew it was around here somewhere. Over here, Miss Potter. I have proof.'

She sped up her pace to catch up with him a few feet ahead.

'This, my dear student, is a dinosaur track.'

She gasped as she looked down, hardly believing. 'It can't be.' She knelt down, not caring if she got scratched or dusty, and looked intently at the fossilised tracks in the ground. One was three times the size of her hand, a three-toed imprint that reminded her of an elephant's foot.

'They can't just leave dinosaur prints in the ground with everyone walking over them. They should be protected or something.'

She couldn't comprehend how a few hours ago she was stubbing her toe in her bedroom and now she was walking in the tracks of prehistoric giants.

'Pretty impressive, huh. I've got a whole other lesson on dinosaurs I can give you another day.'

'I can't wait,' she said, genuinely meaning it, as she snapped a photo of her outstretched hand inside the footprint. She needed evidence. Lily would never believe it otherwise.

ABBIE WALKED BACK to the car a few steps behind Kyle,

exhausted but exhilarated, and extremely impressed at his orientation skills. She flopped into the seat, feeling the tired muscles in her legs after the unaccustomed exercise, and Kyle roared the Chevy back into action for their return journey.

'Does this thing have Bluetooth?' she asked, earning herself a dirty look from the driver's seat. 'Okay, you're preserving the classic feel, I get it. It's just I want to play you some songs from the band I'm booking for the last home game of the season. I heard them live one of my first days in the city in Rose's bar, and now they've had a number one single on the Billboard chart, but we know them, so they're going to come and play.' She clapped her hands with excitement as she told him and he looked at her and smiled so genuinely it sent shivers all the way through her.

She used her phone speaker to play him Memphis Black's hit single, 'Whispers for the Road'. As the bass and drums kicked in and the perfect melting pot of Marley and Betty's voices filled the car, a feeling of complete happiness came over her. She'd had the perfect day with an amazing man and, right at that moment, she couldn't imagine any other path for her life than what had happened to bring her all the way out here.

Looking out the window she saw a sign for the town of Moab, which was visible in the distance, and was just about to suggest they find somewhere there to eat before heading home when an awful noise started coming from under the bonnet. The sound of metal bashing together and cogs grating had her gripping the seat.

Kyle, too, looked worried and he quickly pulled over onto the hard shoulder of the road and turned the engine off.

'Oh, shit,' he said, looking at her. 'This could be a problem.'

CHAPTER 15

A N HOUR LATER, they were sitting in a diner on Main Street in Moab. The love of Kyle's life had her own life hanging in the balance at the hands of a local mechanic, who'd said he was sure he could get it fixed by the following lunchtime and had a buddy of his bringing in a part from out of town.

Which left them needing to stay in Moab overnight.

They had made a quick stop at a store on Main Street for overnight essentials and were refuelling after a day that had completely taken it out of Abbie physically. She really had to find a local gym. It was embarrassing.

She looked over the table to the other side of the booth where Kyle was fully focused on his steak and fried eggs. She couldn't eat her pancakes with bacon and maple syrup fast enough either. She knew technically that it was a breakfast dish, but she had found the beauty of American diners was no time was a bad time for pancakes.

Halfway through his meal, Kyle finally paused for breath, resting his hands either side of his plate on the scuffed-up table.

'I'm so sorry, Abbie. This was meant to be a fun day and now we're stranded hours from home and it's ruined your weekend. I feel so bad.' He looked utterly deflated.

And he'd called her Abbie. This wasn't good.

'Don't be an idiot.' She reached across the table and rested her hand on top of his. 'I've had the most perfect day and we don't have to go to work tomorrow so there's no need to freak out. Jesus, what a punishment having to stay in this area longer.' She looked him straight in the eye and smiled encouragingly, and saw him relax a little.

'Okay, well, if we're staying here, then I'm going to make sure we have a good time. Let's finish up and go find somewhere we can stay tonight. Since the back seat of my car isn't an option.'

She was relieved Kyle's sense of humour seemed to be back and was excited at the thought of spending some extra time with him. But she felt anxious in her stomach at the elephant in the room – they were staying here overnight together, and she wasn't sure what he expected.

The rest of the dinner passed in relative silence. She was relieved that it never seemed to be awkward when they weren't talking, as she felt like she was getting away with not voicing her nerves. She felt sure he'd see right through her if she was stuttering her way through a conversation. After paying the bill, he led her back out onto Main Street.

'There isn't a lot here and it's pretty old-fashioned,' he said. 'But because so many people visit this area to explore the national parks, the good thing is there are hotels everywhere. There's one just up here that's not bad.' He pointed ahead of them.

Abbie nodded and continued to walk alongside.

Reaching the hotel, they stepped across the welcome mat out on the street and through the revolving door. It was a traditional hotel, the doors made of wood with gold metal detailing and a dark red carpet with a gold fleur-de-lis pattern in the lobby leading up to a mahogany reception desk.

Approaching the receptionist, Kyle gave her his dazzling smile. Abbie could see the woman practically swoon on the spot. They wouldn't have a problem getting a room here. At the thought of the room situation, she felt her cheeks warming up and her hands get clammy. Why could she not just say to him that she wanted to have separate rooms? She knew it was because part of her wouldn't mind if they didn't.

Kyle looked at her for about the fifth time since they'd left the restaurant, and a small smile flitted across his lips. He winked at her before turning back to the receptionist, who wore a name badge that said 'Susan'.

He unleashed full Kyle upon Susan. The woman didn't stand a chance.

Abbie audibly sighed with relief when she heard him ask for two rooms for the night. And at the same time her own shoulders dropped, so did those of Susan, whose smile beamed that little bit brighter when she realised her two new guests were not 'together'. Abbie supressed a giggle.

As they headed towards the lift and waited for it to arrive, Kyle turned to her.

'You can stop stressing now. Do you really think I'd

force you to share a room with me? Firstly, I wouldn't treat a lady like that, and secondly, I can tell you're not falling for my charms that easily.'

He looked almost sad as he said that, and the worry that he thought she wasn't interested in him at all reignited her earlier panic, albeit for a different reason. As she hurried to try to explain, he held up his hand.

'You don't need to explain, England. You know I like you, but I'm not that guy.'

The lift pinged open and they headed up to their rooms.

Abbie spoke to break the silence. 'Meet in half an hour to hit a bar?'

'Your best idea yet.' He grinned and she skipped to her room to try to fix the sweaty mess she'd become after the hot day in the desert.

WITH A GIN and tonic in her hand and watching Kyle sip at a bottle of Budweiser, Abbie felt completely calm again. They'd come to a bar a few doors down from the hotel. It reminded her a bit of The Live Joint with its ramshackle interior, but it didn't have the stage or band posters adorning the walls. The music was thanks to the jukebox in the corner, the paper inside showing the song choices yellowing and curling at the corners. Johnny Cash was playing quietly through the speakers, the country song perfect for this bar in the middle of nowhere.

One wall was covered with hundreds of beer mats, while the counter had foreign currency notes pinned to the front of it, covering the whole length. Kyle explained how it had become tradition for any overseas tourists to pin a note. Before they even ordered a drink, Abbie took five pounds from her purse and added it to the collection. She wanted to leave a little piece of herself here as she would never forget Moab.

Now they sat at a wooden table in the corner at the back of the room. It was quiet, with only a couple of other tables occupied. They settled into the cosy bar and it was as easy as always to talk to Kyle.

'Does your dad still come out here with you sometimes?' she asked. She was curious as Kyle hadn't talked about either of his parents until today.

'Not so often. My parents were older when they had me and they're in their mid-seventies now, so it's harder to get him out to do the things we used to when I was younger. They live up near Park City now and have quite the social life there with all their friends.' He smiled. It was obvious how besotted he was with them as he carried on talking about their good life in the mountains.

Abbie told him about her own parents and all about Lily. She also found herself spilling out the story about the footballer at her old club, and how the whole incident and aftermath had been a factor in her decision to make the move.

Kyle was appalled, and she had to reassure him that she had not been upset or hurt. It had simply exacerbated her need to leave and find a new challenge anyway. It made her heart lurch how protective he seemed to be of her, like he was about his parents and his youth team. He made her feel safe.

He started explaining how he made sure when he worked with the kids in his youth team that he gave them some life lessons if they needed it.

'Once, I walked in on some of the older youth players, college age, talking about what they'd done at the weekend with a bunch of girls. Sport is about discipline and, if their parents aren't going to teach them, then I sure am. The first thing my mom taught me, before I even went to school, was that you don't put your hands on a girl unless she's happy for you to do it,' he said matter-of-factly.

'You can't be real.' Abbie smiled, and he raised his eyebrows. 'I'm still trying to find the bad bits. You take it so seriously working with those kids and it's amazing. I don't know if I'd have the patience.'

'You would,' he said. 'You're a bit of a badass yourself, coming in here and whipping that club into shape. Hank is over the moon with you.'

She clapped her hands. 'Oh, I hope so. I'm trying. Oh my god,' she said, an idea sparking in her mind. 'I think I have an idea.'

'Wait,' Kyle said. 'Let me get us another round.'

As he dashed to the bar, her mind went into over-drive, and as soon as he returned to the table she started explaining.

'You work so hard with these kids. What if we did something where the fifteen that show the best attitude and aptitude over a certain period of time get the chance to fly to England to do a training camp with a Premiership club there? I'm pretty sure I could swing it with my old boss and it would be a reward for hard work.'

Kyle loved it. He absolutely loved it.

They talked it over and started to plan how the kids would earn their place and how it would work.

'This is amazing, Abbie, I can't believe you came up with this.'

'Well, what can I say?' she teased. 'That's why they pay me the big bucks.'

Laughing, they left the bar and walked the few feet to the hotel. They had a long drive back tomorrow, as long as the car could be fixed.

As they went up in the lift to the fourth floor, she leaned into him, the warming effects of the alcohol and the activity of the day making her sleepy. He guided her out of the lift and followed her to her room, which was next to his.

'Are you following me to my room, Mr Miller?' she asked as she located her key in her bag.

'I'm just making sure my tipsy friend manages to get in okay,' he answered.

She turned to say goodnight. Leaning up to kiss his cheek, she brushed his warm stubble and was overwhelmed by the electricity between them. She lingered at his cheek, then slid her lips across to meet his own and felt his whole body respond as he moved closer to her. When she wrapped her arms around his neck, he knotted his hands around her waist and deepened the kiss, his tongue darting in to meet hers, and she was completely lost in the moment.

As he pulled away to look at her, she remembered Kitty's warning and came back down to earth. She let go of him and turned to put her key in the lock.

'Sorry. I think it's time for me to go to bed.' Not giving him time to respond or change her mind, she hurriedly entered the room.

Inside, she lay down heavily on the bed, her mind racing. It had been a long time since she'd kissed anyone, and that kiss had blown her mind.

SITTING IN THE hotel breakfast room the following morning, nursing a strong coffee to go along with the slight headache she had, Abbie felt herself blush as Kyle walked in. He saluted her, then joined her and poured himself a black coffee from the jug on the table. Stirring in a sugar, he told her the mechanic had texted to say the car would be ready in an hour.

As he studied the menu, apparently lost in thought as he decided which eggs to go for, she couldn't believe that he could be so calm and seemingly unbothered by what had happened last night.

The kiss had been pretty incredible. It had stirred

feelings in her that she'd forgotten she was capable of, yet she had broken it off.

The waitress came over and Kyle ordered a huge plate of eggs, bacon, sausages, hash browns, mushrooms and tomato. Abbie's stomach was feeling the effects of at least three too many gins and she ordered the same.

'So, let's talk about that kiss.'

Kyle looked straight at her, and it took everything in her not to spit out the mouthful of coffee she had just taken. American men were so... forward. Right this second, she would have done anything to be sitting opposite an uptight, emotionally stunted, overly polite British guy who wouldn't have dreamed of ever mentioning it again.

'You're clearly not going to start, so I will,' he said. 'I like you. You know this. I've loved every minute of getting to know you. Then every time I think we're heading somewhere you shut down and seem standoffish. I don't know if you've had bad stuff in your past or you're just not sure about me. Maybe you're worried because we work together. Right now, I'm getting a lot of mixed signals, but that kiss was pretty phenomenal and I don't think I was the only one into it. So, I'd just like to know what's going on here.'

Fucking hell, he was upfront.

And he was staring at her intently.

He wasn't going to let this go.

Time to put on the big girl pants. She took a deep breath.

She was saved momentarily by the waitress bringing their orders, and as Kyle started to make a dent in his plate, he motioned for her to talk.

'You're right, about everything.' She shrugged. That wasn't going to be enough, she could see. Her Britishness squirmed inside at being forced to talk about all of this.

'That doesn't answer any of my questions.' He raised his eyebrows and lifted his coffee cup to his lips.

'You're not wrong that there's something between us. I think you're brilliant. You've been amazing ever since I arrived, and I've loved all the time we've spent together. But yes, I'm nervous. It goes against everything I feel about you, having got to know you a bit, but I'll admit I've heard a few things that make me question if it would be a good idea. And because we work together, if it turns out things weren't a good idea, that makes it messy.'

She was wringing her napkin in her lap as she said this, hating the unpredictability of where this conversation would go now.

'And what exactly are the few things you've heard?' he asked, making air quotes to emphasis the few things.

She blew her cheeks out before starting again.

'I kind of heard that I wouldn't be the first girl you'd befriended at work, and also that you kind of liked the ladies and I maybe wouldn't be the only one if something happened, and even if something did happen it maybe wouldn't last because of all the others.' She knew she was babbling and mentally slapped herself to shut up. She felt sick as she said it. She didn't want to hurt him, but he had asked. She was surprised when he burst out laughing and had to hold his stomach.

'Kitty,' he stated through the laughter.

Abbie hesitantly nodded and waited for him to stop laughing. She had no idea what was going on.

'I'm sorry about her, Abbie. She's basically okay, but she sometimes gets a bit jealous where I'm concerned and it's crazy. You could maybe have called me a player in college, but who isn't? That isn't me now and I genuinely like you. I've never had any kind of hook-up or relationship with anyone at work ever before. I mean, for god's sake, the only women there for the past few years have been Kitty and Tina from the cafeteria.'

She was still confused.

'Why would Kitty be jealous? She always seems mad at you.'

He briefly closed his eyes and sighed. 'It's such an old story. We went to high school together and I took her to prom. I felt bad for her. She was one of those girls who was always lonely, and our parents were friends. I found out from my mom that no one had invited her, and I wasn't dating anyone so I asked her. I thought I was doing a nice thing but then she was really mad at me when I told her after that I didn't want a relationship with her. I guess it was the wrong thing to do.'

Abbie was surprised, but everything then fell into place. Kitty had been nothing but nice to her but always became prickly whenever Kyle's name came up.

'But this was over ten years ago now?' she asked.

'Sixteen years ago. And, apparently, she's still mad at me about it. I'm sure when she meets her Prince Charming it'll all be forgotten, but I'm sorry you got caught in the crossfire.'

Abbie hesitantly asked her next question. 'If she's still mad at you about it, surely if anything happens with us, she'll be angry at both of us? And that wouldn't be easy, with us all working together.' She looked down and noticed she had bunched up both of her hands into a ball.

Kyle sighed again. 'You know what? She's a grown-up and neither of us have done anything wrong or would be doing anything wrong if things develop. Which, I'm going to lay it on the line here, I hope they do.'

He gazed straight at her as he said this and she felt her last bit of resolve melt away. She wanted to explore this thing with him and she couldn't keep pushing her feelings away.

She slowly nodded at him and he shifted his chair so he was sitting right next to her. Her breath quickened as he cupped her face with his hand and brought his lips down to meet her own.

He tasted of coffee and she melted into the gentle kiss.

They were brought back to earth by the ping of his mobile phone and, remembering where they were, they separated and smiled at each other.

'My beauty is fixed. Let's go home?'

She nodded yes and they intertwined hands as they headed out.

CHAPTER 16

D URING THEIR LONG drive back to Salt Lake City, she
and Kyle chatted constantly. Any walls she still had
up to keep him out had been battered down that morning
at breakfast. He had been honest with her and everything
now made sense. With those last barriers coming down,
her feelings for him had flooded to the surface. She had
been trying to keep them at bay, but now she was a goner,
good and proper. Trying to play it cool wasn't going to be
easy, but he didn't seem to want that. He was as open as
ever and pulled her into him on the bench seat as they
drove home, his right arm draped around her shoulder,
only lifting when he needed to change gear.

When he dropped her home, they shared another kiss
but she didn't invite him in, feeling she should probably
put up some kind of pretence that they should 'date' a bit
before dragging him kicking and screaming to her
bedroom.

She managed to save the whole story to tell Rose the
next night, as they went to watch a big rock band from
Germany play at The Saltair. They were taking it in turns
to write up the reviews, or writing them together when
they had the time, and it still didn't feel like work. She
kept expecting to feel the dread of having to go to another

gig like she used to, but she enjoyed doing this with Rose. Because there wasn't much money involved, it was all purely for the love of the music and the writing and, more than anything, the brilliant friendship she and Rose were continuing to grow.

Sweaty and exhausted from dancing right in the middle of the crowds in the pits, they headed out to Abbie's car to drive back to Rose's place. They were both flooded with adrenaline from the gig and there was no way they could sleep anytime soon so they decided to write up their blog that night.

Rose had taken on the responsibility of updating their gig listings as she proclaimed she had more time during the day than Abbie, and it was better to use her time wisely or else she would just buy things she didn't need. She had managed to get even more venues to agree to a cut of the ticket if they were bought after linking from The Salt Scene, and they had already earned a few hundred dollars over the past month. It was pretty incredible for an idea that had been born without a strategy over quite a lot of the Malbec region's finest.

As they refined their blog post, giving a four-star review to the five-piece that shook the floor of The Saltair with their gritty anthems and vibrating bass, Abbie casually asked Rose if she might be able to ask the promoter of the gig they were attending the following night for an extra ticket. It was going to be at a smaller venue in the city that had a night on for up-and-coming local singers and bands, with a line-up of five acts.

'Yeah, I'm sure it'll be okay. That's one of the places that's been all over us as we've been sending clients their way. What's the name? I'll ask them to add it to the guest list.' Rose barely looked up as she replied while tapping away.

'Um, it's Kyle Miller,' she said, feeling her cheeks glow.

Rose's head sprang up and her fingers paused in mid-air.

She yelped with glee when Abbie filled her in on what had happened at the weekend, asking for more and more details of who said what and who gave what facial expression when, analysing every minute detail until Abbie didn't have any more to give.

Abbie was exhilarated. She didn't remember feeling this excited and having all these butterflies when she was with Josh. Thinking back, she was always trying to please him and feeling anxious if she felt like she wasn't, whereas, with Kyle, she felt that she could be completely herself. She was excited to bring together her two favourite people in Salt Lake City, and she only had to wait a day for it to happen.

THE FOLLOWING NIGHT couldn't have gone better. The three of them grabbed a small table in the centre of the room, still with a clear view of the small stage, but not so close that they couldn't have a conversation. It was as if

Rose and Kyle had known each other forever. They swapped stories about the city they had both lived in their whole lives, not believing they hadn't crossed each other's paths before as they talked about mutual places they had hung out and people they knew.

Abbie and Rose then told Kyle all about how The Salt Scene had come about that night in The Live Joint where they had celebrated the idea over tequila, and about some of the great bands they had seen over the past few months.

A young singer from the south of the state took to the stage with his guitar, and Abbie and Rose were entranced by his gravelly voice as he sang a cover of an Aretha Franklin song, followed by two of his own compositions. Rose scribbled some notes in her battered book as Abbie searched for him online to link to the piece they would later write. As she looked up, she saw Kyle watching her intently, his dark eyes making her stomach flip.

He leant over, whispering into her ear. 'It makes me so happy to see you so excited doing something just for the love of it. Reminds me of how it felt when I first kicked a ball around a field.'

His low voice sent vibrations through her as his lips brushed her ear. It was everything she could do not to jump him on the spot.

Rose proudly told him how local places were clamouring to partner with them and how she now had venues up in Park City asking her to add them to their listings. To Abbie's complete surprise, she revealed that the Sundance Film Festival had been in touch just a few hours before to invite them to their music programme for the following year. That would mark Abbie's anniversary of arriving in the city and the end of the time she'd committed to; she wondered if she'd still be there or not.

Sundance Film Festival. Lily would be so impressed.

Kyle went to buy celebratory drinks while Abbie and Rose squealed at the unlikeliness of the whole thing.

As soon as he was out of earshot, Rose spoke breathlessly. 'Oh my god he's gorgeous and amazing and how in the hell did you managed to restrain yourself from ripping off his clothes immediately when you laid eyes on him?'

'I'm not quite sure myself,' Abbie replied as they both collapsed into giggles.

They then had to pretend they were laughing at a meme on Rose's phone when Kyle arrived back at the table.

After dropping Rose home, Kyle drove Abbie to San Giovanni's, which she guessed was going to be their place. She'd already admitted she had no food in the house as she was too busy getting ready for the move and with work to bother cooking, so he said he wanted to make sure she had at least one good meal that week.

After an extravagant welcome from Rafaele, they settled down in the cosy corner the waiter had seated them in. Over steaming bowls of spicy tomato pasta, warm crusty bread and huge, juicy Nocellara olives, he looked at her thoughtfully.

'You know something, England. I'm proud of you. It can't have been easy for you to move so far from home, and you seem to be grabbing life with both hands. And, you were right, Rose is brilliant.'

She grinned. 'I told you! I can't imagine how anyone would think otherwise, but I'm thrilled that you got along.' If everything kept going in the right direction, Kyle and Rose might be seeing quite a bit of each other.

She filled him in on her conversation with her old boss, Dave Jones, and how she had proposed sending some of the Utah Saints youth team to England in the summer for a training camp. Dave had thought it was a brilliant idea and said they could run a week-long programme which would end up in a match versus the London Town FC youth squad. If they timed it right, they could do a return trip where the LTFC kids visited Utah. He said it would be a good chance for him to check she hadn't gone too American on him and that she was being looked after. Abbie secretly thought it probably had more to do with him getting away from Margaret Jones for a week, who was probably the only person on earth who could scare the living daylights out of her husband.

'This is absolutely amazing! In fact, I'm going to email Kitty right now and get her to book us an appointment with Hank so we can pitch him the idea. I'm sure he'll love it, and the kids would love it even more; you know already from them that the Premiership is where they look for their heroes and this would be an amazing possibility for them.'

They talked about what she missed most about England and she told Kyle that it was really only the people. If living in Salt Lake City had taught her anything, it was that it wasn't the place you were that made something home, it was the people you were with. She told him more about her parents and about Lily. And about Polly and how happy she was now, living with Damian the artist. She told him all about their old flat in Camden and what it was like living in London.

She couldn't imagine picking Kyle up and dropping him in her old neighbourhood – he was too outdoorsy. Her mind flashed back to him showing her how to snowboard and leading her expertly through a freaking desert. He would be too constrained in a city like London. And that pickup truck would never fit in the local supermarket car park.

Then, and she didn't know what made her do it, she told him about Violet. She told him about her best friend since university and how she suddenly seemed to be avoiding Abbie. How it was the only thing marring what was an amazing decision to come here to America and how it hit her at different points in the day and was making her feel anxious.

In his usual Kyle way, he seemed concerned but practical.

'Babe, send her an email. Just ask her what's going on. I'm sure it's nothing you've done, maybe she's missing you and finding it hard to keep up with the time difference.'

It was what Abbie had thought herself but it didn't take away from the fact she was missing her best friend like crazy. Especially at a time when she had some exciting news that the Violet of a few months ago would have been eager to hear.

Kyle continued trying to soothe her. 'I had a friend that did a similar thing a few years back. It turned out he was getting a divorce and needed some space to handle things.'

'I know you're right and there must be an explanation. It's just, if something is going on, I want to be there for her like she's always been for me,' she said. He reached across and squeezed her hand.

He drove her home after that and, feeling like they had got even closer as they opened up to each other more, Abbie invited him in for a coffee.

As she stood at the kitchen counter spooning instant coffee into two mugs and waiting for the kettle to boil, she felt the warmth of his presence behind her. He reached around her, took the teaspoon out of her hand and placed it on the counter, then softly put his hands on either side of her waist and turned her round to face him.

Clasping her hands in his own he met her gaze, and her stomach fizzed as she lost herself in his dark eyes. He took a step forward, gently but firmly pinning her to the counter with the weight of him. Her body responded instantly to his touch, electricity flowing between them, and she arched her back to bring them even closer.

So slowly she thought she would explode, he lowered his head and grazed his lips along her own, then traced her jawline and collarbone with light kisses.

She reached up and twisted her fingers into his dark hair, and he wrapped one arm tightly around her back, his lips finding hers again.

As the kiss intensified, she didn't want to wait any longer, and she could feel he didn't either. She freed her hands, tugged off his t-shirt and let it drop to the ground.

'Shall we move this somewhere more comfortable?' he asked, barely taking his lips away from her.

She nodded, and he lifted her off the floor in one move and carried her along the hallway to the bedroom, Abbie murmuring directions as they went.

From high in the sky above the mountains, the moon shone through the open blinds and threw a glow on the otherwise dark room.

Kyle placed her on the bed, never once stopping the kiss, and trailed his hand along her body.

Pausing and propping himself up on his elbow, he looked at her intently. 'Are you okay? You're sure?'

'I can't remember ever being this okay,' she replied, pulled him back towards her.

Afterwards, he wrapped his arms around her as she nestled onto his chest, and they slept entwined until the sun peeked through the blinds and woke them.

He took his time with her again the following morning. It was the best alarm call either of them could have asked for.

'Good morning,' he murmured after they lay in satisfied silence for a while, the two of them facing each other as they snuggled under the covers.

'Is there something better to say than good morning? I'm not sure it does justice to how I'm feeling right now,' she replied as he leant down and pressed his lips to her forehead.

'A morning beyond compare?' he offered.

'Faultless,' she responded. 'I do have a question for you, though.'

'The answer is, "that thing I did is definitely legal."'

'You're an idiot,' she said laughingly. 'Although my question was – is there *anything* you're not phenomenal at?'

'Hmmm, the million-dollar question. We haven't found anything yet, although timekeeping might be on the list if we stay here much longer. We're going to be late.'

Grudgingly, they got up for work, and she groaned in mock protest all the way to the bathroom. As much as she wanted to forget the outside world existed and drink in Kyle for several days, real life was calling.

He brought her a cup of coffee after she got out of the shower, and they kissed like teenagers until they got in their separate cars to head off for the day.

She didn't care what the day had to throw at her. She was on top of the world.

CHAPTER 17

B EFORE SHE KNEW it, Wednesday had arrived or, as it was noted in her diary, moving day. As Kyle lifted the last of her suitcases with ease into the back of his pickup and clicked shut the tailgate, Abbie reached her arms up around his neck and kissed him. He snaked his arm around her waist and pulled her in tight.

Kissing her on the forehead, he looked her up and down. 'You even look cute in your decorating gear.'

'This isn't decorating gear.' She swatted his arm, pretending to be offended as she looked down at her soft, pale blue denim dungarees which she had teamed with a distressed Rolling Stones tee. 'These are my favourite dungarees, so you better get used to them.'

'Dungarees are for toddlers and farmers. And last time I checked, you weren't either of those.'

'You're still getting to know me. You don't know half of my skills yet. Maybe I throw the best tantrums you've ever seen. Maybe I'm a crack sheep herder or highly adept at delivering foals.'

'I think I can fairly confidently say that, although you're amazing and clever and creative and incredibly skilled at some things that I personally am benefitting from, sheep herding and delivering baby foals are not in your portfolio of talents. I still think you're hot, though. Even in dungarees.'

He kissed her again then got into his truck to drive over to the new house with her boxes and cases and wait for the furniture to start being delivered. She was staying for the final inspection with the estate agent, then she'd join him.

She had no clue how she would have done this move without him. It made her slightly nervous that they were doing things together that normally wouldn't happen this early in a relationship. They weren't even 'officially' dating, she guessed, but equally, it all felt so right and he seemed to be relishing the chance to help her. She guessed he secretly liked being a bit of a hero, and it made her laugh.

Alone in the apartment, she walked from room to room around the place that had been home for the past few months. Thinking back to how it felt packing this time compared to how it had been in London, she was pleasantly surprised how a few short months could change things so considerably.

Sorting her things in London had almost been a detox. She had thrown out the old and exorcised some of her demons, ditching the clothes that had been a mask to hide her away from the world and throwing out unhappy memories of Josh. She could never forget that scan of her lost baby. It would be imprinted on her mind forever, but the thoughts were becoming less frequent and less guilt-laced.

She pushed the thought away as she looked out of her bedroom window out to the Wasatch Mountains. This place had changed her and, for the first time in a long time, her future felt full of possibilities. She was happy.

She remembered the morning after she arrived, walking in to discover this ridiculous bedroom and throwing herself on the bed, squealing. And she remembered how she had finally christened it a few nights before with Kyle in the most spectacular of fashions. She'd definitely never forget this place. For old time's sake, she took a run and jump at the bed and threw herself on it.

If Kyle said she looked like a toddler in her dungarees, she might as well act the part.

The doorbell sounded, and she scrambled up to answer it. She was met by a tall, willowy blonde in a two-piece grey skirt suit, the type who looked like she got out of bed with her hair blow-dried to perfection and never got a broken nail. Abbie was immediately intimidated by this put-together woman, but felt more at ease when the estate agent gave a wide smile that reached all the way to her piercing blue eyes and introduced herself as Karen Warren.

After inviting her in, Abbie stood in the kitchen. 'I'm so sorry I can't make you a coffee. All my stuff is packed and gone already.'

'Don't worry,' Karen smiled. 'I've already had two espressos this morning. I can go thirty minutes without.'

Karen briskly walked around the apartment with her iPad, while Abbie sat feeling like a spare part in the kitchen. She texted Kyle as she was waiting:

If the furniture arrives before I get there please build the bed first x

Karen walked into the kitchen as Abbie was giggling at his reply. She put her phone on the counter.

'Abbie, the place is perfect. Thanks for making my job easy. It's such a shame you couldn't stay on longer. We love having tenants like you and now I have to try to find someone who'll appreciate it as much as you clearly have.'

Abbie frowned in confusion. 'I thought you already had someone moving in here next week.'

Karen sighed. 'Unfortunately not. The person who originally rented this place for you said right at the start that she was pretty sure you'd stay on longer, so we didn't market the place. Then we were informed a couple of weeks ago that you wouldn't extend. It's a great place, though, I'm sure it won't take us long. We have some viewings over the next few days.'

'I did want to stay. There must have been some mis-communication because we were told it was rented. I don't understand what happened.'

She looked back at her phone as a text pinged in, and then had no more time to think about whatever was going on with the apartment as it was Kyle telling her the furniture was arriving. She said her goodbyes to Karen, wishing her luck in finding someone quickly, then hopped in her car and drove over to her new house.

She would talk to Kitty at work and try to figure out

what had happened. But no matter where the confusion lay, she didn't care because needing to move had brought her closer to Kyle, and she had found her dream home.

'YOU THOUGHT YOU needed to save this damsel in distress, but you had no idea that she was, in fact, the Queen of Flatpack in disguise.' Abbie stood next to the bed brandishing a Phillips-head screwdriver after securing the final base slat. She had found a gorgeous Cotswold cream wooden bed frame with a high cushioned cream headboard at the warehouse that looked as perfect as she'd imagined it would in the turret room.

'Well, let's see if it's still in one piece when we've finished with it and then decide how good at building you are.' He winked at her as he started removing the plastic from her new memory foam mattress.

They lifted the mattress onto the base, then she shrieked as he grabbed her and threw her down on the bed.

'Stop! Stop!' She giggled through his kisses. 'As much as I could lie here all day, this place will never be liveable if we don't get a move on.'

'Spoilsport,' he teased as he jumped up and left the room.

As she put sheets, pillows and a duvet on the bed, she could hear Kyle downstairs moving her sofa into place. She had picked a soft dusty-grey corner couch and a whole lot of lighter grey cushions. It was one of those sofas that you melted into, and she couldn't wait to get the house in order so she could enjoy some serious Netflix time.

She emptied her suitcases of clothes onto the bed. She knew that would be a great incentive to get them sorted so she could get into her bed. Sure enough, she stepped up the pace and put everything away in the built-in closet and in the chest of drawers and beautiful dresser with huge mirror she had bought to match her Cotswold cream bed. Putting the throw cushions she had bought for the window seat in place, she looked around, proud of her work.

Then she joined Kyle downstairs. He had fixed her new TV to the wall and built her bookshelf. It was all coming together fast, and the furniture looked even better in the spaces than she'd imagined when they went shopping.

She had bought a table with four chairs for the open plan kitchen/diner in the same light cream as the kitchen cupboards and, as she pushed the chairs underneath, she sighed with happiness. It already felt like home.

Kyle brought the kitchen boxes in and together they unpacked them, putting everything away in cupboards and drawers until the job was complete.

'We make a great team, hey?' He pulled her toward him with the belt loop of her dungarees.

She smiled. 'Any two people who can be in a room together while doing flatpack and not have a massive argument are obviously meant to be together.' Jesus, what did she just say? What was it about him that made her lose any kind of filter? What idiot talks out loud about being meant to be together when they've been dating for all of three minutes?

He silenced her thoughts with a kiss and she felt relieved he hadn't yet gone running for the mountains.

By nine o'clock they had everything else unpacked and in cupboards and drawers, and were sitting at her kitchen table eating Chinese delivery food straight out of the boxes. Dirty food was just what the doctor ordered after smashing the move out of the ballpark. She was doing really well learning her American sport clichés, she mused, as she dug into beef and broccoli in oyster sauce.

They spent their second night together that evening and it was even better than the first. She woke up in the early hours to find his arms wrapped tight around her and his head nestled in the crook of her neck. She watched him sleep for a few minutes before falling back asleep in his arms, only to be woken the next morning by the sun shining in through her new bay window.

He wasn't next to her but she heard him clattering around downstairs. Pulling on a t-shirt, she went into the kitchen where he was frying bacon and a plate on the table was piled high with pancakes.

She could get used to this.

'Why don't I drive you into work, England?' he asked as he speared a fork into the bacon, transferring it onto a dish then setting it on the table next to the pancakes. 'We can get a coffee on the way, and then I'll drop you home tonight?'

'You're on,' Abbie said, as she hungrily loaded her plate. She wasn't sure she took a breath as she wolfed it down.

Wondering whether to go for seconds, she caught sight of the time and the decision was made for her. She raced upstairs to get dressed. If she was going to roll in with Kyle, it was probably better not to make it completely obvious by being late.

SITTING IN FRONT of Kitty, Abbie was practically bursting as she explained the plan with London Town Football Club and the youth team trip overseas, for the training camp and to play a match against her old team. She and Kyle had pitched it to Hank earlier that day and he'd practically leapt out of his chair in excitement. He told them to go full steam ahead on it, and to use Kitty to plan logistics and help out wherever needed.

Then he had asked Abbie to stay behind after and told her how happy he was with her work. 'You're making waves with the board,' he said. 'Everyone is impressed with the positive changes you've made in just a few short months, and the board feels their decision to bring you here from England, with your experience, is paying dividends. If you need anything, come directly to me.'

She was buzzing as she explained it all to Kitty, who

seemed very excited at the prospect of a trip to London to chaperone the boys.

After discussing the plan so far and what she needed Kitty's help with, she went to make a move back to her own office, but Kitty stopped her.

'I guess you must have moved by now? Did it all go okay? I'm sorry I couldn't help but I had some family commitments the last few days that clashed with your moving date.' She looked so apologetic, Abbie didn't have the heart to tell her that she would have paid her not to help so she didn't take away the opportunity for one-on-one time with Kyle.

'It all went fine, thanks. I found a nice place and I'm all moved in. No drama whatsoever. I couldn't have asked you to help after everything you've done for me.'

Then she remembered the strange conversation with the estate agent.

'There is one thing, though, Kitty.'

'Yes,' she said, smiling her wide toothy beam. 'How can I help?'

'I don't need anything. It was just a bit weird. When the estate agent came to do the final inspection yesterday, she said that they didn't have anyone moving in and she wished I could have stayed. I said there must have been some confusion or misunderstanding, as they told you they had tenants?'

Kitty looked frozen momentarily then put her hand to her chest, tears springing to her eyes. 'Abbie, I'm sorry, you have to forgive me. I've done something awful.'

Shocked, Abbie sat back down in the chair. 'What on earth is wrong?'

Kitty looked down at her hands, wringing them together on the desk. 'I lied to you. Or rather, I didn't tell you something. You see, they did have a new tenant but then that person pulled out. I knew by that time you had already found somewhere else so I didn't want to tell you and upset you. I know how much you loved the apartment. And now they've inconvenienced you by making you stay for the inspection when I told them to come to me. I'm so sorry, Abbie, this whole situation is far from how I wanted it to go down.'

Abbie breathed a sigh of relief. She'd had no idea what Kitty was about to confess to, but it wasn't all that bad, and she clearly felt guilty.

'Honestly, don't worry. It really isn't a big deal and it did me a favour. I thought I loved it but I love my new place even more. It's a beautiful house with views of the mountains, a bit closer to the city centre. I moved yesterday and I promise you I'm happier than ever. I only mentioned it as I was a bit confused.' She gave Kitty an encouraging look and saw the worry start to fall from her face.

'I really am sorry. I should have told you when I found out. Can you forgive me?'

Abbie laughed this time. 'Please don't worry, it's not a drama. You've been nothing but helpful since I started and you've sorted out so many things for me. You, of all people, I am grateful to. And I really do love my new place even more than the apartment. You'll have to come for dinner to see it sometime.' The words were out of her mouth before she was even sure she meant them.

Kitty clapped with excitement and then paused, a flash of hesitation crossing her face.

'I know you're getting yourself sorted now, but I did wonder if you needed any help with your car. It's on a lease so I can get the dealer to fix it quickly and provide you with a courtesy car while it's in the shop.'

'My car is fine,' Abbie said, confused.

'Oh. It's just I happened to be passing the window when you arrived this morning and I saw you get out of Kyle's truck. I know he helped you move so I figured maybe he picked you up if he knew you were having car trouble.'

Abbie felt a pang of anxiety, and she knew this wasn't the moment to tell Kitty about her and Kyle. It was too soon, and she still wasn't sure how she would take it, given what Kyle had told her.

'He's helping me pick up a piece of furniture after work later and he thought it would be easier if we just had one car, so he picked me up on the way to work this morning.' She scrambled for an explanation, hoping she sounded calm and collected as the lie fell out of her mouth.

'You've been spending a lot of time with him, haven't you?' Kitty looked nervous as she quietly asked the question and Abbie felt guilty. She didn't want to hurt someone who meant well, even if she was quite intense.

'A bit, but he's just been really helpful. He knew someone who helped me find the new house quickly, and he's been great with some of the heavy lifting. He's been a good friend about it all,' she said definitively, hoping the statement would stop this conversation becoming even more awkward than it already was.

Kitty rubbed her hand over her face, her usual unflappable manner gone as she looked visibly agitated. 'That's Kyle, alright. Mr Helpful. You remember what I told you, right? I'm just trying to look out for you.'

Abbie squirmed inside. The conversation was going in exactly the direction she didn't want it to.

'You don't have to worry, we're just friends. I don't know many people out here and you've both been so good to me. I'm a foreigner, thousands of miles from home, and meeting the two of you has really helped me settle in.' She went to stand, but Kitty held her hand up and told her to sit down.

'I wasn't going to tell you this because it's extremely personal. But I can't watch as he takes you for a ride.'

Abbie felt sick. This conversation was happening whether she liked it or not, and she knew she didn't want to hear whatever was about to come out of Kitty's mouth. She crossed her legs tightly and felt the muscles in her thighs and calves tighten as she waited.

'He was Mr Helpful at high school too. Our parents knew each other and I think our moms got talking and he found out, somehow, I didn't have a date to prom so he decided to invite me. We went to prom and it was the most amazing night. I had this baby blue dress that my grandmother had bought for me. He bought me a corsage and picked me up in his dad's car and we danced all night, and talked, and I got to know him more than I had in four whole years of high school.' Kitty looked straight at Abbie. 'I really liked him, and he said he wished he'd gotten to know me better earlier too.'

She clasped her hands together and her voice got harder.

'He was my first that night. He knew how important and special that was to me. And then he completely screwed me over.'

Abbie felt the blood drain from her body and a knife twist in her gut. He had lied to her.

She pulled herself together enough to get some words out.

'Kitty, I'm so sorry that something like that happened to you, it's awful. But you have nothing to worry about. I'm not interested in Kyle that way. Sorry to dash out but I must get back to my work, I've got a whole stack of things to do.'

Heading down the corridor, she swerved into the walk-in stationery cupboard and sat down heavily on a stool, tears pricking at her eyes.

She'd been a complete idiot, falling for the stereotypical charming, handsome guy who swept her off her feet. He must be laughing at how stupid she was. How had she not read the signs?

She furiously typed out a text.

Violet, I have no fucking clue what's going on with you but I've been sleeping with a complete prick over here and it's all gone tits up. I have so much to tell you. So many good things are happening here, but I also need my best friend right now. Please, please call me. A xxx

She pressed send then ordered an Uber. She'd work from home that afternoon as there was no way she was getting in a car with him.

After she'd gathered her things from her desk and waited for the taxi to arrive, she tapped out another text.

Michael, please can you get Violet to call me. I don't know what's going on but I've had nothing but one-word answers from her, if anything at all, for weeks now and I'm worried. If you can tell her I really need to talk to her I'd be really grateful.

Getting into the taxi as it pulled up, she roughly pulled on the seat belt and clenched her jaw as she thought about what to do next.

CHAPTER 18

PICKING UP THE remote control from beside her on the sofa, Abbie turned up the volume on the TV even more. She didn't even know what she was watching, she was just trying to drown out the noise of Kyle knocking on the door and calling her name.

She'd been flicking through channels for the past hour, not able to focus on anything as she tried to process her anger. This was a new feeling for her. With Josh, he made her feel so worthless and she was desperately sad for years after he left her.

With Kyle, she was angry as hell.

He had duped her, pulled the wool over her eyes, played her. However you wanted to say it, he purposefully didn't tell her the truth, despite having every opportunity. Now she couldn't believe she had trusted him, and she was embarrassed like crazy about being made a fool of.

It hurt because she had opened up for the first time since Josh and yet, here she was, back on a sofa, fighting back tears and alone again. Without even Violet to meet and get drunk with and verbally pull Kyle to pieces.

He'd been trying to call her for the past hour, she guessed ever since he went to meet her for lunch and she wasn't there. She refused to read the texts he was sending and had turned her phone to silent. Then, five minutes ago he turned up at the door, knocking and calling for her to open up. He knew she was there because the curtains were open, so he could see her through the window. She refused to turn around to look at him.

'Abbie, let me in. I'm really worried,' he called through the door. 'I don't understand what's going on, but if you're hurt or upset or something has happened to someone, let me help.'

She snorted.

Let him help? That's what got her into this situation in the first place. Letting him help her with her housing problem. Letting him help her get to know the area. Letting him help her get her heart broken all over again.

It fell silent and, a few moments later, she heard his pickup fire up. Her head whipped around to look out of the window, where she saw the rear of the truck pulling away at breakneck speed. She didn't think he would give up that easily. At least she could turn the TV down again, with the reality stars currently screaming at each other.

At times like this, when your best friend was apparently avoiding you, you couldn't bear to talk about the whole drama with anyone else and you had sacked off work for the afternoon, the only thing she could think to do was hunker down in the kitchen and boil the kettle for another cup of tea while she silently raged. She hoped she'd feel slightly less angry in the morning, as she couldn't avoid work simply because she was an idiot and Kyle was a wanker. She didn't think those were applicable circumstances on the sick leave guidelines.

Staring into space as she sipped at her tea, her eyes widened as she heard a key in the lock of the front door, followed by Kyle's voice calling her name. She could hear him go into the lounge and then, finding it empty, he barrelled into the kitchen. Beads of sweat were dripping from his face and he looked like he had seen a ghost.

He ran straight up to her, knelt down and put his arms around her. 'What's happened? Tell me. I'm worried.'

She stiffened under his touch and he loosened his hold and stood up, taking a step back with a frown as he studied her unsmiling face.

'She told me, Kyle. And don't I feel like the idiot.' When she finally spoke, her voice came out clear and firm.

'Who told you what?

'Kitty. She told me that you slept together. That you took her fucking virginity, for god's sake. When you told me that all you did was take her to prom to be a nice guy. And all the time it was a hell of a lot bigger a deal than that. How could you lie to me?'

As he closed his eyes and let his head fall back, his shoulders drooping, she knew Kitty had been telling the truth without him even having to admit it.

He took a deep breath through his nose, his chest expanding, and opened his eyes before he started speaking again. 'Abbie, we were eighteen. We were kids. It was a really long time ago. I didn't purposefully not tell you. It's just that it honestly isn't a big deal. It was a one-time thing that lasted all of about two minutes and that was the end of it.'

She looked at him.

'Are you sure it was like that for her? She pretty much told me you broke her heart. She warned me about you at the start but I completely ignored her, and now I find out you've been lying to me. What am I supposed to think?'

Pulling out a chair and sitting opposite her, he took her hands in his. She tried to shake him off but he held on.

'Abbie, I'm not going to let something I did sixteen years ago mess up this thing that we're just getting started with. I was eighteen years old. I was about to head off to college. After the prom she asked me if it meant we were boyfriend and girlfriend, and that was the last thing I wanted. I let her down as gently as I could and told her I couldn't be with anyone as I was moving out of state. I didn't have feelings for her then and I don't now. I can't believe she would actually tell you something that happened so long ago. We've all grown up now.'

She stayed silent. She didn't know what to believe. She knew there were two sides to every story and it sounded like Kitty had had a big crush on him and maybe he just didn't understand how heartbroken a teenage girl could get. But he'd still lied to her.

'Come on, Abbie.' He squeezed her hands in his. 'You can't tell me that you don't have a past. And we've only been dating five minutes. I wouldn't even have expected us to talk about anything like this yet.'

She felt sick to her stomach. Yes, she had a past. And he didn't know the half of it. And wouldn't know.

But then she felt stupid. She hadn't even told him about Josh. And surely a hidden ex-husband was quite the secret?

'Oh god, you're right. Don't get me wrong. You still should have told me. I felt so fucking stupid sitting there stressing to her that we were just friends so she didn't need to worry about my wellbeing, and then she came out with that. I had to hide every emotion I was feeling and get the hell out of there. But, of course, I have a past.' She paused, drew a breath and then continued hesitantly. 'If it's not going to make you run a million miles, I was married once.'

She kept her head low but looked up out of the corner of her eye to see his reaction.

He looked surprised but not particularly bothered.

She lifted her head a bit higher.

'See? You just dropped on me you're a divorcee and I'm cool as a cucumber. Everyone has a bit of baggage, but what do we do? Let it control us and live in the past, or get on with life? It's there to be lived.'

'Agreed. Although I would just like to say that in the life we are living, you don't have to work directly with the person whose heart your boyfriend smashed to smithereens as a teenager. That would be me who's living that reality.'

'Oh, we're next level. Did you just call me your boyfriend?' He put his finger under her chin and lifted it until she was looking at him, then wiggled his eyebrows at her.

She felt her mouth twitching. 'Did we have our first fight?'

'I think we did, England. Did we survive it?'

'TBC.'

He looked at her, not taking his hand from her chin. 'No more secrets, hey?'

Her stomach lurched and she averted her gaze. 'I think you owe me a lot of pancakes and bacon for what you put me through today.'

'I'll make you some later. For now, get your ass upstairs.'

STILL WRAPPED UP in her duvet a few hours later, Abbie contentedly sank further into the pillow. Kyle had gone back to work and she was going to make up for her lost working time that week later, but she allowed herself some extra time to relax after the tension of what had happened.

She opened her eyes when she heard her phone ringing and grabbed it from the bedside table. She scurried to answer it when she saw it was Violet.

'Oh my god, she's alive,' Abbie squealed down the phone. She was feeling pretty euphoric after making up in the best way with Kyle, and she almost forgot that she'd been annoyed at Violet for doing a disappearing act.

The familiar Irish lilt came clear across the line, as if she was in the next room and not thousands of miles away.

'Babe, I'm sorry I haven't caught up with you. Things have been a bit mad at home. But I saw your text and wanted to check what the hell was going on.'

Delighted that she could finally fill her best friend in on what had been happening the past few weeks, she began to regale Violet with her story. From snowboarding in Park City, to finding dinosaur prints in Moab. And from the first kiss to the most recent and everything in between.

Violet was making the right noises but wasn't asking questions, allowing Abbie to tell the story with minimal interruption. 'But didn't you message me saying you needed me because he was being a prick?' As usual, Violet didn't mince her words.

Abbie hesitantly told her the story about Kitty, but how they had made up and got over it just that afternoon.

Violet made encouraging noises and said she was glad it was all sorted out.

Abbie frowned. This wasn't Violet. She would have asked for every minute detail, interrupting Abbie's flow at least once every thirty seconds, and she would have been absolutely livid at Kyle's lie.

'Can you please tell me what's going on, Violet? I don't know if I've upset you or it's something else, but you're not being yourself and it's scaring me.' She said it quietly. It felt like she didn't know the person she was talking to, so it needed careful handling. She had no intention of falling out with her best friend.

Suddenly, the silence on the end of the line was filled with quiet sobs.

'Oh my god, what's happened? Are you ill?' she pleaded, feeling sick to her stomach.

'No, no, I'm not, nothing like that. I've just been putting off telling you something because I know it's going to upset you.' Violet got the words out through her tears.

Abbie continued with the calmest voice she could, even though she was panicking like crazy. 'You can tell me anything, Vi. You're my best friend. Always have been, always will be. And, Jesus Christ, you know all my shit. There's nothing you can say that's going to upset me.'

She heard Violet take a deep breath.

'Michael and I. We're… we're having a baby, Abbie.'

Abbie felt her heart leap, and she screamed. 'Vi, this is absolutely the best news I think I've heard in years. Why the hell would you think that would upset me? I'm basically going to be an auntie.'

'Are you really not upset?' she asked, the tears still audible in her voice.

'No, of course not, you idiot. Why would I be upset? You guys are going to be the best parents ever.'

'I thought, with what happened to you with the pregnancy and how you've felt since, that it was insensitive of me to tell you about the baby. It wasn't planned, but then when it happened, we realised we were happy about it.'

Abbie shook her head. 'You total idiot. The two are not the same thing.'

'But when you found out Josh was having a baby with his new wife you ran to the other side of the world. I was so scared you would run away from me when you knew I was pregnant. Michael was so mad at me when he found out I've been avoiding telling you. He figured it out when you texted him, and he told me if I didn't call you, he would cut off my pickled egg supply. And I can tell you, I will murder someone without those pickled eggs.'

Abbie spoke through her laughter. 'Josh is a separate deal altogether. That news was just the final push I needed to get my arse in gear. But moving here wasn't really because of that, not in the end. And Vi, I've been feeling less guilty about it all since I've been here. It's hard to explain but I feel almost liberated from that period of my life. I have these moments every now and then but most of the time, it's better.'

'Oh, Abbie,' Violet sighed. 'When are you going to believe me that you shouldn't feel guilty at all?'

'I'm not sure if that's ever going to happen. But anyway, this isn't about me. I want a blow-by-blow of how you found out, how you told Michael, how he reacted, how your mother reacted. Tell me everything!'

Two hours later, Kyle walked in to find Abbie and Violet still on the phone having their very overdue catch-up.

She shooed him out of her room.

'Be gone to the kitchen, please. Violet and I are talking the finer details about you and I don't need you in earshot.'

He grabbed a pillow and swatted her with it before heading out of the room to let the two friends continue to forensically analyse his ass.

THE FOLLOWING MORNING Abbie got up early. She had to do some catching up after her lost midweek day.

First though, she clicked onto the blog. Rose had been to a big gig two nights ago and posted another review and Abbie wanted to take a look through the comments. She rubbed her eyes to make sure she wasn't seeing things. Over two hundred comments joining in on the chat about Kings of Leon coming to town. Some people had gone to the same gig and wanted to join in with their own mini review, and some just wanted to get in on the discussion about a band they loved. And it was wholly positive. This thing was really getting some traction.

As she clicked off the internet, her thoughts turned to the thing she had been trying to ignore since she made up with Kyle, but knew she couldn't much longer.

Kitty.

She knew what it was like to be young and have a crazy crush on a guy. What girl didn't? But it seemed that whereas most girls laughed off their teenage crushes a few years later when they realised the school heartthrob wasn't all that, Kitty's teenage crush, and the rejection that came with it, had hit her hard and she hadn't got over the upset it caused her.

Abbie didn't blame her, but it did make things difficult where Kyle was concerned. It was still early days for them and, as much as she didn't want to lie to Kitty, it didn't feel right to tell her they had started dating.

Abbie knew she was being a bit selfish in deciding that to avoid a potential scene. But equally, Kitty still seemed so angry at what had happened all these years later, and she didn't want to be the one to upset her.

For now, she felt the best course of action was discretion. No more cosy journeys to and from work together. They needed to keep their relationship between themselves until they figured out if things were for the long run. And if they were? Then they'd figure out how to break it to Kitty without breaking the poor girl. She'd told Kyle her thoughts and, for now, he said he understood.

One way of taking Kitty's mind off of speculating, which she had clearly been doing, would be to make sure she was really involved and invested in the work they were doing together. She'd been so excited about the trip to London with the youth team. Abbie was sure Kitty could do a great job of planning that. After all, she was queen of the social committee and loved nothing more than organising the staff away days.

She opened up her laptop again and tapped out an email to Kitty, apologising for going home early yesterday and explaining that she had felt unwell but would be back that morning. And that the first item on the agenda was to take Kitty to a nice lunch so they could go over the trip planning and Abbie could thank her for all the help she had given her since she arrived. She added that she was so excited they were working together and she couldn't wait to show her around London.

She couldn't help but feel that she needed to silently apologise for what Kyle did to her sixteen years ago. And the fact she was hiding their relationship from her.

A nice lunch and a trip to London would surely go some way towards easing the guilt?

CHAPTER 19

PARKED UP IN the middle of Arches National Park on a Saturday lunchtime, Abbie stretched her arms out, smiling. After another Friday night game, she and Kyle had set off for a weekend out of the city. She was giddy to be back in this magical place again, and this time they were organised. They had overnight bags and had driven down in Kyle's pickup. The truck was only two years old, and she was hoping this meant they wouldn't get stranded again. As much as she loved his classic Chevy, she thought maybe he should treat it with more reverence and not take it on four or five hour drives in oppressive heat in the middle of a desert. The poor thing had been overworked.

Although she knew they were heading back to Moab, Kyle hadn't told her where they were staying, only that it was a surprise he was sure she'd love.

Before that, they were going to explore the park more. Kyle pulled a bag out of the back seat of the truck and passed her a blanket to lay on the ground. It was really hot again so she picked a spot that was shaded by one of the impressive arches and surrounding rocks, and Kyle joined her with the food they had bought on the way.

After a lunch of cold meats, cheese, crunchy bread, potato salad, olives and fruit, they started out on another hike. They were exploring a different part of the park today, with more of the same arches and desert she had seen before, but it was still jaw-dropping and it didn't feel any less surreal and awe-inspiring than the first time. He took them walking much further this time and it was a full five hours before they returned to the car, Abbie, hot and bothered from the heat and feeling every muscle in her legs and Kyle, as usual, looking like he hadn't broken a sweat.

Then he drove them to another spot in the park to watch the sun set before heading to their digs for the night. They sat down on the soft dusky blue blanket, a red rock arch between them and the horizon, and he put his arm around her waist and drew her closer. She snuggled in, the warmth from his body welcome as the evening air started to cool. She was feeling tired after their day of activity. Although it made her very aware of how she hadn't worked out all that often in the UK, she always felt healthy when they were doing something active. Discovering Kyle's Utah was good for her.

Wordlessly, they watched as the sun started to dip towards the horizon. A fierce, burning orange, it threw an unbelievable light onto the desert that glinted off the rocks. She hadn't taken any pictures when they watched the sun rise the first time they visited, as everything had been such a surprise, but this time she reached for her phone and snapped a few photos of the special landscape. She didn't want to forget it, and she also wanted to send them to Violet. She knew she hadn't been able to do this place justice when she described it during their phone call, but maybe Violet would understand if she could capture even a fragment of its magic with a camera.

She could feel Kyle looking down at her as she took the final photo, and turned her gaze to him. Her stomach flipped as their eyes met. She had fallen for him hard.

'Abbie?' he said, sounding like he wanted her permission to continue.

'Yes?'

'This trip. It's an apology of sorts for the mistake I made not telling you the truth about Kitty.'

'You don't need to apologise,' she said, swatting at his hand. 'We talked about this.'

'I know. But I need you to know that I'm not playing around with your feelings and I'll prove it. I'm serious about where this is going.'

She was done for. She leant over, pressing her lips to his before settling back into his arms to continue watching this magical sunset.

As the last of the sun disappeared over the horizon, he ushered her back to the truck. He'd said their lodgings were around a twenty-minute drive, so it would already be dark when they got there.

Happily, she climbed up into the passenger seat and, after he started the engine, she scanned through radio stations. She loved doing that, and since she moved there, she'd discovered new songs and artists she liked this way. She was pretty sure it annoyed Kyle that she skipped past his favourite station, but they were still early enough on that he didn't say. And until that time came, she planned to take full advantage of the musical freedom.

'Did you enjoy today?' he asked after they'd been driving a while, the crunching sound of the tyres on the gravelly desert floor beneath them.

'Hated it,' she replied, deadpan, before breaking into a grin. 'Wasn't it obvious?' she enthused. 'I loved it. Again. This place is phenomenal.'

'I was hoping you'd say something like that. It makes it easier to tell you we're not leaving yet.'

She smiled, raising one eyebrow. 'Kidnapping me and keeping me hostage in a cave?' she asked. 'I could be down with that.'

'Nearly. I was planning to keep you there.'

Her eyes followed where he was pointing to and she gasped.

Up ahead was a transparent dome-shaped tent lit up by a firepit near the entrance. As the truck crunched along and they got closer, she could see a full double bed set up inside the tent and strings of fairy lights running from the top of the dome downwards.

'What do you think?' he asked as he applied the handbrake and switched off the ignition. The thrum of the powerful engine gave way to absolute silence.

'I don't even know what to say. This is unbelievable. How did you do this?'

'Ah, you know me. I know a guy who knows a guy. Shall we go in?'

Her surprise gave way to excitement and she threw

open the car door and scrambled down, skipping towards the tent. She paused at the entrance and waited for Kyle to join her. Taking his hand, she shook her head in disbelief.

'I can't believe you've done all this. It's insane. Did you know I've never been camping before?'

'Honestly, England, that's shocked me more than the fact you're a divorcee. How the hell have you never been camping?' He looked at her like she had just announced she was marrying her dog and moving to Jupiter.

'We just never did it when I was a kid. Then, when I was a bit older and my friends were going to festivals, I couldn't imagine anything worse than sleeping on the hard ground in the cold with kids throwing up right outside the tent. And then I got married when I was twenty-three, and I had to be an adult and live in a posh flat in the part of London where all the banker wankers live. So, it just sort of never happened.' She shrugged her shoulders.

'Thank god I came into your life to show you what you've been missing. Although, just to get things straightened out, this is absolutely not camping.'

She looked at him quizzically.

'You have a double bed. And a heater for when it gets cold. And a generator for electricity. And around the corner of that rock there's a small unit with a toilet and a shower with hot water. This, England, is the ultimate in upmarket glamping.'

She walked into the dome and looked around. There

was the double bed right in the centre, and a huge rug. There was an empty wooden trunk for them to put their things in, and behind the bed was a small fridge and a wicker hamper.

Kyle pulled a bottle of champagne out of the fridge and carried it to the bed with two flutes, then beckoned for Abbie to sit with him.

'You really are making the apology of a lifetime,' she said as she sat down on the soft cream duvet. The turquoise, burgundy and dark grey pattern showed Native American symbols including feathers, arrows, headdresses, tepees and eagles.

'This is all so beautiful, Kyle,' she sighed as he handed her the glasses. She laughed as he made a lunge for the flutes in her hands when the bottle threatened to overflow, bubbles peeping above the neck.

Filling the glasses to the brim, he put the bottle on the floor and then raised his glass towards her. Abbie clinked her glass with his as he made a toast.

'To the best girl I know. Gorgeous, intelligent, and incredibly forgiving.'

She laughed and shook her head at him. 'Flattery will get you everywhere.'

'That's exactly what I was aiming for.' Their eyes met as they took a sip of the champagne.

She looked around again and admired the woven rug on the floor. It was bright blue with a pattern of the outline of yellow four-pointed stars.

'That star is a Native American symbol, too, like the

bedspread,' Kyle said. 'It originally described a huge meteor shower in the US back in 1833 that they called The Night the Stars Fell.'

She looked at him.

'Who even are you, Kyle Miller? You are this cliché of a perfect man, bringing me to the most perfect places and knowing all this perfect stuff.'

'I could say the same about you. In case you hadn't noticed, I'm pretty crazy about you. I've been bringing out the big guns with my pride and joy Chevy and showing you all the best places I know to try to impress this intelligent, beautiful Brit who came literally crashing into my life. Also, don't think I haven't noticed how you're overcompensating for me with Kitty by being incredibly nice to her. You're kind as well. Where did *you* even come from?'

'Liverpool, by way of London,' she quipped, and they drained their champagne.

'Okay, England, lie down.'

'Already? You haven't even fed me yet. If you want to treat me like a wanton sex slave, you need to feed me to keep my energy up.'

'Don't worry, I'm feeding you. And I'm not stripping you just yet. Just lie down and look up.'

She did as she was told while he got off the bed and clicked a switch which killed the fairy lights, plunging the tent into complete darkness.

As her eyes adjusted, he lay down next to her, taking her hand and sending his gaze upwards.

'Wow.' It was all she could say.

Above and all around the dome were thousands upon thousands of bright white stars filling the clear black sky. With no artificial light from the desert, the stars could put on their best show. It was absolutely breathtaking.

Now the transparent tent made sense.

Although, she mused, she wasn't quite sure how she felt about the coyotes and deer looking in on what they would be getting up to later.

As Kyle sizzled bacon in a pan over the firepit the next morning and Abbie sat on the ground with a mug of coffee, he looked at her, clearly deciding whether to speak or not, and eventually decided on the former.

'I'm intrigued, England.'

'About what?'

'How the hell a guy could let you go. I don't understand.'

She took her time before answering, considering what she was going to say.

'If we're being honest, it upset me for a long time. A good couple of years. I can say now that it feels like that period was a lifetime ago, and I wouldn't change what happened because I would never have come here if we'd stayed together. We were really young when we got married – I was only twenty-three. I never got a straight answer out of him but he just upped and left one day.

Told me he couldn't do it anymore. So, I don't really know, but probably we got married too young and he outgrew me before I had the chance to realise that I probably would have outgrown him too.'

'What an idiot,' Kyle huffed. 'Although, selfishly, I'm glad you're here.'

She smiled. 'We were extremely different people. Josh worked in finance and wore swanky suits every day and had a lot of obnoxious friends that I didn't like. He equally didn't like my friends. The girls drank too much and swore too much and were far too normal for his liking. I also think he always had a weird thing about me and my family being from the north of England. I always thought his parents kind of looked down on me. We just weren't meant to be, long-term. I know that now.'

'I nearly proposed once.'

She rubbed her hands together with glee. 'I love this. Now I'm not the only one having to tell uncomfortable and embarrassing stories about my past. Spill.'

'Are you kidding?' He waved the spatula at her. 'You literally know I took a girl's virginity.'

'Yeah but, like you said, you were kids. It was a long time ago. I want to know about more recent humiliation.'

'Jesus, England, you're brutal.'

'Spill,' she shouted.

'I was even younger than you were. My girlfriend would have practically been a child bride.'

She looked at him, frowning.

'Coming from an area like this, it's a small place. You

get used to people going to college, meeting someone, getting a job, getting married to whoever they met at sixteen or eighteen or twenty and doing the whole normal life thing. So, when I was in Indiana, I had a girlfriend who was a freshman like me. She was called Kim, she was from Florida and was studying political science. We met in the student bar. We dated for quite a while and I was all set to propose because I thought that was what we had to do next. Some other couples had already gotten engaged while we were at college.'

'Childhood sweethearts. This is such a cute story. What happened?' Abbie had her elbows rested on her knees and her chin in her hands, all ears for what he had to say next.

'Sophomore year, we left school for spring break and she went to Mexico with her friends from Florida. Next thing, she had hooked up with a local waiter, dropped out of college and moved to Cancun. I never knew what happened to her next, although I did hear a rumour she was a tequila girl in a local bar.'

Abbie burst out laughing. 'No fucking way. That isn't true.'

'I swear on my Chevy's life it is,' he laughed, handing her a plate of bacon and sausage.

'Oh my god, were you heartbroken?' She didn't like the thought of someone hurting him.

'Nope. I realised I didn't really care all that much and decided to make the most of my remaining years in education to have some fun before I had to become a grown-up. What I had saved up to buy the ring, I used to buy the Chevy.'

'That is a ridiculous story.'

'That's college life, baby. Two of my buddies here from Utah did meet their wives at college, though. They're each two kids and a dog deep in life already.'

'It's so nice you have lifelong friends close by. Says a lot about you that you guys have been friends pretty much your whole lives. I'm looking forward to meeting them.'

'Are you missing your friends from home?' He moved away from the fire to sit opposite her, eating from his own plate of breakfast.

'Yeah, I am. The time difference makes it more difficult. We're trying, and we're emailing and texting, but obviously, it's not the same as seeing them. But don't get me wrong, I'm loving it here and you and Rose have made all the difference. I could have been anywhere in the world, but it's the people you meet who make places special. It could have been really lonely.'

'Tell me about them. Obviously, I know a bit about Violet already.'

'Violet will always be my best friend. We met at university, and she's brilliant and fierce and is going to be a bloody brilliant mum. Then there's Polly. I met her when we moved in together after I separated from Josh, and she's hilarious. She's a musician, she frequently changes her hair colour and she was one of the only people in London who managed to meet guys in actual real life on a regular basis and get dates. That was until she met this artist called Damian, fell madly in love, and now they're happily living in our old place together. It's funny, Rose kind of reminds me of a mix of them both. Maybe that's why I was so drawn to her.'

'You look so happy talking about them. You're beaming.'

'I am. When you live far away from your parents, like I did when I was in London and they were in Liverpool, your friends become your family and they're both the best girls. I lost touch with the people I worked with in the music industry as when I was with Josh, we didn't really do anything unless it was with his friends. Then, when we split up, I kind of hibernated. But those two have been the best.'

'Well, I can't wait to meet them. They clearly have great taste in friends.'

Abbie suddenly had an idea. 'I'll show you what they look like.'

She grabbed her phone from inside the tent and clicked onto Facebook. She showed Kyle pictures of Violet and her from university days, right through to her leaving party in London. She showed him photos of Michael and explained how the job at the Utah Saints was all down to him. And she found a variety of snaps of Polly showing her with red hair, blue hair, black hair and green, so Kyle could see the whole spectrum of colour. Then she showed him her mum and dad, and Lily, and her heart felt full as she shared the people she cared about most in the world with the man she was falling in love with.

She couldn't believe how lucky she was.

CHAPTER 20

CLUTCHING HER NOTEBOOK, Abbie walked into Hank's office. Six months had flown by and now she was having her formal review.

Even though she knew she'd been doing a good job, and Hank had regularly praised her, she couldn't help but be nervous. Being in Salt Lake City had changed her life for the better more than she could have dared to imagine, and she didn't want to lose it.

'Sit, sit, sit, Abbie. Do you need a coffee? I'll get Kitty to grab you one.'

'I'm okay thanks, I'm good with this water.' She shook her water bottle at him and sat down.

The last thing she wanted nowadays was to have Kitty do anything that could be seen as waiting on her, or imply that she was less senior. She certainly didn't want him to ask Kitty to fetch her a coffee.

She focused fully as he started to speak.

'This is really just a formality, Abbie. We've been so impressed with you. We know that you were thrown in at the deep end, living in a foreign country and working in something brand new, but you've attacked this challenge full force and we're already seeing results. Your team love working with you, and since you launched The Half-

Time Show, our ticket sales are up an average of seventeen per cent per game. That's no coincidence. Our numbers were at a plateau the last three seasons until this initiative launched.'

Abbie didn't know what to say. She had taken a massive risk and it was paying off.

'I'm so happy it's working, Hank, and I'm loving working here. I'm looking forward to going big for the final game. And then the trip with the youth team to London should be really helpful and rewarding for them. Basically, if you'll have me, I'd love to stay.'

'It's a deal.' He reached over the table, grinning, and shook her hand so hard it nearly took her arm off. 'Is there anything you need from us? Anything else we can do to support you?'

'I don't think so. Everyone has been great, thanks. I do have an idea for next season, to create a fan club to get the local community engaged with the club from an early age so they grow up supporting the Utah Saints. That way, if you're always encouraging the kids as well, they'll go through their lives as an engaged supporter and get their friends involved. Once I've fleshed it out a bit more, I'd love your feedback on that.'

'It sounds awesome. What would we do without you around here now? You're just a ball of energy, aren't you?'

It was funny hearing someone describe her that way. He wouldn't have recognised her a year ago. He definitely wouldn't have called her energetic.

'If we're all set here, I'll get your paperwork drawn up

to say you've passed your probation with flying colours.'

'I think we're set,' she replied, then picked up her things and practically skipped out of the office.

She walked straight into Kitty, who asked her how it went.

'Really well. I've passed my probation and he wants me to stay. I'm so thrilled,' she said, hugging Kitty in a moment of uninhibited happiness.

Kitty seemed surprised but hugged her back, then beckoned her into her office to carry on talking.

'I'm super stoked for you,' she said as they sat down. 'It's been amazing having you here. And I'd never be planning a trip to London if it wasn't for you.'

'We're going to have a lot of fun. Before then, though, it's the final game of the season in exactly two months, on the fifteenth of October, and I'm about to sign the contract with the band this afternoon.' She wiggled her eyebrows at Kitty, the hint of a smile on her face.

'Who? Someone I've heard of?' she asked, leaning forward on her chair.

'I think you will have. Memphis Black?' Abbie waited for a reaction.

Kitty's eyes opened wide. 'Oh my god, are you kidding? I love them. I downloaded their new album just last week. How did you get them?'

'I hope everyone's reaction is the same as yours. I met them just before they blew up, so they've done a good deal for us. They're super excited at playing in a sports arena actually, and Kevin, the drummer, loves football so he's buzzing. They've not done that before. I'm dealing with their agent now, they're so big time.'

'Fame has gone to their heads already?' Kitty asked, leaning forward even further.

Abbie laughed. 'No, not at all. They're just on tour and busy, and they'll be doing the game during a few days off, so it's easier if I talk to their agent while they're on the road. They're really nice people. You'll meet them when they're here. In fact, you can take care of them for me on the day if you want?'

She really shouldn't keep trying to people-please with Kitty. But it was like she couldn't stop – words just came spilling out of her mouth.

'I'd love that! We're going to have the best time over the next few months. I'm really happy you came here, you know, Abbie. It's so nice to have a proper friend at work, and I'm enjoying the projects we're doing together so much.'

'Me too,' she said, throwing Kitty a genuinely grateful smile. 'I couldn't have done it without you.'

Kitty clapped her hands together. 'We have to celebrate. You're over here all alone and you just got some great news from your boss and I want to make sure we mark the occasion. No excuses, tonight, we're going out. I'll plan something and send you an email later with the details. Okay?'

What could she say? She couldn't tell Kitty about the person she most wanted to celebrate with, so she found herself nodding along in agreement.

A COUPLE OF hours later she watched with her arms folded as Kyle practically bent double laughing across the table from her in San Giovanni's. He had said there was no other place to celebrate than their favourite Italian restaurant. They had escaped for lunch together so she could tell him properly about the meeting with Hank, and he was now in hysterics as she relayed how she'd been roped into celebrating with Kitty that evening.

'Let me get this straight,' he started, before collapsing back into laughter.

She felt her mouth twitching but fought to stay straight-faced.

'You're celebrating passing your probation by letting Kitty take you to a jewellery-making class?' He was in fits of laughter again before he could let her answer.

She swatted his hand and fought her own laughter. 'Stop it. She put loads of thought into it. She said she thought it would be nice if I could make myself a piece of jewellery to always remember the day by. She means well. It's a really nice gesture.' She felt awful that Kyle was teasing Kitty.

'She's uptight and overzealous. But she seems to have taken a liking to you, so if you want to mark this occasion by making a friendship bracelet, go for it.'

'I don't want to, idiot. But I could hardly say no, and

she thinks I don't have anyone else here to celebrate with. She was being sweet.'

Kyle sighed. 'Look, Abbie.'

It was never a good sign when he called her by her proper name. She braced herself. She knew what was coming. This would be the third time he brought it up.

'I know you're trying to protect her feelings, or whatever it is you're doing, but she's going to find out about us sooner or later and she'll be more pissed if she thinks her new BFF has been keeping stuff from her. It's like a Band-Aid – the quicker you rip it off, the less it hurts. You're going to drive yourself crazy keeping this a secret much longer. Every time that door opens your head flies around so fast you almost give yourself whiplash.'

'I know,' she nodded.

'And also, I slept with her once, sixteen years ago. When we were teenagers. I think you're making this into a much bigger deal than it actually is.'

Abbie ran her fingers through her hair. 'I'll do it. I promise. I'll find a time.'

He raised his glass of orange juice. 'Okay, enough lecturing for now. I want to raise a toast to my beautiful, brilliant England, who I knew didn't have anything to worry about today, but she's British and modest and doesn't know how great she is, so she worried anyway. Here's to the future.'

Happy tears pricked her eyes. This was definitely a day to remember.

Kyle clinked his glass to hers and said, 'We'll celebrate

properly later in the week. And there will not be a bead or an earring in sight.'

AFTER THE JEWELLERY class, Abbie managed to persuade Kitty that they really should go for some drinks, and Kitty had excitedly said she knew the perfect place where she'd been going for years. It wasn't the kind of bar Abbie would normally go to but they served alcohol so, at that moment, there was nowhere better.

While Kitty was in the bathroom, Abbie looked around. The bar was completely devoid of personality. It was a long, thin room and everything was white. A bench ran the length of the back of the room with small, low tables and cushioned cubes forming the table areas. On the opposite side was the bar, the bright lights on its frosted plastic front illuminating the rest of the room. The barman, wearing a Hawaiian style shirt somewhat unironically, looked about fourteen and the wire-bound, laminated cocktail menu had photos of the wide variety of multicoloured concoctions that they specialised in.

He was making piña coladas for them. Kitty had insisted Abbie have one, as it was her favourite drink. Abbie could see the cocktail umbrellas and neon straws at the ready to add the final flourish. Had David Attenborough really not got the plastic straw message this far? This kid was wholly responsible for killing some turtles tonight.

The saving grace was that she had organised for Rose to meet them later. She was on an early shift at work and would join them when she finished.

As Kitty retook her seat on one of the white cubes, Tom Cruise's lovechild put the cocktails on the table in front of them. Kitty held her glass up.

'I want to propose a toast. Congratulations on your permanent role!'

Abbie felt like a bitch as she brought her glass up to meet Kitty's. She had sat judging this place for the past five minutes when Kitty had made this effort to make her feel at home and like she had a friend.

She ran her fingers across the beads of the bracelet around her wrist. They had indeed made friendship bracelets at the class, and Kitty had looked like she was having the time of her life.

Yes, they were different, and she wasn't Violet or Polly or Rose, but Abbie really should value her the same as her other friends. She went to speak but Kitty spoke at the same time and Abbie told her to carry on.

'Now you're here for the long-term, we really need to get you on the dating scene, right?' she asked, although Abbie felt it was more of a rhetorical question. She was proved right when Kitty carried on talking without giving her a chance to respond. 'I have this friend from my church group who says she knows this guy around our age who said he loved the British accent the other day. So, we thought we could set you up!' She clapped her hands excitedly and Abbie's stomach sank. She knew she had to say something. And, as Kyle said, she needed to rip off the plaster.

'Actually, I have some more good news to share with you!' Abbie delivered it in the most upbeat voice she could muster, hoping that she could project onto Kitty that this was a good thing.

'You met someone!' Again, it was more of a statement than a question. 'Tell me all about it. Where did you meet him? When? Is he American?'

Abbie smiled her widest grin, a smile that she knew didn't quite reach her eyes, and took a long drink of her cocktail. In fact, when she put the glass on the table, it was half empty already. Dutch courage was a real thing.

'Yes, he's American. It's such a funny story and couldn't be more unexpected.'

What was this weird giggle coming out of her mouth? She sounded like an animal being strangled.

Kitty looked at her strangely. 'You seem nervous, Abbie. Is everything okay?'

'Totally fine, completely okay. Oh, god. Okay, I'm going to tell you. I've been worried about this because the last thing I want to do is upset you or cause any weirdness because you're a friend.'

Kitty wasn't smiling anymore. In fact, she was looking at her stony-faced, legs crossed and arms wrapped tightly across her body.

'You're babbling. Are you sure you're okay?'

'Yes. Sorry, Kitty. Honestly, I'm a bit nervous.'

'You don't need to be nervous with me. You can tell

me anything. I'm here to help you, remember? Your first friend in Salt Lake.'

'Okay. I've been on a couple of dates with Kyle.'

She decided to take the Kitty approach and not let her respond, but carry on talking.

'It's early days and you don't need to worry about me. I didn't want you to find out another way and think I was keeping anything from you. And I know you probably don't even really care as you guys went to prom about a hundred years ago but, you know, it's the girl code so I really wanted you to know even though there's not all that much to know.'

She took in a deep breath and waited for Kitty to respond. She was completely unreadable.

Then Kitty smiled at her. It looked strained, but then Kitty never really looked relaxed. Abbie twisted her hands together in her lap, the silent seconds feeling like hours.

'Abbie. It's fine. Like you said, we went to prom a long time ago. I only warned you about him because I didn't want you to get hurt. I just want you to be happy. I had kind of guessed anyway.'

'Are you sure?'

'Absolutely. Please don't give it a minute's thought.'

As though an angel had been sent from above to save her, at that moment, Abbie saw Rose walking through the door of the bar and jumped up to beckon her over.

She had explained Kitty's unique nature to Rose already and, to her relief, when Abbie introduced them, Rose immediately embraced Kitty and told her how much she had been looking forward to meeting her, how much Abbie had talked about her, and how she knew what a great friend she had been since Abbie arrived in the US.

The timing couldn't have been better.

Abbie dashed to the bar to order another round of sickly-sweet cocktails, leaving them for a few minutes to catch her breath and slow her heart rate down.

She didn't think that whole breaking news went excellently, but it could have been worse. At least she had ripped off the plaster and it was out there in the open. Kitty might not be over the moon about it, but Abbie was sure she'd get used to the idea. And she'd make sure to keep Kitty excited about their projects and the trip to London.

The rest of the evening passed without incident. Abbie was quieter than she usually would be, but Rose did a great job of asking Kitty lots of questions, which was clearly making her feel good as she was positively glowing being the centre of attention.

As they headed home, Abbie sank deep into the seat of the taxi she was sharing with Rose.

'So, you finally told her, huh?'

'Yeah, you picked up on that?' Abbie turned to face her friend.

'I heard you when I was coming into the bar. Figured I arrived at a good time.'

'The best,' she sighed.

'Strange chick.'

'Kitty is a bit prickly sometimes but, like I've said to

Kyle, she's helped me so much. I just think she's maybe had some weird things in her life that stop her from being totally relaxed or something. I've been trying to work it out. Tonight was nice, though, she seemed to like you.'

'She was tolerating me. I kept seeing her glance at my tattoos, and she definitely thought I was about to steal her purse at any moment.'

Abbie stifled a giggle as they pulled up outside Rose's apartment. 'She's not that bad, honestly.'

'She's not who you should have spent tonight celebrating with. Get home to your guy.'

Rose kissed her on the cheek, and Abbie redirected the taxi to Kyle's house. She needed a hug.

CHAPTER 21

'HAPPY BIRTHDAY TO you. Happy birthday to you.' Abbie grudgingly opened one eye as Kyle woke her up with his dreadfully out of tune singing. She had finally found something he wasn't good at.

'It's so early, why are you waking me up?' She threw the covers back over her head.

He pulled the duvet halfway down the bed and started up his rendition of Happy Birthday again.

'Alright, alright. If I wake up, will you please stop singing?'

'It's a deal. But I won't stop fussing around you. You need help now you're thirty. And it's not early, it's ten o'clock.'

She finally opened her eyes, with the full intention of smacking him, but stopped when she saw he had brought them breakfast in bed. There was toast, eggs and bacon, two steaming cups of coffee and two mimosas in champagne flutes. A single-stemmed pale pink rose in a vase sat next to a card and a small package neatly gift-wrapped.

She genuinely felt she did not deserve this man. He was a dream come true. And she hadn't even been looking for him.

'You didn't need to do this,' she exclaimed, nearly

knocking over the tray as she reached to grab him.

'Woah, steady there. I brought you breakfast in bed. I did not agree to a full deep clean of the bedroom if you destroy it. And, of course I had to. You only turn thirty once. And I really want to take advantage of it because they don't call them the dirty thirties for nothing.'

She rolled her eyes at him before turning her attention back to the tray.

'Can I open it?' She touched the package, looking at him before picking it up.

'That's what it's there for.'

She carefully peeled off the tape from the silver wrapping paper and took out a black velvet bag. Loosening the drawstring, she emptied the contents into her hand and gasped as she saw it.

It was a beautiful, delicate silver bangle, about half a centimetre wide, etched with the same four-pronged star pattern that had been on the rug they saw when they camped at Arches.

'Do you like it?' he asked nervously, and she realised she had been holding her breath.

'Are you serious?' She slid it onto her wrist and reached over to kiss him. 'I love it. I can't believe how much thought you put into this. I'm so incredibly touched.'

'It's nothing really, and there was a method to my madness,' he said, moving closer to her on the bed. 'I had to get something to replace that awful friendship bracelet you made with Kitty.'

She laughed, despite herself. 'You're an arsehole. But one with incredibly good taste in jewellery, so I'll let you off.'

'What do you want to do today, birthday girl?'

'First I need to speak to my parents. I've got sixteen messages asking me to text them as soon as I wake up so they can call me. Then I'm easy. The weather's good, maybe we could go to the park?'

'You don't want to do anything special?' He frowned.

She shook her head, screwing up her nose. 'I've never been one for making a big song and dance about my birthday. It'll just be nice to be outside and take it easy. We haven't had a lot of relaxation time recently.'

'True.' He nodded. 'But I do have dinner reservations for us and I'm not having any excuses. It can be a chilled day but we're still celebrating properly tonight.'

'Deal. Now, can I finally eat my food?' She motioned towards the plate with a fork.

'Fuck it, it's cold already. Get dressed. I'm taking you out for breakfast.'

ABBIE FELT KIND of groggy as they pulled up outside the restaurant that evening. They had walked around the park for hours in the sticky September heat, and she had been so tired after a busy week and an active day that she fell asleep on her couch afterwards. When Kyle came to pick her up for dinner after stopping at his own place to get changed into fresh clothes, he had luckily come a bit early and woken her so she had time to get ready and not miss their reservation, but she still felt exhausted. She was sure some food and a glass of wine would perk her up, but she was looking forward to a fairly early night.

The restaurant was new to her, not somewhere she and Kyle had been before, and she was excited for another new experience with him.

When Kyle stated his name, the waitress ushered them towards the back of the large room, and to her surprise, Abbie could see they were being led to a private dining area beyond an emerald green curtain.

She momentarily paused, rubbed her eyes, then screamed in disbelief when she rounded the curtain and saw some amazingly familiar faces. Violet, Lily and Polly screamed too and almost knocked their chairs over in their rush to scramble around the table to reach her, embracing her in a rugby-style scrum.

The rest of the restaurant must have been deafened by the sound of the four screeching girls. Abbie couldn't believe her eyes. Suddenly, she didn't feel so tired anymore.

'What the hell are you doing here? How? What? I don't understand.'

She kept a firm grip on Lily, her head turning from Violet to Polly and then to her sister, before she started all over again, still struggling to believe they were all here in front of her.

'It's all down to him.' Violet pointed at Kyle. 'He's

better than a teenage girl at Facebook investigation work, and he tracked me down to get us all over here. He thought a special birthday was worth a surprise, and we were all happy to have an excuse for a little holiday.'

'Mum and Dad really wanted to come, Abs, but Mum couldn't get the time off work and Dad had tickets to the game today, and they said they'd see you at home for Christmas, which isn't long away. They did send a present though.'

Lily pushed a gift into Abbie's hands. She looked even more grown up than when Abbie had left just eight months ago.

'I'm so happy to see you, Lils. Great timing just before you start university, right?'

'Yep, and you won't believe this. Polly only upgraded us all to first class on the plane. It was dead posh, Abs. They gave us pyjamas to wear and a three-course meal and a dead nice toiletry bag to take away and everything.'

She looked fit to burst. Abbie stared at Polly, confused.

'You did what?'

Polly shrugged, as if it was nothing. Abbie knew they had never worked out how she managed to earn her money, but this seemed certifiably crazy. 'You can't take it with you. I thought our first collective girls trip needed a bit of luxury.'

'But you can't afford that. None of us can.'

'My great-grandfather invented Tarmac. I can do anything I want for my friends.'

At this, Abbie, Violet, Lily and Kyle all looked agog. Abbie's jaw dropped open. It took Violet to break the silence. 'You what? How the hell have you never mentioned this?'

'It never came up. Now, drinks?'

The four girls burst out laughing as Kyle continued to watch, bemused. Abbie giggled looking at his face. He didn't know what he had let himself in for.

As they took their seats at the table, Abbie noticed there were three empty chairs.

'I took the liberty of inviting a few more of your friends,' Kyle said. 'I just asked them to give us a few minutes so you could catch up with the others first.'

She clasped his hand.

'I cannot believe you did this for me. I am so overwhelmed right now. But thank you.'

As she kissed him, her final guests appeared from around the curtain. Kitty walked in, clutching a gift bag and a silver helium balloon with 'THIRTY' printed on it. Following right behind, Rose beamed as she walked hand-in-hand with one of the most beautiful women Abbie thought she had ever seen.

After embracing Kitty, she turned to Rose, who was bursting with pride as she finally introduced Abbie to her girlfriend.

'Abbie, Stella. Stella, Abbie. I am so excited that you're finally meeting. I feel like I've been talking so much about each of you to the other one, and you each must have thought I was making the other one up.'

It was a whirlwind of chatter and introductions and laughter, and Abbie couldn't imagine wanting to be anywhere else in the world. She wasn't sure she had ever felt quite so loved and she had Kyle to thank for making this happen. And her amazing sister and friends to thank for flying halfway round the world, albeit in first class.

When everyone was settled and the initial shock had died down, she went to the bathroom with Violet. She had noticed the small bump through her dress, and wanted a few minutes alone to hug her and appreciate the fact her very best friend was four and a half months away from becoming a mother.

As soon as the door was closed, Violet squealed. 'Oh my god, he is fucking gorgeous. You hit the jackpot.'

Abbie laughed. 'I want to talk about you. Can I touch it?'

'Of course you can, you eejit. I've been saving something else to tell you as well. An extra birthday present really.'

'What?' Abbie exclaimed, grabbing Violet's hand.

'You're the only person Michael and I agreed to tell. It's going to be a surprise for everyone else. We're having a little girl.' Tears of happiness sprang to Violet's eyes. She wasn't normally emotional like this and it made Abbie feel incredibly moved.

'Oh, stop crying or I won't be able to finish telling you the rest of the surprise.'

Abbie dabbed her tears away before wiping away Violet's from under her eyes with her thumbs.

'We want you to be her godmother, Abbie. If you'll have us?'

That was it. Abbie burst into happy tears, with Violet joining her. 'Yes, yes and yes a million times. This is the best birthday present ever.'

'Right, stop being so soft, I want more information on this hunk of a man out there. He's gorgeous, he clearly adores you and he seems like he's got a good head on his shoulders. He can't possibly be all those things and not have any bad points. What is it? Does he snore like a pig? Leave his dirty pants on the floor?'

Their happy tears turned to laughter before Abbie's face became serious.

'He does seem too good to be true, Vi,' she said. 'He's pretty much the perfect boyfriend and I'm waiting for something to go wrong because I know I don't deserve this and I'm hiding this huge secret from him. But things are so good that I'm being selfish and I don't want to ruin it.'

'Absolute nonsense!' Violet said loudly. 'You deserve this more than you know and you have to stop thinking that way. What happened, you've got to stop punishing yourself for it, the blame doesn't lay with you quite frankly. I know you've been putting this brave face on since you've been here, but I know you and I know it still bothers you and it just can't go on forever. Also, you're not being selfish. It's incredibly personal and it's your choice if you tell him or not.'

Abbie half smiled, not wanting to ruin the amazing

evening after Violet had travelled so far.

'Right, it's your thirtieth birthday and there's a room full of people out there waiting for the star of the show, so let's get back out there.' She grabbed Abbie's hand. 'You're allowed to be happy you know. It's insanity if you feel any kind of guilt for that. It's completely misplaced.'

Abbie squeezed her hand and nodded, not sure if she really believed the sentiment, but with a determination to enjoy the evening.

They re-joined the group after touching up their make-up, Kyle looking at her quizzically as she beamed at him upon returning to the table. She would tell him the good news later, but for now, she wanted to savour every moment of this night. He had been right that morning. You only turned thirty once. And if this was what her thirties had in store, she couldn't wait.

Polly, Rose and Stella seemed to be getting on famously. They were swapping stories about bands they liked, music they thought the others would like, tales of being in a band, their best tattoos and everything else in between. It was a true meeting of minds and Abbie knew now that she was right about what drew her to Rose. She was the perfect blend of Polly and Violet.

Kitty was seated between Violet and Lily. Abbie could hear her colleague asking lots of questions about London and Violet animatedly answering. Lily was getting in on the act too. She was shortly moving to the capital to study at university, so, as a typical teenager, that meant she was already the fount of all knowledge despite having spent the grand total of a week there in the past three years. Abbie giggled to herself. She really didn't need to worry about Lily at all. She was going to be absolutely fine.

And it was so nice to see Kitty more relaxed. Abbie had imagined she'd be more on edge in a larger group, but it was like she'd come to life. She was smiling from ear to ear, and there didn't seem to be any awkwardness over the Kyle situation. He had been right, she just needed to get it out in the open, and it hadn't turned out to be a big deal after all.

Abbie herself had Violet to her left and Kyle to her right. She reached over to take his hand and noticed that he had been watching her watching everyone else. She hoped her face conveyed to him exactly how she was feeling right now. She felt like the luckiest girl in the world. Looking around the table, she had the best friends and family a girl could wish for. And a boyfriend to die for.

Two hours later they all sat, completely stuffed. The family-style restaurant had served a modern twist on all-American food and the courses kept coming and coming, filling the large table so there was no room for even one extra plate. They had, except Violet, consumed a lot of bottles of wine and now, with them all propping up the bar in the main restaurant, Abbie could see that the jet lag was starting to kick in fast on her visitors from England. She indicated to Kyle that they should get them home and they all started to say their goodbyes.

When she reached Rose and Kitty who were, likely

due to the buckets of pinot noir, inconceivably chatting at the bar, she noticed they were talking to a guy. He was tall with angular features, around forty, and looked as if he were completely smitten with Kitty.

'Abbie, this is Cody,' Rose said. 'We just met him, and he and Kitty have so much in common. Cody, this is Abbie, it's her birthday so you really have to thank her or else you might never have met our wonderful Kitty.'

Abbie stifled a laugh. She knew exactly what Rose was up to. She hadn't had the chance to tell her it wasn't an issue anymore, and Kitty didn't care about Kyle.

Leaving them to it she hugged everyone goodbye, promising to meet up with Rose later in the week before Stella left again on tour.

She hauled herself into the passenger seat of Kyle's truck, looking in the back where her visitors were struggling to keep their eyes open.

'Jet lag's a killer right? In fifteen minutes, we'll be home. And then you can all get to sleep so you're fresh for a day of exploring tomorrow.'

Kyle had told her during dinner that they were all leaving on Tuesday evening, but he'd booked the next two days off work for her so they could spend time together. He also told her he wasn't going to stay at her place, so the four of them could split themselves between the two bedrooms. He really had thought of everything.

She practically had to carry Lily up the stairs when they got to the house. She was on her last legs, and Abbie well remembered that feeling from her first few nights in the city. She put her sister with Polly in the guest bedroom and showed Polly where everything was. Lily fell unconscious on the bed within seconds still wearing her clothes.

Then she settled Violet in the bed in her own room. She fussed around, making sure she was comfortable until her friend swatted her like a fly, telling her to leave her alone. Abbie gave her one more huge hug before leaving her to sleep.

Heading downstairs, she joined Kyle, who was watching some generic sports programme on the TV. She snuggled in next to him, her head nestling perfectly into his chest as he wrapped an arm around her.

'I don't even know how to say thank you for what you've done for me today,' she whispered quietly into his chest.

'I can think of a few ways.' He picked her up and put her in his lap, his lips meeting hers in the most gentle of kisses, then tracing down her neck and across her collarbone. 'Happy birthday, England.'

'You can't do this to me, we have house guests.' She giggled.

He groaned. 'I know. I don't know why I did this. I should have put them in a hotel and kept you all to myself. How do you feel about the backseat of a truck?'

'Get home and take a cold shower.'

He laughed, getting up to head home. 'Sleep well, beautiful, and enjoy tomorrow. And again, happy birthday.'

After he kissed her goodbye, she lay on the sofa, wondering if it was too late to take him up on the offer of the backseat of the truck. Giggling, she prised herself off the comfy cushions and upstairs, where she watched Violet softly snoring, her heart full from the evening. Kyle had excelled himself.

CHAPTER 22

THE NEXT TWO days passed in a whirlwind of activity, chatting and laughter. Abbie, Violet, Lily and Polly toured around the city, with Abbie proudly showing them all the things she'd discovered when she first arrived.

They visited the site of the imposing Mormon church and Temple Square, they went for walks around Liberty Park, and they all got their credit cards out for a visit to the big mall. Abbie was happy to be in a position to hand over a wad of dollars to Lily and tell her to go wild and get new clothes for university. She took them to Park City and to The Live Joint, where they got to meet Rose again and see an up-and-coming band that were performing as part of a tour across the country.

They ate so much food. She took them for Mexican and Italian and pizza and burgers. They ate breakfast burritos as they sat looking at the mountains from the park, and they fell into bed exhausted.

Abbie wished more than anything she could have taken them to Arches, but there wasn't enough time. They would have to visit again.

As she was taking her make-up off on Monday evening, she noticed Violet studying her intently in the mirror. She spun around, grinning. She still couldn't believe her best friend was there, and it made her heart want to burst every time she looked at Violet's neat little baby bump. She was so tiny and wearing the bump well, although Abbie still couldn't imagine what she would look like as she got further along. She couldn't imagine her petite friend carrying a full-size baby. It didn't seem possible.

'You look so happy, Abs. And you look well. Really well. Despite all the crap you obviously eat here. When was the last time you ate a vegetable?'

'We ate salad for lunch, you idiot.'

'America has twisted your mind quickly. It doesn't count as salad if it's plastered in five thousand calories of dressing.'

'Don't be a calorie bore, Vi, it doesn't suit you. Or are you practicing your nagging skills ready for motherhood?' Abbie turned back to the mirror to finish removing her mascara.

'Do you miss it?' Violet asked quietly.

'Home?'

'Yeah.'

Abbie paused, wanting to get her explanation right. 'I miss you. And I miss Lily and Polly and Mum and Dad. And, this might sound odd, but I miss being able to walk around because you have to drive everywhere here. Weirdly, though, I don't miss the actual place. If being here has taught me one thing, it's that it's about the people around you and not where you are. Kyle's been really important for me learning that. Without him and Rose, I honestly don't know how it would have gone. I might have come home already.'

Violet beckoned for Abbie to sit with her on the bed, then took her hand. 'I'm very, very pleased it's all going well here. And I'm over the bloody moon you've finally got back in the saddle. Especially on such a nice, quality thoroughbred.'

Abbie laughed. There was nothing like a British sense of humour.

'Selfishly, though, I wonder how long you think you'll stay here. We miss you so much. You are planning to come back at some point, right?'

Abbie paused, not sure whether to update Violet on something that had happened at the end of the previous week. She decided to tell her. She hadn't told anyone else. She definitely hadn't told Kyle.

'It's funny, Vi. I honestly haven't been thinking long term. I got here, I've been making the most of it and things have been happening. I know it's still pretty early days with Kyle, but he's amazing. I'm loving my job. The city is cool and I'm discovering new places around here all the time, so it still feels really new.'

'But?' Violet always knew when Abbie was holding something back.

'It's not really a but, however, I got offered a job back in London on Friday. It was completely out of the blue and made me think a bit, that's all. If it was something I wanted to consider.'

'Wow, Abs, that's mega. What was the job? Another football club trying to poach you?'

Abbie shook her head. 'No, it's crazy. You know I've been writing this blog with Rose here? I got contacted by a big music website and magazine publisher, and they wanted to hire me full-time as a gig reviewer and features writer.'

Violet's eyes opened really wide. 'The baby just kicked then. Quick, feel.'

Abbie rushed to put her hand where Violet was pointing, and there it was. The gentlest of little prods through Violet's stomach into her hand. Tears sprang to her eyes. It was one of the most beautiful things that had ever happened to her.

'Little one is excited, thinking that her Auntie Abs might be coming home,' Violet whispered.

Taking her hand again, Abbie spoke carefully. 'I turned it down.'

A sad smile found its way to Violet's lips as she nodded. 'It's okay, Abs. You're happy here. You're thriving. I can see.'

'It feels like this is where I'm meant to be right now. I've fallen in love with Kyle, not that I've told him that yet. I feel alive again.'

'I know. And I'm so fucking happy for you I can't explain. It just kind of sucks that it's happened so far from home. I desperately miss you. I guess I'll just have to take some more trips out here to visit when I'm on maternity leave, won't I?'

They fell asleep that night hand in hand, Abbie feeling conflicted that the most important parts of her life were split by thousands of miles, but ultimately knowing where she needed to be at this point.

IT WAS ALL over far too quickly. Violet, Lily and Polly had a flight just after lunchtime as they were connecting in New York on their way home. It meant that, after a quick breakfast and a final walk around Liberty Park, where there were stunning views of the Wasatch Mountains and the most beautiful blue sky for them to photograph, they had to leave for the airport. Violet had to get back to work, as she had nearly run out of holiday days for the year, and Lily had some preparation classes to take before her degree started. Polly's band had two gigs later in the week and Damian was opening an exhibition of his paintings at a pop-up art fair in Shoreditch that she couldn't miss, so she was excited about the week to come.

After checking in for their flight at the counter where, despite everyone's protests and shouts and even an attempt at physical restraint, Polly once again withdrew her platinum credit card and upgraded everyone for the plane journey home, the four went to a café before security for one final drink together.

While they were in America, Lily had received the news that she was moving into student accommodation not too far from where Polly lived. Abbie felt a bit better about saying goodbye to her sister knowing that Polly had promised to keep an eye on her.

When they couldn't leave it any longer to go to security, Abbie took it in turns hugging each of them. She knew she was gripping on for dear life, each hug lasting a lot longer than Violet, Lily or Polly were probably comfortable with, but she wanted to squeeze every last bit of them before they returned to England. All four of them had tears streaming down their faces by the time they eventually let go, and Abbie's heart hurt as she finally waved them goodbye and headed back to her car to go home.

Sitting in her bedroom later that afternoon, after cleaning and tidying the whole house to keep her mind off of the place now feeling so empty, she finally stopped to think about the past few days. She felt a hole where they had been but she treasured every minute that she had enjoyed with them.

She probably would never have spent that kind of quality time with Polly back in London. They were always like ships passing in the night. She had learnt more about Polly's unbelievable family history in the past three days than she had in two years living together. And she had seen new depths to her. A kindness, a protectiveness and a generosity that, now she thought about it, were always there, but had been a little bit masked by the multicoloured hair and nocturnal lifestyle that Polly led. That she could be so kind to be looking out for Lily made her feel like her sister would be just fine in the big, bright lights of England's capital city.

Lily. She was just gorgeous. And getting feistier and

more strong-willed by the day. Abbie couldn't remember being as confident and fearless at that age as her little sister. Yet she still had that childlike excitement about everything. When Abbie drove them over to Park City to show them the cute little streets and explain it was where the famous film festival took place, Lily's eyes remained on stalks the whole time they were there in case she managed to spot Tom Holland, who apparently had a new film out soon. No explaining that the film festival wasn't happening for months would dull her hope. Abbie loved her even more after spending these days together, and her sister and Polly got on like a house on fire.

And Violet. What could she say? If it wasn't for Violet she may very well still be sat crying in her old bedroom, clinging on to old sorrow and grief, hating her job and wearing some pretty terrible clothes. Violet had hauled her up, inspired her to make a change and supported her when she needed it. And Abbie was determined to return that support in the most important role she had been given in her life so far. She knew asking her to be godmother wasn't something that Violet would have taken lightly – her strong Irish roots meant she was one of the only people Abbie knew who still went to church on a fairly regular basis. And Abbie wouldn't let her down. She hadn't figured out yet how she could be the best god-mother possible with the distance between them, but she knew it was about more than just physical closeness.

She started to cry, but it wasn't through sadness. It was a release of sorts. She could relax knowing everyone was okay. And even though she was crying because she already missed them, she was also crying with happiness as she felt so unbelievably lucky she had so many amazing people in her life.

And this was, in a big part, thanks to Kyle. After everything she'd heard about him and how she'd tried to fight her feelings, it was him who made this trip for her friends to visit her happen, and who went to all this effort to bring a bit of home here for her. She was so lucky.

A noise behind her made her start, but when she swung her head around to look at her bedroom door there was nobody there. It must have been one of the doors downstairs slamming. She'd opened the windows and it was a breezy day.

The sound, though, brought her back to the present and she dried her eyes and reapplied her make-up.

The visit from Violet, Lily and Polly had lifted her. She hadn't realised that she'd been feeling homesick, but now she was reinvigorated and was sure the feelings would keep her lifted through until Christmas when she could visit home again and see her parents.

As she was chopping salad twenty minutes later to go with the grilled steaks she planned to cook for dinner, she heard a knock on the front door. Putting down the knife, she opened the door to see Kyle standing there.

'Why are you knocking? I texted you to let you know I left the door unlocked and just to come straight in. I was vacuuming a bit earlier so I didn't want to not hear you arrive.'

He looked a bit hesitant. 'I didn't see it. Sorry.'

'Don't worry, come in anyway. I'm getting dinner ready.'

He paused in the doorway so she ushered him in and reached up for a kiss. 'Is something wrong?'

'No, nothing. Did the girls get on their flight okay?'

She carried on slicing cucumber as she explained the sad farewell and how she'd received a text to say they were taking off and were already two glasses of champagne deep into their first-class experience. 'I think it's safe to say they're absolutely fine.'

'Are you?' he asked, taking a sip of the Budweiser he'd taken out of the fridge as he marinated the steak next to her at the counter.

'Me? I'm fine. Why?'

'I was just worried you might be upset saying good-bye.'

'Well, yes, of course I am. That's my sister and my two closest friends, and I probably won't see them now until Christmas. But it means the world they came here. And it means the world you organised it for me.'

She reached up to wrap her arms around his neck and he hugged her tightly back, burying his head in the crook of her neck, breathing her in. It was all she could do to stay upright as her legs went to jelly.

Just two days apart and this was what happened to her. She needed help. She was taken.

The embrace was over all too quickly and he headed into the garden to throw the steaks on the BBQ.

SHE WAS WOKEN at five thirty the following morning by her phone ringing. She quickly silenced it and ran out of the bedroom so as not to wake a slumbering Kyle.

Wearily looking at the screen, she pressed answer when she saw it was her mum's mobile. That was strange in and of itself as she always called Abbie from home, and compounded by the fact that she had only spoken to her mother the morning before, when they caught up on her birthday week and all the things she did with Lily when she visited. Her stomach flipped as her instinct told her something was wrong.

'Mum, are you okay?'

The soft sound of her mum's voice started to fill her ear and she felt a wave of homesickness.

'Yes, love. How are you? I bet you're enjoying a nice quiet house now the girls have come back home.'

'I'm okay, Mum. It's pretty early here, I've just got up. Is everything okay there?'

Her mum paused momentarily. 'Well, love, I don't want you to worry at all because he's in the best place, but we're at the hospital at the moment with your dad. He's just getting a few tests, nothing to worry about, but I knew you'd not be happy if we didn't tell you.'

'Tests? What tests? What's happened?' Abbie asked urgently, a sick feeling hitting the pit of her stomach and tears springing to her eyes.

'Don't get upset, love, I don't like the thought of you

being so far away and I can't give you a hug if you're crying.'

'I'm getting upset because I don't know what's going on, Mum. I'm worrying. Tell me, please,' she begged, pacing the living room.

'Okay, but remember, he's in the best place with brilliant doctors and nurses. They've been fussing over us ever since we arrived. He woke up in the middle of the night feeling a lot of pressure on his chest.'

'Oh my god, he's had a heart attack?' Abbie shrieked, the feeling of panic deepening with every second.

'We don't know that at the moment. They're doing tests because chest pain can mean a few different things and, although some of the symptoms point to a heart attack, none of the tests so far have shown the right markers for it to be that. It's just a waiting game while they look at a lot of different things.'

Abbie did everything she could to stop herself from bursting out crying. 'Okay, Mum. Look, I'll get on the internet as soon as I'm off the phone and come home. I can get a flight tonight and be home tomorrow morning.'

'No, no, love, I don't want you to be going to all that expense and leaving your job when we don't even know what it is yet. I promise you I'll call you later on. He's up and talking and saying he wants to go home as it's all a big fuss over nothing.'

'Have you told Lily?'

'Yes, I have. She landed this morning, and she's hanging out at Polly's house today while she waits for news.

Polly, bless her, hasn't got work today so she's looking out for her.'

'Oh, thank god. I'll call her and check in. Mum?'

'Yes, love?'

'I love you and Dad so much. I feel so far away right now.' She started quietly crying, her hand gripping the phone, not wanting to say goodbye.

'And we love you. We're so proud of you and what you're doing, and you're having these adventures that we would never have been brave enough to try. Don't feel guilty about being there, this would have happened no matter where you were.'

'I know, but I can't help but feel that I should be there helping you, though, and be there in case, in case…'

'Stop it now. Get yourself into the kitchen and make yourself a cup of tea and please don't worry until we know that there's actually something to worry about. I promise I'll call you as soon as the doctor's been in to see us.'

After saying goodbyes, Abbie sat on the sofa in shock, her eyes wet with tears. She started when she heard the door open, and Kyle looked at her with fear written all over his face.

'What's happened, babe?' he asked while dashing to sit next to her and took her into his arms.

She crumpled into him and started crying harder, haltingly explaining the phone call she'd had with her mother.

'And I feel so helpless being here so far away,' she finished, as a fresh burst of tears hit her. 'I'll never forgive myself if something happens to him.'

'Okay, babe, I need you to breathe,' Kyle said, holding her tight. 'I know this must be scary, but your mom's right. We can't worry until we know what we're dealing with, and then we can make a plan. If that involves getting you home as quickly as possible, that's what we'll do.'

'We can't worry?' Abbie almost shouted, and pulled out of his embrace. 'It's easy for you to say. Your parents are a drive away and they're healthy. My dad's in the hospital and realistically it would take me two days to get to him. I can't not be stressed right now.'

'I know, I know, come here,' Kyle soothed. 'I'm sorry, I know I'm not in your shoes but, believe me, I can imagine how you're feeling. Do you want to stay home today? I'll talk to Hank and explain what's happening.'

'No, I'll go mad if I stay at home,' she said, finally slowing her breath a little. After a pause, she continued, 'I'll come in with you and try to keep my mind off it a bit by keeping busy, but I'll pack a bag and bring my passport in case I need to go to the airport straight from work.'

Wordlessly, Kyle put his arms back around her and pulled her in close.

THE MORNING AT work felt like it lasted a week. Every time Abbie checked the time, feeling like hours had passed, it was only a few minutes since the last time she looked. She couldn't concentrate on any task and simply flicked between computer programmes and web browsers in a bid to pass the morning.

Kyle brought her some lunch at noon but she couldn't eat a thing and tossed the sandwich unopened into the bin.

She had texted her mother on and off all day, so she knew her father was stable and not in any immediate danger, but there was still no news on a diagnosis and the torment was eating away at her.

Finally, just after two, her mother's number flashed up on the phone again, and Abbie trembled as she answered.

'Mum? How is he?'

'He's going to be absolutely fine, love.' Abbie's shoulders dropped as she recognised a smile in her mother's voice. 'He's had a gall bladder attack. One of the symptoms can be mistaken for a heart attack, as he had very severe heartburn.'

'Oh, thank god!' Abbie exclaimed. 'So, he's going to be okay?'

'Yes, love. They're giving him some medication and will see how he gets on. It might go away on its own, and they'll only need to look at removing stones if it happens again, but it's all pretty straightforward if that does happen, from what they're telling us.'

'I'm so relieved. You have no idea how worried I was, Mum. I've got a bag here at work so I could dash to the airport if you needed me.' Abbie felt like the air was suddenly easier to breathe in. She had no idea how tense she'd been.

'If I'm being honest, I was a bit worried too, but I should have known it was just your dad making a performance. It was bin day wasn't it, I think he was wanting to avoid putting them out.'

Abbie laughed for the first time that day and felt the stresses start to melt away.

'I love you, Mum. I'll come home soon for a visit, yeah? I'm missing you.'

'That would be lovely, Abs, but don't you worry about us. I promise you, we're fine.'

Abbie texted Kyle as soon as she hung up to let him know the good news. She might just be able to go to sleep that night.

CHAPTER 23

TWO DAYS LATER and Abbie was in her kitchen again preparing dinner, when Kyle knocked on the door. She'd barely seen him in the past couple of days as their workloads had been heavy, and she'd gone to a gig with Rose the night before.

As always, she reached up to kiss him, but it felt odd. He didn't seem to be kissing her back with any enthusiasm and his body felt rigid. He'd been distant since the incident with her dad, and she was worried. His text replies were short and not the usual warm or flirty tone.

This strange mood made her anxious but she hated confrontation so she zipped around the kitchen, finishing the spaghetti carbonara she'd made for them and dishing it out into two large bowls, the steam rising off the pasta as she placed the bowls on the table.

Kyle ate, but barely spoke during dinner and she felt sick to the pit of her stomach. The awkward atmosphere was building and she couldn't let it continue any longer.

'Babe. What's wrong? Is everything okay with your family?' Her hands were shaking as she broached the subject, not sure what was going on.

He sighed and carried on looking at the contents of his bowl. 'Abbie, I need to talk to you.'

Oh, god. He'd called her Abbie again. Never a good sign.

'Okay, what do we need to talk about? Do you want more pasta?' She started to get up from the table to avoid whatever it was he was going to say as she already knew she didn't like his tone.

He put his hand on top of hers to stop her. 'I'm good. Sit down.'

She could barely believe what she was hearing over the next ten minutes. He delivered a stuttering, hesitant monologue that she heard only bits of as she sat, silently, trying to understand what was happening.

'It's not you, it's me…'

'I just need to focus on my career right now…'

'You haven't done anything wrong but I can't be with you at the moment…'

'I think I'd better leave.'

She managed to blurt out, 'Yes, I think you better had. Get out.' Then she turned around and faced the sink. She felt his presence watching her for a moment before he got up and left.

It didn't matter. The words. The clichés. They all added up to him walking out the door as she felt herself shrinking more and more into an abyss.

What the hell had just happened?

Two days ago, he had comforted her when she was a mess worrying about her dad. They had been having the greatest time. She knew she had snapped at him after she got off the phone from her mother, but surely, he wasn't so fragile that a comment when she was in a highly stressful situation would have driven him away?

As she stared at the door that he'd closed on his way out, she felt bereft. She needed to talk to someone. This didn't make any sense. Not Violet. She would be asleep. Rose. Yes. Rose. She grabbed her mobile and found the number, slowed by her shaking fingers fumbling on the keypad.

Her friend answered after two rings and had to ask Abbie three times to repeat herself as she didn't understand what she was trying to say through the crying.

'I can't believe it's happened to me again. He's just finished it with no real explanation. I thought everything was fine, we were having an amazing time, and he said it's over. What's wrong with me? It can't be a coincidence that the same thing has happened twice, can it?'

She knew she sounded hysterical, and Rose sounded worried at the other end of the phone, but her whole existence in her new city had just been turned on its axis.

'Calm down, Abbie, I'm coming over to your place now. Just sit down and wait for me.' She heard a door close and figured Rose was already leaving her apartment.

'What am I going to do, Rose?'

Her heart hurt as she continued to sob.

CHAPTER 24

THE FINAL MATCH of the Utah Saints season was upon Abbie before she knew it. The past four weeks since Kyle broke up with her had been confusing and upsetting, and even though Rose had been a rock, she had felt very lonely at times as her day-to-day life had changed from the easy routine she'd got into with Kyle.

She'd tried to start a new structure and was taking things day by day. Although she was desperately sad, she didn't want to fall in the same trap she'd plunged into after Josh, and she had enough going on to fill her hours. Before she left England, she'd thought she might start exercising when she got to America, but that hadn't happened – until now. It was Rose who suggested it. She had a friend who ran to keep his mind clear, and it worked wonders for him. So, every morning for the past three weeks, Abbie had laced up her running shoes, put some upbeat music on her headphones and run for thirty minutes through Liberty Park. The first ten days she hadn't wanted to get out of bed, but had forced herself. The last ten days she hadn't even tried to talk herself out of it. Up, dress, run, shower, get ready for the day.

She had thrown herself into work, focusing to a level she didn't know was possible, and even travelling twice in the past three weeks to away games in different states. Hank didn't need her to do it, but she said she wanted to keep stepping up and would go if he agreed. He was more than happy for her to join the team in St Louis and Seattle, and she had taken the chance to explore these new cities. The weekends were the worst, so filling her time with football games was a great distraction.

And thank god for the blog. Every night that Rose wasn't working in The Live Joint, she had organised for them to go to a gig somewhere. And, when she was working, she insisted that Abbie go to the bar to keep her company.

It meant that some of the benefits of the running were being negated by alcohol on more nights of the week than she would normally drink, but she was limiting herself to one or two a night and was feeling good.

Luckily, she hadn't seen Kyle much. They were obviously and actively trying to avoid each other. He hadn't come near the marketing office, and she had stayed away from places she thought she might bump into him. She had driven out for lunch every day to avoid a possible meeting in the canteen and asked Kitty to go to him directly with any questions or information about the youth team trip to the UK.

She hadn't told Kitty about the breakup. If she was honest, she was absolutely mortified. Kitty had given her fair warning and told her some extremely personal information to try to keep her safe, and she'd ignored her entirely.

She also didn't want Kitty feeling sorry for her. They had the big finale today and the youth team trip next month and she needed Kitty focused. But, more than that, she needed herself focused. She was scared that Kitty's reaction would throw her off the course she had set for herself, of getting through this.

She didn't want to sink again.

All her focus right now was on today, the big final. The players themselves had a job to do. They had enjoyed a steady season, and if they won today, they'd finish third in the championship. That would be their best result in history and she could feel the nervous excitement through every corridor. From the cleaner who had worked there for fifteen years, right up to Hank, everyone was on tenterhooks.

She was excited about The Half-Time Show today. Children from the local hospital were coming to take part in the penalty shoot-out against the mascot, Eric the Elk, and of course, there'd be the big performance by Memphis Black. Rose was arriving shortly to support her, and because she didn't want to miss seeing the band they'd watched all those months back at the bar play an arena.

It was only an hour now until kick-off and her usual nerves had started coursing through her. She likened it to having a birthday party when you were a child. Would anyone turn up? Would everyone have a good time? Even though this was the sixteenth running of The Half-Time Show, she couldn't help but feel a little anxious, especially with the band being by far the biggest and most well-known of any that had performed this season.

In fact, the game was a sell-out, and Hank put a lot of that down to the buzz around Memphis Black's appearance. His four children were all big fans, and couldn't wait to see them play today. He'd requested a private meet and greet for them which, of course, Abbie had hastily added to the plan.

With forty-five minutes to go, she started to panic. The band had been due to arrive fifteen minutes ago, but there was no sign of them. She called Kitty.

'Have you heard from the band or their agent? I'm worried they're not here yet, and we need to get all their equipment ready in the tunnel.'

'I haven't heard from any of them, Abbie. You hadn't asked me to speak to them.'

'I didn't specifically ask you but you've double-checked with all the bands at the last ten matches for me, so I didn't think this would be any different. You spoke to them originally about their requirements, right?'

'Yes, but then because you knew them, I figured you would do it. Sorry, Abbie, I feel like I've done something wrong here. Have I?'

'No, of course you haven't. I'm just getting concerned. Don't worry, I'll call them myself.'

Hanging up, she located the agent's cell phone number and punched it into her phone. He answered quickly, although the line was noisy as he was clearly at some sort of gig.

'Hi, yes, it's Abbie Potter here. From Utah Saints. I

booked Memphis Black for a performance at our last home match of the season here at the Salt Lake City Arena.'

'Oh, hi, Abbie, how can I help? Do you have a re-scheduled date for them?'

'Sorry? I think the line is bad. I'm trying to find out where they are. They're late.'

'Abbie, I'm really confused. You cancelled, about a month ago? Emailed to say how sorry you were but the boss had a change of plan, and you understood that meant you'd lose your deposit. I replied to you confirming. I can send it to you again?'

'No. Wait. Cancel? I didn't cancel. I didn't do this. This must be a mistake. You've made a mistake. I don't know what's happening but I guarantee I didn't cancel.' Her voice had gone up an octave and her hands were shaking, beads of sweat appearing on her forehead and the palms of her hands as the panic rose. 'I need them here.'

'Look, I'm sorry if there's been an issue at your end, but I definitely have that email. I'll send it on to you now. I'm sorry, Abbie, but the band booked a new gig for today after you cancelled, and they're in California now.'

'I didn't cancel.' She realised she was shouting, but she didn't know what to do. None of this made sense.

'Sorry, there's nothing I can do at this late stage. I have to go, one of my bands is about to go on stage at a festival. Talk soon.'

'But what am I supposed to do?' Abbie shrieked, but she was talking to herself as he'd ended the call.

Rose walked in at that exact moment, and her eyes widened as she saw Abbie in such a state.

'What the hell has happened? Has he done something to you?'

'Who?'

'KYLE.'

'Oh god no, he's the least of my problems. I have a half-time show in exactly seventy-five minutes and no fucking band.'

'What the fuck?'

Abbie explained the current predicament as well as she could, considering she had no idea what had happened.

'Oh, fuck.'

'Yes. What am I going to do, Rose? I think I'm going to get fired.'

'Nope. That's not going to happen. I've got an idea.'

Within minutes Rose had called Stella, who was now on the case to get a local band. She knew them all, and was confident of success.

Thirty minutes later, a four-piece called The Flightless were en route to the arena.

Abbie left Rose with Kitty in the car park to welcome them and get them set up while she went to find Hank.

As she could have predicted, the news did not go down well.

'You what? You mean to tell me that the band people bought a ticket to this game specifically to see, the band that is the reason today is a sell-out, aren't coming?'

'I need to look into what happened, Hank. The agent

says he has a cancellation notice from us in writing. None of this makes sense to me, but I've done what I can, and we at least have some music for half-time. I don't know what else I can do at this stage. I can't get them here. They're in California.'

She threw her head back in frustration, looking at the ceiling of the tunnel where she was publicly having a conversation in raised voices with her boss.

At that point, Kitty walked by. 'Mr Henderson, if I can say, Abbie really has done her best to fix this by getting her friend's band here. They've arrived and they're ready to play. They had one song in the top ten a few months ago so they're not completely unknown. Okay, they're not Memphis Black, but they'll put on a good show.'

'Ladies. I don't have time for this. I need to go and talk to the team. We have a game to win and then I have four children to console because they're not meeting their favourite band after all. And Abbie, you'd better figure out how we're going to respond to all the complaints that will be headed our way.'

With that, Hank Henderson the Third marched off in the direction of the dressing room and Abbie's heart sank. She felt sick.

They did win the game, which was a small mercy, and The Flightless were brilliant. But she couldn't feel happy about either as she left the stadium at the end of the day to go home.

The following day she stayed in her pyjamas. She

didn't run in the park. And she didn't do any work on the blog. She felt utterly useless. And she turned over and over in her mind what had happened the day before. Had the agent made a mistake with the bookings and didn't want to admit it? All she knew for sure was that she had an inbox of complaints and calls for ticket refunds, and a very pissed-off boss.

ABBIE SPENT THREE hours on Monday morning personally writing back to all the complaints, explaining that their disappointment was understood but their tickets specified that the line-up was subject to change, hoping that they enjoyed the top-ten charting band The Flightless, and giving them a voucher to spend in the club store.

She was utterly deflated, although Kitty had told her that Hank calmed down slightly after his seventeen-year-old daughter declared that he was the best father in the universe for making it possible for her to meet the lead singer of The Flightless, because her picture with him had the most likes she'd ever received on Instagram.

A new calendar invitation popped into her inbox from Kitty, inviting her to a meeting that day with her and Hank to discuss the youth player trip to the UK. She felt her shoulders relax a little. At least there was that project to carry on with, and hopefully Hank would forgive and forget what happened with Memphis Black. She was still waiting for the email to come in from the agent, so she suspected he might be covering for making the booking error himself, or maybe it was a genuine mix-up, but either way, there was no point in dwelling on it. It had happened and she couldn't change the past. She could only focus on the future, and with any luck, Hank would now get youth player fever. If she could make this field trip next week a success, hopefully it would regain his trust in her.

Sitting in the meeting a little while later, Kitty cleared her throat before beginning to speak.

'Sorry to call you both at such short notice, but we have a problem that couldn't wait.'

Abbie's head shot up to look straight at Kitty. She hadn't been told of any problems and she didn't want to hear about anything like that for the first time in front of their boss. 'What do you mean, Kitty? I thought we were on track with everything?'

'I'm sorry, Abbie, we'll have to pull the trip. All the visas were refused for the youth team and I've tried everything but it can't be fixed in time.' She looked stricken but Abbie didn't have time for consoling as she felt panic rising for the second time in three days.

'I don't understand. We've already booked flights, hotels and coaches, and you said the visas were under control. What's happened?'

'I'm sorry, Abbie, and I'm sorry, Hank, but apparently there was something wrong on the application forms, and they just can't fix it in time at the visa office. I feel terrible.'

Hank banged his fist on the desk, causing both Kitty and Abbie to jump in their seats.

'All I'm hearing is a lot of hot air. Abbie, you had ultimate responsibility for this project, and you should have been all over it, checking up on every element. Kitty can't be blamed for this. She was trying to help and support your workload. I'm happy for her to do that but she's not trained like you are in this area, and she can't be held ultimately accountable. The buck stops with you.'

Kitty started crying and apologising over and over. Abbie spoke through gritted teeth. 'Don't worry, Kitty. Hank's right. It's not your fault. I should have got this.'

Dismissed from Hank's office, Abbie trudged back to her own. She wondered what was going to happen to her. Would she be fired? She didn't understand how everything had unravelled so quickly. Kyle, her work. It was like the world was still punishing her for what had happened in her past. She was stupid to think she could simply start again and everything from before would disappear.

She left the office bang on the dot of five and headed straight to meet Rose. There was no gig to cover tonight, but they had planned to meet for a pizza and a beer, and dear god, did she need it.

After she had relayed the awfulness of the day to Rose, she sat pensively, anxiously picking at the label of her beer bottle.

'I'm thinking of going home,' she sighed, utterly dejected.

'You can, there's nothing urgent to do on the blog. Get a good night's sleep and we'll chat tomorrow.'

'No, I mean home, home. Back to England.'

'You can't!' Rose exclaimed. 'No way would the Abbie I know give up after a little mishap. Everything will be forgotten before you know it. These things always blow over.'

'I don't know about that. It's two mishaps, and neither of them were very little. Hank is absolutely furious. And I bet Kyle is too. I haven't heard from him but he was so excited for the kids to do this programme in England, and it's all ruined because I took my eye off the ball.'

'That's not true and you know it. It was an accident. A mistake. They happen all the time.'

'Yeah, but they can't happen on that big a scale when I'm meant to be responsible. It's been the mother of all fuck-ups.'

Rose looked at her. 'What's really going on?'

'I don't know. I just feel with everything that's gone wrong the last month maybe I was living in a false illusion here. Something happened to me back in England, when I was married. I always felt guilty about it, and moving here I kind of managed to squash it. But now I'm thinking maybe it'll always be something I have to live with and I was just pretending here with this new life that it would go away. And, Violet is pregnant. Do I really want to be thousands of miles from my best friend and godchild?'

'I have no idea what you're talking about that you have to live with, and I'm not going to pry if you don't want to tell me. But I don't think you should make any hasty decisions when you're upset. You're too emotional right now.'

Abbie hugged Rose tight. Her mind was whirring at a million miles an hour. She needed to sleep. But first, about five more beers.

CHAPTER 25

A S ABBIE WAS getting ready to go to work the next day, not entirely sure if she had a job to go back to, she heard a knock at the door.

She quickly finished applying the mascara on her left eye, then ran downstairs. It felt like a punch to the stomach when she opened the door and came face to face with Kyle. He looked shocked as she visibly recoiled and started apologising for the early visit.

'What do you want? I'm going to be late for work.'

'I heard about what happened on Saturday at the game, and then yesterday from Hank, and I wanted to come to see you.'

'Oh, so you can pile in on me as well. Go on then, say what you need to say. I don't blame you for being pissed off.' She stood there with one hand resting on the door and the other on her hip, waiting for the inevitable attack.

'God no, Abbie. I'm worried about you, that's why I came here. I don't care about the trip, but it seems like something is going on and I feel responsible and, for fuck's sake, will you let me in? I don't want to have this conversation with you on the doorstep.'

She felt temper building deep in the pit of her stomach, the likes of which she couldn't remember ever having.

'You feel what? Responsible? You mean guilty more like. I don't need you coming over here treating me like some charity case to make yourself feel better. This has nothing to do with you.' Her voice was rising and she could feel her jaw clenching.

'I didn't mean it like that. And of course I don't think you're a charity case. And I'm not trying to make myself feel better. Look, let me come inside, England. Please?'

She looked at him and his pleading, sorrowful eyes and waved him into the living room. She couldn't sit in the kitchen with him. The place where he unceremoniously dumped her. She hadn't made carbonara since.

'Shall we sit?' he asked hesitantly.

She pointed to the armchair. 'Be my guest.' She perched rigidly on the edge of the sofa, hands in her lap, playing with the charms on the bracelet her family had given her before she moved. The bracelet Kyle had bought her was deep in the recesses of her jewellery box. She couldn't look at it. It hurt too much.

'Tell me what happened,' he said. 'None of this makes sense. You don't make mistakes like this, and I don't believe you would have done any of it on purpose. I've told Hank he needs to calm down.'

'I took my eye off the ball. It's my fault. Things have been really busy and Kitty has been helping me loads. I just wasn't checking things that I should have been, and I assumed things I shouldn't have, and some things fell through the net. I still can't explain how the band was cancelled, but their agent still hasn't forwarded me this alleged email he claims he received, so maybe it's a good old communication fuck-up. I thought Kitty would double-check everything with the band like she has for the last ten performers, but she thought I was doing it because I knew them. What can I say?'

'Okay, and what about the London trip?'

'Again, I have no real idea until I look into it more. Apparently, the visas weren't applied for correctly.' She shrugged. 'All I know is I screwed up big time, Hank is furious, and Kitty is a nervous wreck because clearly my management skills are pretty fucking abysmal too. I'm going in today but I don't know if I have a job, in all honesty. And maybe I don't deserve to have one. Maybe it's a sign.'

'You're being crazy,' he said, his voice louder than normal. 'You've worked your ass off since you've been here and you've been amazing. For the club and for me. You belong here and I'm not going to have you blaming yourself. Everyone makes mistakes, but it seems that Kitty wasn't exactly on her A game either.'

'She shouldn't have to be. She was only supposed to be helping me because I bit off more than I could chew. And these weren't mistakes, they were massive fuck-ups that have cost the club a lot of money and embarrassment. The opposite of what my job is. Let's face it, I'm just not good enough.' She slumped into the couch, a realisation hitting her at that moment. Everything in the past nine months had been a façade. She had run away, just like

Violet said, but nothing had really changed. She was still the same Abbie Potter, simply making a mess of a different thing in a different place.

'What? No, Abbie. That's just not true. You are a phenomenal person, and I'm going to help you figure this shit out.'

'So phenomenal you dumped me.' She said the words quietly, the feelings of inadequacy flooding back from all those years ago, wounds that she thought were healing nicely suddenly ripped open and raw.

'I…' He stopped, seemingly not able to continue his sentence.

'What? Realised the exotic foreigner wasn't all that interesting after all? Certainly not for the great Kyle Miller.'

'Jesus Christ, no. That wasn't it at all. I thought you wanted to go home. I thought you were homesick as hell. So, I thought if you didn't have me to worry about, you could make the choice you needed to make.'

She laughed. A strange laugh that she didn't recognise as coming out of her own mouth. 'Nice excuse, Kyle. I've never said anything to make you think I was so homesick I was considering going back to England. In fact, quite the opposite. I've told you exactly how I feel about being here. But if that's how you want to justify it, that's fine. I don't need explanations. Nobody has given me any before.'

He looked wretched. 'I'm not bullshitting you, babe. The night you took the girls to the airport, I let myself in.

I was going to surprise you. But I heard you crying. So hard, I thought you were going to cry your whole guts out. I didn't know what to do so I left for a while, then came back and knocked at the door. And then your dad. I know he was okay in the end but you were so distraught that you weren't there, feeling guilty about being so far away when he could have been really sick. That's when I knew it wasn't fair of me to keep you here. Not when you so clearly needed to be with your friends and family in your home country. I care so much about you. I need you to be happy.'

She sat silently, taking in what he'd said. She didn't believe him. She had been so honest with him about her feelings, and he was choosing to interpret an inevitable sadness at saying goodbye to Violet, Lily and Polly as an easy out for breaking her heart. She figured it made things easier for him in his own mind that way.

He broke the silence. 'I want you back, England. I was an idiot. If you really don't want to go home, I want to be with you. I've never wanted anything more.'

She had never seen him look so vulnerable. Her heart hurt and she was so confused.

'Tell me what's really going on, then. Sorry, but I don't believe that you did that because you were trying to make things easy for me. Things were good between us. Fuck, they were great. I was having the best relationship I'd ever had with you, then the break-up happened totally out of nowhere. There's something you're keeping from me.' She crossed her arms and waited, and he sat silently

271

as though weighing up whether or not to speak.

She was horrified when she saw him tear up and put the heels of his hands over his eyes. Dashing over, she crouched down on the floor next to where he was sitting and rested her hands on his knee. 'What's the matter? Tell me. You're scaring me.'

He wiped his eyes, composing himself, and took her hand in his, but wouldn't raise his eyes to her.

'Do you remember when we went camping, and I told you about my old college girlfriend?'

'The one who ran away to be a tequila girl in Cancun?'

'Yes. I wasn't entirely upfront with you about that. When I said I didn't care all that much, it wasn't true. I really loved her, and I was a mess for a long time after she upped and left. I numbed the pain with one-night stand after one-night stand, and I've never opened myself up to committing to anyone since. Then I met you, and it was like an explosion in my heart. I wanted you from the second I met you and the more I got to know you, the more I wanted to be with you. I've never felt like this before, not even with Kim. So when I heard you crying and I thought you were torn between here and England, I got scared that you'd leave. I ran before you could run. There you have it.' His head fell back as he looked at the ceiling.

'I wasn't going to leave you. I was the happiest I had ever been.' She threw him a sad smile.

'I know I was an idiot and I should have told you

what I was thinking. Let me help you sort this mess out. I want to make it up to you.'

She got to her feet, needing to put some physical space between them. 'I need a minute. The last few days have been a lot. Stay here, I'll go and make us some coffee.'

She walked dazedly into the kitchen, filling the kettle and putting it on to boil. Mechanically, she took two mugs from the cupboard and scooped in instant coffee from the jar.

Did he really mean it? He couldn't. He hadn't shown at any point in the past month that he regretted his decision. She hadn't heard a word from him. Those weren't the actions of a man in love, surely?

Now, all of a sudden, he showed up like a knight in shining armour when she was at her lowest. To what? To save her? Did he have some kind of issue where he always needed to be a hero? Right at that moment, though, she felt like she could do with saving.

She was petrified of facing Hank and dealing with whatever the fallout of the past few days would be.

After she dealt with Kyle, she would call Violet. Her best friend would know what to do about this whole mess. She was terrified at the thought of losing this job she'd come to love so much, but equally felt like it was probably exactly what she deserved. Didn't Kyle say he'd already spoken to Hank? Maybe everything would be okay. But she felt so off-kilter and her gut instinct was screaming all the bad things.

She finished making the coffee and headed back into the lounge where Kyle stood, facing away from her, studying something in his hands.

'Coffee's ready,' she said, holding a mug towards him.

He didn't move.

'Kyle?'

'What's this?' he finally asked, turning and holding a small piece of white card in his hand.

She frowned, trying to work out what he had, then had to scramble to keep hold of the mugs in her hands when she realised he was holding the scan that she'd tucked inside one of the books that had been sitting on the shelf in front of him.

'That's a baby scan,' she said carefully as the blood ran cold through her body.

'I know that. I'm just wondering why it's a baby scan with your name at the top of it. Do you have a kid back in England you've been hiding from me?'

She closed her eyes. This couldn't be happening. It felt like her whole world had gone to shit in a matter of days. The universe had obviously decided to pull the final rug from under her.

'Sit down, I'll try to explain. I'm warning you, though, you'll probably hate me after this.'

He hesitantly took his coffee from her and returned to his spot on the armchair. She sat opposite on the sofa again and swallowed.

'This isn't easy for me, Kyle. Violet is the only person who knows this story. Not even my family know. I'll tell you everything then you can decide what you think of me. If it's anything like I feel about myself, I know how this is going to end. You were right all along not to want me.'

He continued to stay silent, nodding at her to carry on. She noticed he was gripping his coffee cup with both hands. It must have been burning his skin but he didn't seem to notice.

She nodded back, took a deep breath, and began to tell him the secret she had carried with her for seven long years.

'You know Josh and I got married when I was twenty-three. We were kids, I was a baby. But we were playing at being grown-ups and playing it pretty well. We were happy, or so I thought. It was in the first year of our marriage that I found out I was pregnant. For me, it was the inevitable next step. We had got married, we had bought the flat. That's what happens next, right? You have two point four kids and live happily ever after.'

She looked at him, waiting for a reaction, but his face was blank. Her hands started to shake as she resumed her story.

'When I found out, I was nearly three months already. I hadn't had any symptoms but I'd been missing periods so I went to the doctors. She asked if I could be pregnant and I laughed because I'd been taking the pill, but she made me do a test anyway and there it was. A hundred per cent positive. I was shocked but actually pretty happy about it. And I thought Josh would be thrilled. He was such a stereotypical city boy, I thought he'd be proud of the fact that he'd managed to defy contraception and make a baby. I decided to get the scan to kind of announce it to him. You see, I told you, we were kids playing at being grown-ups and I didn't even stop to think he might want to be there for something so important. I did the scan with Violet.'

'Then what?' Kyle asked. 'Did you lose it?'

'In a way, yes.' A single tear escaped from the corner of her eye and she quickly wiped it away. She didn't want him feeling sorry for her. She didn't deserve sympathy.

'I told Josh and he went crazy. He thought I must have stopped taking my pill or not taken them right for it to have happened, and he accused me of being reckless and trying to trick him into having a kid without agreeing. And he absolutely didn't want a baby. He said we were way too young, he still had so much he wanted to do in his career. We couldn't afford for me to be off work. He wanted us to travel before becoming parents. There were a hundred reasons he came out with. He said we simply weren't ready for that stage in our life and we had to sort it out before it was too late. He booked me into a clinic to terminate two days later.'

'And you didn't fight?' Kyle asked, visibly shocked.

'I'm not trying to blame Josh at all but, by that point, I kind of did as I was told. We went out with his friends; we didn't see mine that much. But I idolised him, so I thought he must have been right. It wasn't the right time for us to do that. But I wasn't strong. You're right. And that's why I know I don't deserve anything good. I don't deserve to be flying in a career or have these perfect times with you. Because what I did was pretty terrible. I didn't fight for that little one. But the worst thing is, even though I am still occasionally sad about it, I don't regret doing it. Because look at what happened. We would have been alone. And I would have been an awful mother.'

'What the hell makes you say that?' Kyle shot around to sit next to her on the sofa, taking her hand.

'I couldn't stand up for myself or a little baby. I'm ashamed of that. But also, the whole saga that played out showed I wasn't good enough. Do you know what gave me the push to make this move to Utah?' She looked at her lap as she asked him.

'Only that you got the opportunity through Violet's partner.'

'That wasn't it. Josh got married last year, and I saw on his Facebook that he and his new wife were having a baby. In fact, it would have been born by now. He or she will be a few months old. And I'm telling you, he's never been happier or prouder of something in his life. He couldn't wait to shout to the world about it. So, you see, I wasn't good enough to be a mother, so he left me to find someone who was. And he wasted no time in making it happen with someone else.'

Kyle tightened his grip on her hand. 'This is a big old piece of baggage you've been carrying around with you. It's heavy. I don't know what to say right now.'

She sighed. 'I knew you wouldn't. Look, can I have

some space? I haven't talked about this in years and I need to process a bit.'

They said an awkward goodbye with Kyle putting one uneasy arm around her before leaving. When she heard his truck drive off, she lay on the sofa. Once the tears started, they were hard to stop, and she lay there for what felt like hours.

When there were no more tears left, she looked at her watch. It was eleven o'clock and she hadn't got to work yet. She downloaded the morning's emails to her phone, and her stomach lurched as she saw one from Hank.

Abbie

After the events of the last few days, I think it would do both you and I good to have a break from each other while I think about the future and if you remaining at the club is something that is going to work for both of us.

I asked Kitty to book you a flight home at the club's expense while I go through this evaluation.

I am sorry it is short notice but the best price was for a flight leaving for London this evening and I attach this ticket to the email.

I'll be in touch soon. Have a safe flight.

Hank Henderson III

Feeling utterly resigned, she went upstairs to pack all her belongings into the cases she'd arrived with. She was clearly not coming back.

CHAPTER 26

S ITTING IN HER parents' living room in Liverpool a week later, curled up in her pyjamas and her dad's dressing gown, snuggled under a fluffy blanket with a cup of tea in her hand, Abbie felt like the last nine months must have been a dream. Salt Lake City, the Utah Saints and Kyle seemed so far away she wondered if she'd made up the whole thing. She knew she hadn't from the regular emails she was exchanging with Rose, but the feeling of being transported into an alternate universe was real.

For the first time in her adult life, she had no idea what to do.

She knew at some point she would have to figure out the logistics of giving notice on her house and dealing with all her new furniture but, with the rent paid for the next three months, she didn't want to think about that yet. It seemed exhausting.

If something was going wrong in her personal life, she had always had her work. And even if things were not ideal at work, like in the final months at LTFC, it was still there.

She knew she should be searching earnestly for a new job, and her parents were too polite to ask when she was going to give up residency on their sofa, but she was exhausted. The fight had left her and she wanted to hibernate.

She vaguely knew it was evening because it was already dark outside but she had no real idea of the time. The TV was on but she couldn't have told anyone what was playing. She knew her family were worried, but she needed some more days to rest. Then she'd pull herself together.

A game show on the television was reaching its conclusion, the families in the final buzzing with excitement that they were up for the grand prize, when Violet burst through the door at a million miles an hour. She was into her final trimester now and her bump entered the room before she did. She looked fierce and ready for battle, despite being over six months with child.

Having had no idea that Violet wasn't at home in London, Abbie wasn't expecting her to visit and sat up, hurriedly brushing the biscuit crumbs from the dressing gown that was pulled around her tightly. She knew this wouldn't be good.

'For fuck's sake, Abbie. This is the second time in a fucking year that we've had to have a come-to-Jesus conversation so let's make this quick. It'll be less painful that way. Get the fuck up and get in the fucking shower.' Violet's Irish accent had never sounded stronger, nor had she ever sounded so cross. 'And hurry up about it because your mammy is on her way home and we're all going to have a talk.'

Abbie was slightly petrified at this miniature whirlwind, and after briefly embracing her friend, she ran upstairs and turned on the water to heat up while she grabbed a towel. Violet meant business, and it was usually in Abbie's best interest so the fastest way out of this was to clean herself up.

When she got back downstairs, Violet had tidied the living room. The used mugs and glasses were washed and put away, the blanket folded on the back of the sofa and the open packet of biscuits nowhere to be seen.

'That's better, you look human,' Violet said, ushering her onto the sofa.

'Don't worry about me, I'm not the one six months pregnant. How are you doing? Well, I know how you're doing because we speak every day, but I wasn't expecting to see you this evening. How did you get to Liverpool?'

Her friend plumped a pillow before leaning back on it. 'There's a fast train from Euston, don't you know. Didn't take much more time than taking a cab across London in rush hour. Now, we need to talk.'

Abbie nodded. 'I know. I know you're going to tell me I need to look for a new job and I promise I will.'

'What about that one you told me about when I visited you? With the music magazine or whatever? Can't you take that job? You can come and stay with me and Michael until you find a new place to live.'

'It's bloody gone to someone else already, some ex-Rolling Stone writer. It's the only email I actually sent a couple of days ago so I could tell you I'd done something, and they replied pretty much straight away saying they'd had to fill the role. So that's a no go.' She shrugged.

'And why have you not done anything else?'

God, Violet could be terrifying. 'I was taking some time here, getting over the jet lag and the shock and all that before the new mission. I'm okay, I promise, I'm not in the same place I was before. I know I'll survive it. I'm just having some bad days.'

'I know you will, darling,' Violet said, stroking Abbie's arm. 'It's just, from everything you told me about that last conversation with Kyle, I don't think you've properly dealt with what happened seven years ago. As much as you've been trying to push it aside, I don't think you can fully move on until you have. You're punishing yourself for something that you shouldn't be and thinking things about yourself that just aren't true. It's affecting the rest of your life. So, I think you should tell your mam.' She said it decisively and matter-of-factly, as if she had suggested Abbie tell her mother what she had for lunch.

Violet's powers of persuasion were even more potent than Abbie thought, and after a fraught conversation in which Violet made far too much sense, she found herself agreeing. Her friend said she wouldn't leave her side and would support her throughout, but Abbie said she needed to do it alone and she would tell both her parents when they got back. Violet wanted to buy some early Christmas gifts in the late-night shopping, so she headed off to the city centre.

When Abbie's parents walked through the door, her dad looked delighted that she had got dressed into something other than pyjamas for the first time in a week.

She stutteringly told them she needed to get something off her chest and, once she started, she found it was easier to tell it a second time around, especially as they gave her encouraging nods throughout.

She'd been unsure what reaction she'd get and was prepared for her parents to be disgusted. But her dad moved closer to her, putting an arm around her shoulder and hugging her tight. She sank into him, exhausted from recounting the same tale she'd told Kyle a week before. Her mum sat on her other side holding both of her hands in her own, and Abbie felt their strength coursing to her.

'I can't believe you've shouldered all this on your own all these years, love. You must have been really suffering,' her mother said gently. 'You did nothing wrong, you know. It's very common. I had a group of girlfriends and we heard terrible stories back in the day from the girls who had to come over here to get sorted from Ireland. We formed an unofficial charity of sorts when we were in our twenties to support young girls travelling over on the ferry. We set up a little stand at the docks so they knew they were welcome, helped take them to the places they were going, and even offered beds if we could.'

Abbie looked at her mum in surprise. She didn't think she'd ever heard her speak with so much conviction.

'Oh, I see the way you're looking. We were quite the rebels back in the day, just you believe. Sisters in solidarity and all that. We wanted to make sure that the ones who wanted or needed the choice had it. It didn't seem fair that we had a choice over here and the girls over the water didn't.'

Her dad stretched out his hand and put it on top of theirs. 'That's how I met her, you know, Abbie. I was walking with my friends down on the docks as we were off to watch a band in a local club, and I saw this stunner of a girl in a miniskirt offering out mugs of tea to girls getting off the ferry. I asked her out on the spot.'

Frowning, Abbie spoke. 'Dad, you told me you met Mum in a pub.'

'Yeah, you were never quite as rebellious as me and your mam. We didn't know how well it would go down finding out we met while she was campaigning for a cause, as it were.'

Talking about something else had eased the tension running through Abbie, and her mother squeezed her hand as she began talking once again. 'Did you talk to anyone after, love? Get some support? Because it can be a real help. Even if you were relieved and agreed with the decision you and Josh made in the end, it's very common to still be carrying around guilt and sadness. And your situation is a bit more complicated because, from what you've said, I don't think you've come to terms with the fact it wasn't a hundred per cent your decision.'

Abbie shook her head no. 'Josh came with me, and we were in and out of there as quickly as they would let us. It was pretty awful as there were protesters outside the clinic yelling at me as I went in and came out. I didn't ask for any help, and to be honest I didn't know there was any kind of support. Once it was done, that was it, there weren't any other appointments or follow-ups or anything. I was very often tearful for the first year, and even now I get like that every so often.'

'I get it, love,' her mother replied. 'Lots of the girls who came here felt the same way. We kept in touch with them by letter. Back then, there really wasn't any support and, of course, most of them had to keep it a big secret. But now there's so much help available, and I think it would do you good to talk to someone. I'll get you in with someone I know tomorrow, if you want? Everything you've felt and are going through is so normal. Let's get you talking to someone experienced who can help you. But this time, I want it to be completely your decision.'

At that, Abbie started crying. But they were tears of relief. Her wonderful, kind parents were absolute rocks. She couldn't have imagined that they had a whole past she never knew about, and how gently they would deal with what happened to her.

She leaped at the offer of help and, within an hour, she had an appointment set up for the following morning with a friend of her mother, who had also apparently also been part of the groundbreaking seventies support group Liverpool Operation for Valiant Endeavours (LOVE). She couldn't wait to update Violet. She would be so proud.

A WEEK LATER, having had a session each day with the

counsellor, Abbie was feeling like a different person. She wished now she had opened up to her parents much earlier, knowing that they wouldn't have judged her and would have helped her heal faster. But she was dealing with everything head-on now and was already more relaxed having got things off her chest.

She now understood that she hadn't grieved her loss at the time, and had buried her sadness, so that sorrow kept resurfacing and affecting the way she felt about herself. She'd felt like she didn't have a right to feel sad when she felt guilt at the same time. Guilt for the termination, and guilt later on for partly feeling relieved that she hadn't had a child with Josh. The counselling had given her some crucial learning that had equipped her to start properly moving forwards.

In fact, she was feeling so good that she'd let Lily, who was home visiting for the weekend, persuade her to go out into the city drinking with her and her friends. Abbie wasn't entirely sure how a night on the tiles with a group of eighteen-year-olds was going to go, but she was up for the challenge.

Her sister had deemed that none of Abbie's clothes were appropriate for heading out – they apparently covered far too much skin – so had shoehorned her into a matching pinstripe crop top and shorts combo with skyscraper heels. Abbie had never worn anything like it in her life, and felt that she looked ridiculous. But Lily was so excited with her creation, and Abbie didn't know anyone in Liverpool, so she decided to throw caution to the wind and to hell with the consequences. Those consequences might be pneumonia and a broken ankle, but at least she was in the UK so there was always the NHS to fall back on.

Lily had been on the phone for the past twenty minutes to one of the girls they were about to spend the night with, talking vital clothing and pub route strategies, so Abbie sat waiting in the kitchen and thumbing through a newspaper. She nearly fell off her chair when she saw the headline on the back page: 'RED CARD FOR SULLY AT LTFC'. She quickly scanned the article. John Sullivan was out of contract at London Town Football Club and her old boss was letting him go. The article alluded to a reputation he had built up of not being the most professional of players and noted that his prospects were looking less than good. Rumours suggested he was moving to Australia for a last-ditch opportunity there, which would surely be a fast track to retirement. Her eyes widened as she read the quote from the manager, Dave Jones.

"To take this club to the next level I need a team of dedicated individuals who can work together to produce greatness. I need everyone pulling in the same direction and showing commitment and passion, and I'm looking at signing a couple of great players in the transfer window who I think could help towards our goals. We're not talking to any players who are shortly to be out of contract."

Wow. That was a gut punch of a quote, and she

couldn't help feeling like some sort of justice had been served. It looked like John Sullivan would have to take a huge pay cut as well as move away from his hunting ground of skanky London nightclubs. She was proud of Dave and made a mental note to get in touch during the week.

The doorbell rang, and she got up and tottered unsteadily to the door, wondering how she was going to last ten minutes on the heels, let alone an entire evening. She threw open the door, expecting her dad had forgotten his keys again. She nearly fell over and had to grab the doorframe when she came face to face with the last person she expected to see on her mum and dad's doorstep nearly five thousand miles from home.

'Kyle!' she exclaimed, her eyes wide in shock.

'England. What the hell are you wearing?'

CHAPTER 27

HAVING DISPATCHED LILY out of the house to meet her friends, a still speechless Abbie changed into jeans and a t-shirt, the vertiginous heels gratefully ditched, and joined Kyle where she had left him in the kitchen.

He had somehow found everything he needed to make them both a coffee and was sitting at the table, looking enormous in the compact room. It was strange to see him out of his normal environment and in her parents' house, but he seemed to have made himself at home. He started talking as soon as she sat down opposite him.

'I couldn't reach you and I had to talk to you. I couldn't let you think whatever you were thinking about me when you left.'

She forced a tight smile. 'I wasn't really thinking any-thing. I was thinking that Hank gave me about four hours to pack all my stuff and get out of Dodge. So, there was that, and trying to figure out how I'd start again back here.'

He frowned. 'But Hank didn't fire you. I've tried calling you, texting you, emailing you and I heard nothing. That's why I had to come here.'

'I dropped my American phone and my laptop back

at my desk on the way to the airport. I knew I wouldn't be going back, so how else would I return them? Hank didn't technically fire me, but it was just semantics. That email made it clear I was gone.'

Kyle shook his head. 'You're wrong. But I've been going crazy not being able to reach you. I was an idiot the last time I saw you.'

'No, you weren't,' she said quietly. 'You had every right to react the way you did. I'm okay with things now, and I don't blame you for feeling the way you did.'

He moved to the chair beside her and took her hand. She let him hold it but didn't return the squeeze. She was feeling completely conflicted.

'Again, you're wrong,' he said. 'I didn't think what you thought I did, I just handled it terribly. First of all, I shouldn't have forced you to tell me such private information. I thought you had a child somewhere that I didn't know about. My imagination ran wild and I panicked and strong-armed you into talking about something really personal.'

Abbie went to interrupt but he put his other hand up in the air to quiet her.

'I have to say this, Abbie. Secondly, I didn't think badly of you when you did tell me. I genuinely didn't know what to say. I was so upset that you'd gone through all that and I didn't know what I could say to make it better. I've never had that kind of personal conversation with a partner before and I didn't know how to handle it. In the heat of the moment, I thought it would be respectful to give you some time but then you were just gone, and I couldn't contact you.'

She turned and studied him, both of them looking at each other quietly and intently. Seeing he was telling the truth, she sighed out a long breath, her shoulders feeling lighter.

'I meant what I said before,' he continued, not letting go of the hand he was holding as if his life depended on it. 'I want to be with you. The two weeks you've been gone, not knowing where you were, what you were thinking or if you were okay, has been the worst time I can remember. Sitting there wondering if you hated me and knowing I deserved it if you did. I had to fix it.'

'You love to fix things, don't you?' she said.

He threw her a sad smile. 'If I didn't mess things up to start with, they wouldn't need fixing.'

'You didn't mess anything up, you were human,' she said, feeling a need to comfort him. 'And coming home has been brilliant for me.'

She told him about what she'd been doing the last week with the counsellor. When she finished, he drew her into him and hugged her tight. She allowed her head to sink onto his chest.

'How did you find me, anyway?' she murmured from where she was nestled into his soft black jumper. 'I asked Rose not to give you my contact details.'

'I know, she told me. It was Violet.'

She loosened her grip and sat straight in the chair to face him once again, looking at him in surprise. 'She didn't tell me she'd spoken to you.'

'She didn't speak to me. She shouted at me. Went absolutely ballistic in fact.'

She scrunched her eyes closed in embarrassment. 'Sorry, she gets quite protective.'

'No, don't apologise. It was what I needed. I sent her a message on Facebook trying to find out where you were because you weren't answering me on there, and she asked for my number. Let's just say I didn't get a word in edgeways for about ten minutes, and I deserved everything she threw at me. And then she gave me your address. I've had it written on a piece of paper in my pocket for ten days, trying to build up the courage to come here and beg you to take me back.'

Her heart sank. How could everything she wanted be in touching distance but, just as she nearly got there, it got pulled back out of reach?

'I'm back in England now, Kyle,' she said resignedly. 'For good. Michael is scouting around for a job for me at the moment. The American dream is over.'

He smiled. 'You know what finally got me on the plane over here?'

'Violet terrorising you? Promising torture? Did she threaten to key the side of the '58 Chevy?'

He laughed, and her heart lurched. She couldn't remember the last time she heard him laugh.

'Hank yelled at me and told me to get my ass to wherever the hell you were hiding, get you back to work, figure out my personal shit and sort it out with you, because if I didn't, I was a fucking idiot. Exact words. Apparently, we weren't as discreet as we thought we were.'

She threw both her hands across her face in embarrassment and he prised them away, laughing again.

She laughed back, but then shook her head, struggling to understand. 'Why would Hank want me back, though? I messed two huge things up and he was so angry. I cost them so much money, and I made them look bad to the fans. I screwed up big time.' She felt sick thinking about it all again.

'No, you didn't. Which, if you hadn't been so defeatist and had brought your phone and computer back to England with you, you would have known.'

'I don't get it,' she frowned.

Kyle took a sip of his coffee. 'I didn't think any of it made sense. I was racking my brain but things didn't add up, so I asked our external IT company to look for an email from that agent. Luckily, he finally sent it last week. When I read it, I knew straight away it wasn't you – it wasn't the way you normally talk. The spellings were American, when you still email me in your perfect little Queen's English.'

She raised her eyebrows in confusion and he continued.

'I asked IT why you didn't get the original reply acknowledging the cancellation. They looked and said that although all your other emails were still on the server, that one wasn't. Which means it was deleted from the back-end system. There's only one person at the club they taught how to do that. So, I took it all to Hank. I didn't want to throw her under a bus, but she intentionally threw you under one.'

'What are you talking about? Who?' Abbie urged, getting frustrated.

'It was Kitty,' he said, anger flashing across his face.

Abbie's hand flew to her mouth. 'I can't believe it!'

'I know. It's crazy. Hank called her into the office and said she had two minutes to admit what she had done in her own words or the consequences would be even worse, because we had all the evidence. She started crying and apologising immediately. I asked Hank if he could leave me alone with her for a few minutes and he agreed. He said he needed some time away from her to calm down. Then she admitted everything.'

'She cancelled the band? Why? Why would she try to destroy the club like that?'

'She wasn't trying to destroy the club. She was trying to destroy you. Well, maybe not destroy you, but she was trying to get you out of the picture. She was more jealous than we realised. She hoped that what she thought were clever little chess moves here and there would make you want to go back home, and she'd be rid of the competition. I told her proper sportspeople didn't play dirty like that. I was so angry. And that's not all.'

'Oh god, what more could there be?'

'I told her she'd better tell Hank she was jealous of your job rather than it having anything to do with me and you because the truth made her look even more of a crazy bitch. I didn't pull any punches with her. So that's what she said to him. And she apologised for cancelling the band and for not even filing the visa applications for the youth team trip.'

'What?' Abbie whispered. She could barely get a word out, she was so shocked.

'Yeah. When we said we knew everything she thought we really did, so she ended up confessing to sabotaging both. I honestly thought Hank was going to kill her there and then. She's been fired, Abbie. And Hank has been trying to get hold of you for days to tell you and to get you to come back.'

'I can't believe this,' she exclaimed. 'I know she's always been a bit strange but I didn't think she was capable of that.'

'Neither did I. I escorted her out of the building myself. She broke down in tears again in the parking lot. She kept apologising, saying she couldn't believe what she'd done. She said you were always nice to her and had introduced her to your friends, and if I had to be with someone, she was happy it was you. But it was too little too late for me. She knew exactly what she was doing when she tried to wreck your career. And she didn't do it once and then feel bad. She did it twice in quick succession. I don't have any sympathy for her.'

Abbie ran her hands through her hair. 'Fucking hell, what a mess.'

'Just a bit. And that's when Hank told me to get my ass on a plane or I'd be fired too. I'm under strict instructions not to return without you. So, what do you say? Want to come back to the club? And to me?' he added quietly.

She paused for a while, watching his face turn from hopeful to uncertain. She swallowed and took a deep breath before answering.

'I think I fell in love with Salt Lake City when I woke up on that first morning and went walking around the park, looking at the mountains. That was just before you knocked me flying, by the way. Then I kept falling in love with it more and more as you showed me different places and I built a life there. I loved working at the club, and I've missed it more than I can say the last couple of weeks. There's some unfinished business and I should probably go back and carry on. But I need a couple more weeks here first. Talking to my mum's counsellor friend has really helped me start to put to bed what happened with Josh and the pregnancy, and I want to work on that some more. It's really important for me to be able to move forward without the feelings of guilt and everything else that was tied up with it.'

'I get it. Do you want me to call Hank to explain?'

'No, I'll do it. I'll call him tonight.'

'And what about me? Will you come back to me?' he asked, his eyes gentle as he looked at her.

Her heart and her stomach fluttered. 'I don't know, Kyle. I'm sorry. Everything has been crazy these past few weeks, and I need to take it step by step. We've had two big issues already, caused by each of us keeping something important from the other, and I just don't know if that means we've got a fundamental problem.'

'No,' he said, his voice low and sure and she felt herself weaken at the certainty in his voice. 'That's not it. We moved fast and we're still getting to know each other. If it wasn't for Kitty, we wouldn't have had any problems at all. Don't throw it all away because someone tried to ruin us.'

'You don't know that. Maybe different things would have cropped up. What's happened has felt more like a plot from a film than real life, and I need some time to process things. I moved to Utah for a fresh start and so much happened so quickly, it's been a lot. I went from living a stale kind of life, still grieving the end of my marriage and living under a cloud of guilt about the abortion, to having a big new job in a new country, a new relationship, meeting new friends and even starting the website with Rose. I took on a lot of things to keep busy, but now I'm sitting down, it's all quite overwhelming. I need to take things slowly, and part one is talking to Hank, getting back to the States and getting my job back on track, which I've only known is a possibility for less than thirty minutes. Please.' She looked at him with pleading eyes.

He rubbed his hands over his face. 'Okay. It's not what I want, though. I want you. I know I hurt you, but I won't do it again. I promise that. I love you, Abbie Potter.'

Tears sprang to her eyes. 'I just need some time.'

Kyle slowly nodded, and she could see him clenching his jaw and fighting back tears. 'And when you've had that time, I'll be there. If you want me.'

She felt as if her heart was going to crash out of her chest, but she knew what she had to do.

CHAPTER 28

ABBIE LOOKED AROUND The Live Joint, which she was visiting for the first time since she got back, thinking how natural it felt to be there. She'd loved returning to her pretty house with the mountain views, and now a few days had passed, she felt right back at home. She'd seen Rose twice since she'd returned, and today she had popped into the bar for some Dutch courage.

'Are you sure about this?' Rose asked as Abbie picked up her keys and her handbag.

'Absolutely,' she said, determination in her voice. 'You know what I learnt from my therapy? You don't always get answers to things in life. You have to learn to live with the fact that things aren't always tied up with a nice ribbon and a stamp marked closure.' She mimed quotation marks as she said the last word.

Rose came with her as she headed for the door.

'I guess I'll never know why Josh really left me, because only he knows what was going on in his mind at the time,' she continued. 'Did he just get bored of me? Was he having an affair? Who knows? I don't and I really don't care anymore. I have zero interest in talking to him. But what I can do is meet Kitty and ask her the questions that I have. I've been passive far too many times the past few years because I felt I deserved some things that happened to me. But now I don't think I did deserve them, so this time I want answers.'

'Okay,' Rose sighed. 'But I really think you should let me come with you. After the shit she's pulled, who knows what she's capable of.'

'There's no way she'll do anything stupid. Hank promised he would write her a reference for her job search and not tell anyone he'd fired her if she met me and behaved. I asked him to arrange it for me.'

'You've gone insane or you're a glutton for punishment, there's no other explanation,' Rose said as she hugged Abbie goodbye on the street. 'Good luck then, and I'll see you later on. We have planning to do!' She grinned as she skipped back into the bar.

A short time later, Abbie headed into the café where she'd arranged to meet Kitty. She pushed down her nerves, reminding herself that she hadn't done anything wrong in this situation and she was the one holding the cards. She saw Kitty straight away before her former colleague had spotted her, and anger bubbled inside her stomach. She took some deep breaths before approaching the corner table. She loudly pulled out the wooden chair opposite Kitty, who jumped at the noise, looking up at Abbie with wide eyes tinged with fear.

'Abbie, how are you? How was your trip home? I got you a coffee. A macchiato, extra hot, just the way you like it.' She pushed a cup across the table.

'Really? That's how you want to play this?' Abbie

snapped as she took a seat.

Kitty visibly recoiled, and Abbie noticed she was tightly clasping her hands together. She needed to calm her temper if this conversation was going to go anywhere. Before she could speak, Kitty broke the silence that was dripping with tension.

'Look, I'm sorry. I don't know how to explain how sorry I am. If it makes you feel any better, I've lost everything. The job I worked at for a long time. The co-workers I thought of as friends. That place was my life.'

Abbie felt her nostrils flare. 'You want to blame that on me?' she said, incredulous.

'No. Gosh, this is coming out all wrong. I'm trying to apologise. What I did was messed up and I'm paying for it. That's what I'm trying to say.' Her lip started to tremble. It was the first time Abbie had ever seen the mask slip.

'Okay, let's start over. I didn't come here to have a discussion that doesn't achieve anything. I came here to get some answers, as I hope Hank told you.'

Kitty nodded.

'Why did you do it? It seems inconceivable to me that you would sabotage my job over a guy you hooked up with once when you were teenagers, but Kyle says that's what you told him. So, I want the truth, from the horse's mouth.' She crossed her arms and waited.

'Unfortunately, it's true, although there is a part I didn't tell him. I messed up and I guess that means *I'm* really messed up. I've never had a boyfriend, and I've kind of fixated on Kyle ever since we were teenagers. When I saw he was really happy with you, I felt the potential that I'd been pinning my hopes on slipping away. I started doing stuff that I am not proud of and that I realise was completely insane. Believe me, I'm shocked at myself, and embarrassed, and I wish I could take it all back.' She looked down at her hands, still tightly clasped.

Abbie shook her head. 'Kitty, you're right. It's insane. What's the part you didn't tell Kyle?'

'The jealousy took on a life of its own. I started to think that you had taken everything that was meant for me. The man, and the job. I didn't tell anyone this, but when your job originally came up, I asked Hank if he would consider me for it. Yes, I was an assistant and I didn't have PR experience, but I knew the club inside out and I was positive I could do it. When he said no and explained they were hiring someone with a soccer and PR background, I totally got it. But then when I figured out you and Kyle were together, I started thinking that you'd taken everything I wanted, and I wanted you gone. I thought if you left, I'd have a shot at getting all the things I thought should be mine. I'm getting professional help, Abbie, because I know this all went way too far and I almost got you fired.'

Abbie couldn't believe what she was hearing. 'That is seriously fucked up. I don't even know what to say.' She took a sip of her coffee, trying to think of a response to the madness she had just heard. She suddenly stopped, looking at her cup. 'You didn't poison this, did you?'

'God no, of course not. I would never.'

'I don't know what you're capable of after hearing that.' A sudden thought flashed into her mind. 'You said you worked out Kyle and I were together. Did you tell me about what happened at prom before or after that?'

'I knew you were together when I told you,' she almost whispered.

'And did you mess up the renewal on my apartment on purpose so I had to find somewhere else to live?'

Kitty's face screwed up, as if she were about to cry. 'Yes, Abbie, I'm sorry. I don't know how I can apologise enough.'

'I can't believe you did all that and lied repeatedly to my face. I moved across the world for this job. I was completely alone, taking a huge risk away from my family and my friends, and you tried your very hardest to screw it all up for me. I don't think I need to hear any more.' She made to stand up but Kitty begged her to sit back down.

'I really am sorry, from the bottom of my heart.'

'Do you even have one, or is there just an ice block in there? I'm pretty sure you're only sorry because you got caught. You didn't just do something once, there were at least four things that I know of that got progressively more serious.'

'I deserved that. All I achieved was screwing things up for myself in a major way, and I'm eating away at my savings in therapy.'

Abbie decided she really had heard enough. 'Kitty,

I'm leaving. I'm not going to stay mad at you because I'm going to put my energy into much more constructive things. All I'll say is I really hope you do get the help you need.'

With that, she turned on her heel and walked out of the café.

ROSE TOOK ANOTHER swig of wine from her glass. 'Wow, you absolute badass, I didn't know you had it in you!'

'Neither did I,' Abbie said. 'I was so angry at her but then I realised I'd got my answers and it wasn't going to achieve anything going around in circles, so I got the hell out of there. I want her in the past, there's too much other stuff to focus on. I'm not fired after all, for one!'

'And the website!' Rose said excitedly. 'We need to talk about it. We're doing so well. We're bringing in enough now in sales commissions and ads that in theory we could both take a salary and leave our jobs. Well, I could replace my salary at the bar; it wouldn't be close to what you're making, I'm sure. So, I think we need a game plan.'

Abbie high-fived her across the table. 'I can't believe it's taken off so quickly – it's beyond what I ever imagined. I've got some ideas for how we could keep growing too. For one, we could do a podcast. The two of us talking about the type of music we like and reviewing gigs and maybe getting some artists on to talk about something like the ten songs they couldn't live without? Anyone who's anyone has a podcast these days.'

'I love it!' Rose shrieked. 'So, does that mean you're quitting Utah Saints and we're going to do this job full-time?' She put her hands together in prayer and Abbie laughed.

'Not quite, but I do have a plan.'

'Go on,' Rose urged her to continue.

'With Kitty ruining my first season here I've got a bit of unfinished business, so I want a clean shot at seeing what I can do this year. But I think you should go full-time on the website and take a proper salary. I'll take a small cut and work on it like I have been doing, and over the next year let's put together a proper business and growth strategy. Then, my plan is to leave football for good at the end of the next season so we can take over the music website world. How does that sound?'

Rose picked up the bottle of wine and glugged straight from it. 'Yes, yes and yes. I can't believe how exciting this is! I'm so glad you came back.'

They hugged and Abbie felt a rush of contentment. She was excited about her plan too – about the next year and then beyond. She wasn't scared of the unknown. She silently thanked the universe for bringing her Rose. The Salt Scene and Rose had given her something she didn't think was possible – a way she could work in the music industry, which had been her first love, and enjoy it rather than find it painful.

'It's such a weight off my shoulders, having this plan.'

Abbie smiled. 'It feels like everything is slotting into place. Who knew when I moved here that I'd fall into a dive bar and it would change my whole future? I can't even imagine never having met you. Salt Lake City would have been shit.'

'Don't think about it,' Rose said, handing Abbie the bottle. 'It's too traumatic, and you never have to worry. I'm here for life.'

'Thank god. It's a shame you have Stella, I'd marry you in a heartbeat otherwise.'

Rose suddenly looked serious. 'No, you wouldn't, because you like men. One man in particular. Are you still holding out on him?'

She put her chin in her hands. 'We're both keeping a respectful distance. Everything was pretty overwhelming, I was just in the middle of dealing with some pretty heavy shit, then there he was in my kitchen and, oh god, I think I might have broken his heart. He told me he loved me.'

'And do you love him?'

She looked at Rose, not saying anything, thinking of Kyle. Her heart wanted to burst out of her chest when she thought of him. Though she'd thought about him a lot when she was still back in Liverpool for her remaining few weeks, since she had returned to Salt Lake City, it had intensified with the memories of times they'd had together frequently filling her thoughts. It had physically hurt when she realised how much she missed him. Of course she trusted him, and of course they'd just had a couple of bumps in the road, all due to the fact that both of them had been hurt before. Nothing so terrible that it couldn't be overcome.

He had taught her to throw caution to the wind every now and then. Fly down a slope on a snowboard. Hike through a desert. Love again.

She met Rose's eyes and ever so slightly nodded her head.

'Then get the hell out of here, you idiot, before that single white female shows up at his place putting on an English accent and takes your man.'

At that sobering thought, Abbie nodded and jumped up. It was time to be fearless one more time.

RINGING THE DOORBELL at Kyle's house, Abbie felt a flurry of nerves as she heard his familiar footsteps approaching. When the door opened, she moved in a sudden panic, tripping and falling backwards.

Kyle dashed towards her as she cried out, but he was too late, and she ended up flat out on the ground, a pain searing through her arm.

The shock sent them both silent until she broke the quiet by bursting out laughing.

'Does this feel like déjà vu or what?' she said, through the giggles.

He sat down next to her, shaking his head and trying, but failing, to suppress his smiles.

She propped herself up to sitting, gingerly checking

her grazed arm. Then she shrugged. 'I'll survive.'

'That's the spirit,' he said, and she smiled at him.

She shuffled over and lifted herself to sit on his lap, checking if he resisted before wrapping her arms around his neck.

He wound his arms around her waist.

'England, you came back to me. Are we good?'

She brought her forehead to meet his, noses touching.

'We're good. I had to go half the world away to find you, but I know that life with you is home.'

EPILOGUE

ABBIE COULDN'T BELIEVE how different Park City was when the Sundance Film Festival was in town. The pavements were packed with people spilling out of the shops and restaurants while skiers and snowboarders walked through the streets with their skis and boards, weaving around film buffs and partygoers. The snow-covered mountains loomed imposingly at the end of Main Street, which was lit up as dusk entered with multicoloured fairy lights strung down its length.

Kyle guided her and Lily into a bustling, noisy restaurant where he knew the owner and had snagged them a table on one of the busiest nights. He'd also called in a favour from a friend and got tickets to one of the movie premieres, and the three of them would be gracing the red carpet just a couple of hours from now.

Lily was shaking with excitement and said she was too anxious to eat, but Kyle ordered her food anyway and told her if she didn't eat anything, there would be no premiere. She dutifully ate a burger and fries, practically licking the plate at the end.

Abbie was going to travel back to England two days later with Lily for a short trip home before the new MLS season started in a few short weeks. Memphis Black would play at the huge opening match, which was already sold out. She was so excited thinking about it.

Her attention was brought back to the present when Lily started rapidly swearing under her breath.

'What's up, Lils?'

'Over there, Abbie, over there,' she said, pointing across the room. 'It's Tom Holland. The actor I'm going to marry. The most gorgeous man in the whole entire world.'

Abbie and Kyle looked over to where she was pointing.

The next minute, Kyle was beckoning to the group and Tom Holland and friends headed over.

'Hey, buddy, how's things?' Tom asked as he greeted Kyle like a long-lost brother with a big bear hug.

Lily sat, mouth agape, mute. Abbie watched the whole exchange amused and confused.

'Great, man, let me introduce you. This is my girl-friend Abbie; she's from your homeland. And this is her sister Lily, who's visiting. Abbie, Lily, this is Tom, one of my best snowboarding students.'

He greeted them both with kisses on their cheeks, and Lily's face flamed red.

Tom and his friends had to leave to get to the premiere of his new movie, but not before Kyle snapped a photo of him with a beaming Lily. She hadn't said a single word in the past five minutes, but as soon as they left, she started babbling while furiously texting on her phone.

'The girls are not going to believe this. I need to put it on Instagram and Twitter and Facebook and Snapchat. Kyle, please can you marry my sister? Then maybe we can have a joint wedding?'

Abbie and Kyle burst into laughter as they watched her tapping away.

Soon it was time for them to leave too. On their way out of the restaurant, Abbie's phone rang and she saw it was Michael. She answered straight away.

'I'm a dad. And you're a godmother. Violet has just given birth. We have our little girl.'

And just like that, the day that had already been pretty amazing turned into a perfect one. She took Kyle's hand on one side and Lily's on the other and walked down the snow-kissed street.

Acknowledgements

Well. Where do I start? Probably with the fact that being in a position of writing acknowledgements for my debut novel is the stuff of dreams. I'm pinching myself!

If you're reading this, know that I am so happy and grateful you picked these characters and their story to spend your spare time with – I hope you enjoyed reading Abbie's adventures as much as I enjoyed putting them down on paper. I'd love to hear from you – you can find me on social media.

Kim Atkins. This wouldn't have happened without you (although I know you'll argue that fact) and I will forever be grateful. From being a very early reader when I was just starting, and giving me the encouragement to keep going, to helping shape my first draft and generally being a tremendous cheerleader, professional rockstar and fantastic friend, there are not enough thank yous that could ever explain my appreciation. All I will say is that the bubbles will be on me for as long as you'll let me! And I hope that every girl with any kind of dream is lucky enough to have a mentor as special as you to help her realise she can make it happen with a bit of elbow grease.

Emma and Ross. My friends and early readers. Thank you! You'll never know how nervous I was throwing this out there, and having your feedback and encouragement meant so much. I know I must have bored you both to tears talking about this and you never once told me to shut up. Saints.

Paige Toon. They tell you to never meet your heroes but they are wrong! As you know, I've been a huge fan of your work ever since your first book and to get accidentally Prosecco tipsy with you and become brilliant friends has been such a gift. You are a truly wonderful person and to have such an inspiration cheering me on and taking a total novice seriously has been such a confidence boost.

Charlie Haynes and Amie McCracken. You ladies are geniuses! You finally made it possible for me to work out how to practically write the bloody thing that had been nagging at me for so long and how to make it happen around working full time. Thanks for all the cheerleading and frank advice. I don't think this would have got finished without a programme like yours.

Lily Wilson. Thank you for designing the beautiful cover. You created something that, when I saw it, I instantly knew it was mine. You are so talented and I feel so lucky to have had you design this before you go big time!

Serena Clarke. Editor of dreams. Thank you for so gently taking me through the process and making it less terrifying than it could have been.

My girlfriends! I really feel lucky to be a woman and have an amazing group of inspirational, badass friends. Thanks to all of you and for the amazing support and encouragement to those that saw me through the writing of this – none of you ever questioned if I could actually do this and that means everything. One of the strong messages of this book is the value of female friendships and having an epic support network and I have that in spades. Karen, Nicki, Lee, Mabel, Lindsay and Jess in particular, thank you for listening to my frequent book writing ramblings and, to you and my other glorious friends, I love you.

Nicola, Nic-Nac, Nikisha-B. You might have noticed that Abbie has a little sister that she loves to the moon and back and would do anything for. That's no coincidence. I'm so lucky to have you, Lennon and Garry in my life and I count my blessings I have you every single day.

Mum and Dad. The hardest acknowledgement to write because how on earth do you put a lifetime of love and thankfulness in one paragraph? Thank you for everything you have done and continue to do for our family. You are, quite simply, the most phenomenal parents a girl could wish for and I hope I make you proud (every now and then, when I'm not going out in inappropriate clothing, sleeping in the bush at the front of your house after drinking absinthe or driving too close to the car in front).

Printed in Great Britain
by Amazon

83504779R00183